SIMPLY DEAD

SIMPLY DEAD

Eleanor Kuhns

This first world edition published 2019
in Great Britain and the USA by
SEVERN HOUSE PUBLISHERS LTD of
Eardley House, 4 Uxbridge Street, London W8 7SY.
Trade paperback edition first published
in Great Britain and the USA 2019 by
SEVERN HOUSE PUBLISHERS LTD.

British Library Cataloguing in Publication Data
A CIP catalogue record for this title is available from the British Library.

ISBN-13: 978-0-7278-8884-6 (cased)
ISBN-13: 978-1-78029-604-3 (trade paper)
ISBN-13: 978-1-4483-0221-5 (e-book)

All Severn House titles are printed on acid-free paper.

Severn House Publishers support the Forest Stewardship Council™ [FSC™],
the leading international forest certification organisation.
All our titles that are printed on FSC certified paper carry the FSC logo.

Typeset by Palimpsest Book Production Ltd.,
Falkirk, Stirlingshire, Scotland.
Printed and bound in Great Britain by
TJ International, Padstow, Cornwall.

ONE

'Rees. Will Rees.' Deeper masculine tones joined the woman's shrill cry. Recognizing the constable's voice, Rees put his musket on top of the cabinet. Six thirty was too early for company and, besides, the events of the past eighteen months had made him cautious. He did not think he would ever recover from the persecution he and his family had suffered in his hometown of Dugard a year ago this past summer.

He opened the door. Constable Rouge and his sister Bernadette, the local midwife, came in from the cold. Rees extended a hand to take their cloaks but Rouge shook his head. 'We aren't staying,' he said.

'What brings you out so early on such a cold day?' Lydia asked, wiping her hands on her apron as she turned from the sink. She inspected Bernadette and then exchanged a glance with Rees. Recent tears glistened on Bernadette's cheeks and her hair hung down from her cap in loose untidy strings.

'We need your help,' Bernadette said, clasping and unclasping her hands. Despite the winter weather, she had forgotten her gloves and her skin was red with cold.

'Coffee? Tea?' Lydia asked, extending her hands to grasp Bernadette's.

'Sit down and tell us how we can assist you,' Rees said. Bernadette and her daughter Hortense, also a midwife although still in her teens, had delivered his baby girl. He glanced at Sharon, lying asleep on a blanket by the hearth. She had just learned to walk and usually faded into exhausted naps a few times each day. Since the family rose before four, Sharon had been running around for two and half hours. Rees suspected Lydia would have liked to join her daughter. Trying to control a busy and active toddler at the same time she took care of the house left her weary.

As she helped Bernadette remove her scarlet cloak Rees urged Rouge to the table. He sat down with his legs astride as though prepared to dash away at a second's notice. Bernadette sat down

next to her brother but jumped to her feet a few seconds later and
began to pace, twisting her hands together.

Lydia went to the fireplace to push the kettle over the flames.
'Tell us what happened,' she said.

'Hortense is missing,' Bernadette said. 'She was called out to
deliver a baby over two weeks ago. Oh dear.' Her words ended
on a sob. Putting her hands over her face she turned her back.
Rees saw her shoulders shaking with weeping.

'Hortense did not come home,' Rouge said as his sister fought
for control. Bernadette turned around, her handkerchief still held
to her face.

'When she didn't come home for a few days, I didn't worry,'
she said, her voice thick. 'Sometimes births take longer than one
expects. But Mr Bennett came into town early this morning and
he said the birth went quickly and Hortense left his farm over a
week ago. Almost two weeks.' She looked up at Rees, her face
contorted with terror. 'What could have happened?'

Once Rees might have wondered if a local tribe had taken the
girl, but even this part of the District of Maine had been civilized
twenty and more years.

'I found her cart,' Rouge broke in. 'Abandoned by the side of
the road.'

'The horse was gone,' Bernadette said. 'Do you see what this
means? She had an accident or something and is lost in the woods.'

'It means somebody accosted her—' Rouge began.

As Bernadette began to speak once again, her voice rising in
fear, Rees raised his voice and said firmly, 'One at a time, please.'

'We shouldn't assume the worse quite yet,' Lydia said as she
put a cup of tea in front of Bernadette. 'Perhaps she was injured
and walked to the nearest farm for help.'

'There aren't any farms nearby,' Rouge said. 'The forest is thick
there, in the foothills of Gray Hill.'

Rees glanced at his wife. His wife was chewing her lower lip.
'Oh dear,' she said.

'There are a few homes on the mountain,' Bernadette said.
'Maybe she found her way to one . . .?' Her voice wobbled to a
stop and tears filled her eyes.

'We're asking everyone to join us in searching for her,'
Rouge said.

'Of course we'll help,' Lydia said immediately.

Rees nodded. 'Have you asked the Shakers in Zion to search?' he asked.

'We didn't think they would agree,' Rouge said. 'We are too much of the World,' he added resentfully, quoting a common Shaker phrase.

'They've been very kind to us,' Lydia said. 'They gave us garden sass and other foods as well as our cow Daisy. I bought the beginnings of a flock of chickens from them. And some of the Brothers assisted Will in putting in a field of buckwheat.' Although Rees did not contradict his wife, he would not have described the Shakers' actions as kind. Yes, the Zion community had been generous to offer Lydia and the children refuge after they had fled Dugard. She had been accused of witchcraft and Rees, accused of murder and in danger himself, had feared for both their lives.

But the Zion community had expected to take possession of the farm Lydia had inherited from her first husband. They had surrendered the property to Rees with reluctance, only doing so after he had identified a murderer among their community and demanded the farm in exchange.

'They owe *you* a debt,' Rouge said now, directing a pointed glance in Rees's direction. 'You solved several murders for them. They have no reason to aid me or my sister.'

'I'll ask them,' Rees said. 'I think they may be willing to join the search for a young woman. Where have you looked?'

Bernadette glanced at her brother. Rouge shrugged. 'I went along the North Road until I found the cart.'

'How did you know it was hers?' Lydia asked.

'I built a cover over the seat to protect her from the elements . . .' Rouge's voice drifted into silence.

Rees stared through the kitchen window. Although a few weeks remained before Christmas the winter snows had begun in November. Several inches already carpeted the ground and he knew more was on its way. While out milking early this morning he could smell snow in the air. And it was cold. Not the icy bitterness of January, perhaps, but no one would want to be outside for very long.

'Where are the children?' Bernadette asked, looking around.

'Walking to school,' Lydia said. This year even Joseph, almost three and a half, had joined his siblings. 'Sharon is sleeping.' She nodded at the fireplace. 'And Simon . . .' She bit her lip and looked at her husband.

'Simon joined our eldest son David in Dugard a few months ago,' Rees said. 'David's wife is increasing and David needed the help.' Almost eight, Simon loved farming as much as David and was already an experienced farmer. Rees missed the little boy's help; that was true. But he missed Simon's presence, especially the funny things he said, with an ache that never seemed to disappear.

'But David was just married,' Bernadette said, momentarily diverted.

'A year ago now,' Rees said.

'I didn't attend the wedding,' Lydia said. 'Remember? I remained here, with Sharon and Joseph.' Bernadette nodded as though that made perfect sense. Rees knew Lydia had wanted to go and would have hauled the younger children with her if it had been safe. But the accusation of witchcraft against her was still alive in Dugard. And, sure enough, Rees had seen Constable Farley creep into the Meetinghouse.

A small structure of local stone, the building contained hard wooden benches that circled a table. Rees had found the absence of a pulpit surprising but the service, or lack of one, was even more so. The congregation, if it could be styled in such a manner, remained silent as they communed individually with God. Rees, his rear aching from the hard seat, compared the silence to the singing and dancing in a Shaker Meetinghouse and decided he preferred the latter. He was not very good at just sitting; he knew that.

As he had shifted uncomfortably in his seat for the third time he saw a shadow, directed from the door, move across the room. He turned around. Farley had tiptoed inside. Remembering the threats this superstitious fellow had thrown at Lydia, Rees felt a tingle of fear, a memory of the terror that had consumed him last summer. But fear evaporated in the blast of rage that swept over him and Rees rose to his feet. He took two involuntary steps in the constable's direction before seeing David's contorted face and pleading eyes. Rees paused, glancing quickly around. Mr Bristol, soon to be David's father-in-law, was staring at Rees in dismay.

He almost pursued Farley anyway but he couldn't interrupt his son's wedding. Gulping, Rees forced himself back into the seat.

He could not think of God or of anything saintly; his thoughts were entirely taken up with the desire to pummel Farley into the ground.

By the time the meeting was over, Farley was gone. And David was married. Mr Bristol had spoken in favor for the marriage although he looked as though every word choked him.

'David and his wife, and Simon of course, are supposed to come and visit for Christmas,' Rees said now. He was not so certain they would make it as the chance of snowstorms became more and more likely. And David's wife was with child; the baby due to arrive in the spring. Rees stifled a sigh. Christmas would not be the same without them.

'How wonderful,' Bernadette said, her voice cracking. He looked at her. Her eyes were watery with unshed tears and although her hands held the teacup, they trembled so much the tea had spilled. A brown stain pooled on the wooden table.

Suppressing his own selfish concerns, Rees said, 'Don't worry, we'll find Hortense.' He cast a quick look through the window once again. He just hoped they found her alive. Turning to Rouge, Rees asked, 'Where is her cart located on North Road?' Since he and his family had moved in to Durham, more or less permanently, just eighteen months ago, he did not know this area well. 'Those farms Bernadette mentioned. Could she have gone to one of them?'

Rouge shook his head. 'The few farmhouses out that way are a fair distance from North Road. Besides, I already inquired at the ones nearest the cart.'

'Maybe she walked back to Gray Hill,' Rees suggested.

'No. Too far. And those . . .' He paused, searching for the right word. 'Those habitations are little more than cabins with a buckwheat field or two.'

'How do they live then?' Lydia asked. Rouge's head swiveled to her in surprise. 'Well, they don't farm,' she said, raising her brows.

'Now, in winter, they survive by hunting. Come spring we might see some of the older men bringing down maple syrup or deer hides to sell in town. The others – the younger men – will be up in the lumber camp cutting timber. When the snow melts, they'll drive the logs down the eastern side of the hills to Falmouth.' He paused and added, 'We don't see them much. They keep to themselves.'

'What my brother means,' Bernadette said, 'is that most of the people on Gray Hill prefer their own company. They don't mix with us.'

'Mon Dieu, some of those men have never come off the Hill,' Rouge said emphatically.

'Hortense would have had to stay with the Bennetts,' Bernadette said, returning to her worry. 'She would have been forced to. We don't deliver many babies on Gray Hill and know few other families.' Her voice quivered to a stop. Even Rees knew she was grasping at straws. Rouge looked at his sister and reached across the table to clasp her hand.

'At least the Bennetts live close to the bottom of the hill,' he said reassuringly. 'She could have made it there.' He stumbled over the words – they all knew Hortense was not at the Bennetts and he directed a beseeching look at Rees. 'Will you come?'

'Of course. And I'll speak to Brother Jonathan as well.' He knew they would need as many searchers as possible.

Lydia smiled at Bernadette. 'Why don't you wait here with me where it's warm.'

'No, no. I must go with my brother.' Her mouth contorted and Rees knew she was trying not to cry.

'Stay here, Dette,' Rouge said, his voice gentler than Rees had ever heard. 'You won't be of any help out there freezing by the road.'

Lydia reached across the table and grasped the other woman's hand. 'Please stay here. And let me get you another cup of tea.'

'I'll meet you on North Road,' Rees said to Rouge, wishing Hortense had disappeared closer to town. It would be easier to find her among the farms where there were open fields and people to talk to. And she would have shelter. In the woods, especially the thick evergreen forest of this Maine Province, she could be wandering in circles and moving ever further from the road. He feared they might already be too late to find her alive.

TWO

By the time Rees met the other searchers by the abandoned cart the morning was half-gone. Thin winter sunlight shone upon the road and upon the crowd of men gathered there without warming the air at all. Rees knew it would still be shadowy and dim under the trees; this December sun was too weak to pierce the interlaced evergreens, especially in the shade of Gray Hill. He tipped his head back. Clouds wreathed the top of the hill in gray mist. Anywhere else, this hill would be called a mountain. But not here, in the District of Maine, where understatement was a way of life.

He parked on the roadside opposite to Hortense's cart and threw a blanket over his horse before crossing the road to join Constable Rouge. The Shaker Brothers stood a little apart and Rees nodded to them. There were many more people here than he expected.

'Why don't we send some of the men north?' He suggested to Rouge as he surveyed the crowd milling around by the abandoned vehicle. 'Just in case she went that way.' He thought the throng should be divided, broken up and sent in other directions. This many people would trample Hortense's tracks. 'Maybe you should take a few men to the homesteads in the woods and question those people.' He paused when Rouge frowned.

'But the buggy is here,' he objected, gesturing to it.

'Yes. And we have plenty of men to search here,' Rees said. Rouge was scowling and looked ready to argue. Rees searched for a reason that would persuade the other man. 'Someone should question the families on Gray Hill.' He rushed into speech before Rouge could start shouting. 'Hortense might have taken shelter in one of those cabins, as your sister suggested, no matter how unlikely.'

'What, go from cabin to cabin? That would take days. And there's no guarantee they will even speak to me.'

'But no one else can do this,' Rees said, attempting a touch of flattery. 'You are the constable. They know you, at least somewhat. And you have the authority. Would they even open the door to me?'

Rouge eyed Rees and shook his head. 'Probably not,' he said. He lapsed into silence but his mouth twitched as he thought over the suggestion.

'I'll accompany you,' said a thin fellow nearby. His fair hair stuck out around his cap and he was missing two of his bottom front teeth. 'They know me.'

'Lucas Bennett,' Rouge said, casually. Since he did not seem prepared to complete the introductions, Rees stuck out his hand and announced his name to Mr Bennett.

'We were hoping Hortense made her way back to you and your family,' he added.

'No,' Bennett said. 'She left us more 'n a week ago and we have not seen her since then.'

'You are correct,' Rouge said, breaking into the conversation. 'Only I can question those people.'

'This is for the best,' Rees said, hiding his smile.

'We can begin with Mr Morton, the shopkeeper. Anyone going up the hill by the road would reach the general store and the tavern first,' Bennett said.

Rouge gathered the men he'd brought from town. After a few minutes of conversation they mounted their horses. Slushy snow flew out from under the hooves as they started forward, adding another set of tracks upon the deeply scarred snow in the center of the highway.

Rees went around to the back of the cart. It had been here for several days at least; the snow lay two or three inches deep on the seat despite the canopy. Still visible in the untouched snow at the road's shoulder were the grooves left by the cart's wheels as the vehicle careened into the gully. He expected to see Hortense's footsteps. But there was nothing. Rees stared at the blank snow for a moment, trying to make sense of what his eyes were telling him. No one had stepped down from the cart here, not unless she had gotten out the passenger side. In that case, where was she?

He looked back at the road. The center of the street was a mush of unidentifiable tracks; Hortense's buggy could have come from any direction for all he could tell.

Rees crossed the gully and looked at the snowy band edging the evergreens. Ice coated the stalks and leaves of the dead vegetation protruding from the snow, looking like the sugar-dusted beignets. No footsteps marked the glittering white here either. Hortense had not gone into the woods, not from here – or anywhere around here – anyway. He stared around him, searching for some sign of the girl's presence. He was fairly certain she had not started walking back to town. The tracks of the men who had come to search for her would have covered hers; that was true. But North Road was consistently traveled and she would already have been found. Yet no one had seen her. Taken together with the missing horse, he began to believe Rouge had guessed correctly; someone had intercepted the girl and abducted her. The absence of Hortense's footprints told Rees that the actual attack had taken place somewhere else and then the abductor had driven the cart here to confuse the issue.

He moved toward the Shaker Brothers. The four of them were huddled together against the cold and Brother Jonathan's nose was bright red. 'Would you go into the woods here?' Rees asked, gesturing. 'Look for footsteps. And spread out, but not too far apart. 'He grinned. 'I don't want to be looking for one of you.' Jonathan inclined his head in acknowledgment. The men walked into the forest and soon disappeared among the trees.

Rees pulled the horse blanket from Hannibal's back and threw it into the wagon. He climbed up into the seat and clucked. They turned in a wide arc so that they faced north and then began a slow walk along the side of the road. He kept his gaze pinned to the shoulder, looking for some disturbance in the thin snow. Although he expected to see something almost immediately, the minutes ticked away and the cold bit through his greatcoat and still the snow in the gully remained unmarked by anything but rabbit and deer tracks. Fat flakes began to fall lazily from the sky. He looked up at the curdled clouds. This snow, although light now, would continue to fall and grow thicker and thicker. Time was disappearing. If Hortense was loose in the woods and wasn't found soon she would die of exposure. Rees found himself hoping she was safe inside even if that meant her captors still held her.

He had almost reached the turnoff to Gray Hill, upon which Rouge and his company had disappeared, when Rees saw wheel marks and footprints on the side. Pulling Hannibal to a stop, he stepped down. Since the throng of searchers had not come by here, trampling the snow, the long channels left by buggy wheels remained crisp and very visible. They looked, he thought, identical in size to the midwife's cart. And footsteps were pressed deep into the snow on the driver's side as though someone had jumped down and begun running. The boot prints were small ones. But, confusingly, instead of going into the woods as Rees expected the footprints went back, toward the turnoff to Gray Hill.

Rees stepped down from the wagon and flung the horse blanket over Hannibal's back once again. Then he crossed over the ditch. He followed Hortense's icy tracks, the stiff frozen vegetation that edged the trees crackling under his leather soles. He'd taken only a few steps when he came upon the churned snow where the girl's tracks met and mingled with larger footprints. The deep prints scoring the snow were too large for a woman and the blurry outlines told Rees they'd been made by moccasins. They blended and overlapped in a way that caused him to wonder if, when Hortense had been caught, she'd been wrestled into submission.

He squatted to peer at the ground. The ankle he'd injured last year ached in protest and Rees rose to his feet once again. There was a second set of big footmarks, slightly smaller than the largest and with the pronounced imprint of the big toe. Hortense's smaller boots marked the snow between the two sets of moccasin tracks. Two men then, one on either side of her. They were not dragging her; her tracks were sharp and even, but Rees guessed they had grabbed her arms to propel her forward.

The marks of the horse hooves occasionally strayed over the footprints of the people, covering them. One of the men had gone back to collect the horse – well, he already knew they'd stolen the beast – and here was the proof. One of the men held the reins of Hortense's horse, drawing the mare behind them. About ten yards to the north Hortense's tracks disappeared but he found the hoof prints of a second horse, one with a broken horseshoe.

Rees went down on one knee to examine the tracks. He did not immediately assume because the men wore moccasins that the local Indians had taken the young woman. Many people wore moccasins. Why, he himself had been known to wear them. But not in winter. Today he wore boots and the wet was already seeping through the greased leather. Moccasins afforded even less protection. He hadn't seen anyone wearing moccasins lately; all of the men he'd met, especially all of the searchers, wore stout boots or shoes.

And where had they taken her? Rees rose to his feet and stared into the thickening snow.

The temperature had dropped considerably in the last hour and the falling snow had become an opaque curtain. Soon the snow would cover the tracks and all signs of Hortense would disappear. He began following the trail left by the midwife's newly shod horse, hurrying before the tracks disappeared. But the kidnappers turned out to the center of the road and the trail disappeared into the mess left by the other traffic.

Now what? He wished his old friend Phillip, an Indian tracker who had worked with the Continental Army, helped him now. Although Phillip had taught Rees something about tracking, the Indian was much more experienced and perhaps he could have deciphered the tangle in the center of the road.

Rees looked around him. He stood within a few yards of the path that led to the top of Gray Hill and, as he stared at it, the conviction that the kidnappers had taken Hortense up the hill grew upon him. He hoped Rouge had found some sign of her.

A sudden muffled scream from the forest froze Rees. He listened hard but heard only the crack of a branch. It was nothing. As he turned away he heard another cry. Was that Hortense? Had she escaped her captors? He began to run toward the trees.

He slipped on the icy surface beneath his feet and fell, right shoulder first, knocking the breath from his body. But he pushed himself upright again and kept going.

Inside the woods the falling snow seemed lighter. Rees slowed to a trot, weaving around the tightly woven firs and the trunks of the bare oaks and maples. He did not hear anything further except for the crunch of his feet hitting the snowy ground and his breath puffing out into the air. Realizing he wouldn't hear anything as long as he made so much noise, he stopped and listened again. The snow hissed down, whirling as the breeze picked up and soughed through the trees. He thought he heard a whimper but could not tell from which direction it came.

He began walking, trying to keep the sounds of his own movements to a minimum. He heard faint sobbing but was it ahead or to his right? The crack of a breaking branch sounded like a pistol

shot. He turned right and tried to watch the ground, looking for
the disturbed snow that would mark someone's passage. He had
to watch his own footing as well; low bush blueberries caught at
his feet and he almost tripped more than once.

He had gone some distance when he spotted footprints in the
snow. Wavering prints left by bare feet marked with bloody spots.
Much of the trail had been brushed out – by skirts dragging on
the ground, Rees thought. He went down to his knee once again
and examined the footsteps. The prints were small, the bare toes
clearly indented into the snow. She was coming from the north,
heading south-southeast. He began following the trail, moving as
quickly as he dared. Barefoot, Hortense, or whoever this woman
might be, would not last long in the increasing cold. Even in a
greatcoat with gloves, boots, hat and a scarf, Rees was shivering.
His booted feet were wet and the moisture had begun wicking its
way through his stockings to his knees. She was tiring too. He
spotted several places where she'd fallen and struggled back up.
And, as he followed the path, he saw more frequent areas of
churned snow where cold and exhaustion had driven her to her
knees. Oh no. Cursing softly, he began to hurry, tripping over the
downed branches and jutting boulders. He climbed a slight
rise, panting with the exertion, and saw her. She had collapsed as
she tried to descend the hill and this time she had not gotten up.
Falling snow already dusted her with white. Rees began to run.

As he feared, the body lying in the snow was Hortense, her
brown hair fanned out across the white ground. Her bare feet were
blue with cold, the soles scored by cuts and scrapes. He shuddered
in sympathetic pain. 'Hortense,' he said. 'Wake up. Hortense.'
Where had she come from? And why had she left shelter when
she was so poorly dressed for the weather? Besides those injured
bare feet, she wore only a thin shawl wound around her shoulders.
Where was her cloak? Something terrible must have compelled
her to flee into the blizzard. 'Hortense.' Rees shook her. Not even
her eyelids fluttered and if it were not for the heartbeat pulsing
faintly in her ashen throat he would have thought her already dead.

He knew he could not leave her here, unconscious in the
snow. He took off his scarf and wound it around her, as far as it
would reach, and picked her up. Then he began the long walk
back to the wagon.

THREE

B y the time he reached the road, north of his horse and wagon, the snow was coming down so thickly Rees could see only a few yards ahead. The flakes had gone from large soft feathers to small flecks of white, falling in a blinding cloud. At least, he thought with an exhausted chuckle, he'd come out of the woods further south than he'd gone in. Hannibal was a shadow; if Rees had been any further to the north the horse would have been invisible and Rees would have been completely disoriented.

Had Hortense lost her way in the woods? If she'd turned west, toward the road, she would have reached it and help far sooner. Instead she'd been caught in the woods, far away from anyone who could rescue her. Or was she trying to stay hidden? Rees thought of the churned snow and the cart abandoned by the side of the road many days ago and wondered what exactly had happened.

As he staggered toward Hannibal, first the horse and then the wagon behind the gelding solidified into view. Now that the end was near Rees was not sure he could make it. Hortense was small and slender but she'd begun to feel like she weighed a ton. His arms ached and the stabbing pain in his back would not let up. 'One foot in front of the other,' he told himself. That was the answer. One foot in front of the other. Finally he reached the wagon and was able to drop Hortense into the wagon bed. Gasping, he unfolded his arms. He groaned as sensation began to return in a prickling burning wave.

She had not awakened and he began to fear he'd reached her too late. He took off his great coat and swaddled her in it, hoping the residual warmth from his body would help her. Oh, it was cold! The freezing air swept through his jacket, vest and shirt as though he were wearing nothing at all. He hurried forward and snatched the blanket from Hannibal's back. It smelled of horse and straw but Rees wrapped it around his shoulders and was glad of it.

'Let's go,' he called to Hannibal and slapped the reins down. The horse jumped forward, eager to go home to a nice dry barn.

Within a few minutes Rees came upon the Shaker Brothers. They'd abandoned the search and were climbing into their wagon. He pulled up alongside. 'I've found her, Jonathan,' he said.

'The others won't know,' the Brother replied.

'If they're smart,' Rees said, looking at the snow swirling all around, 'they will have taken refuge with someone on the hill. Otherwise, they are already on their way back.'

Jonathan lifted a hand in response and the two wagons started forward.

The snow was building up rapidly on the road and Rees was glad to follow the Shakers' wagon. They'd hitched two horses to their vehicle and still the animals were struggling to plow through the deepening drifts. Rees followed a few feet back, driving in their tracks. When they arrived at the intersection of the Main Road with Surry, the Shakers turned right for Zion and he turned left. He found the going much more difficult. Hannibal struggled and Rees could hear the horse wheezing with the effort. He was tempted to climb down and walk but he would have an even more difficult time than Hannibal. Finally the house came into view. As he pulled into the yard he began shouting, 'I found her. I found Hortense.'

Lydia and Bernadette rushed outside. Rees pulled up by the front porch and jumped down from the wagon. By now Hortense – and Rees's greatcoat – were completely covered with snow. He picked her up and carried her inside.

After rubbing Hannibal down and offering him a bag of oats as a special treat, Rees joined the others in the parlor, a room they'd closed off for the winter. The fire Lydia had lit when Rees had brought in the still unconscious Hortense was only now beginning to send some heat into the frigid space.

Lydia had put every quilt she owned over the girl. Although the parlor did not feel cozy to Rees, Hortense was warming up. The snow on her hair had melted and her wet brown locks looked black against her bloodless face. Bernadette knelt beside her daughter, rubbing those cold white hands. A bowl of stew sat close to the midwife, though Rees couldn't tell if Bernadette was planning on eating it herself or had been spooning it into Hortense's slack mouth.

'How is she?' he asked.

'She may lose a few toes to frostbite,' Bernadette said, looking up at Rees, 'but I think she'll live. You saved her. I can never repay you . . .' Her voice trembled to a stop.

He nodded although he was not so sure the girl would survive. Hortense had traveled a long way on bare feet in the snow with only a thin shawl to cover her. But he knew better than to voice his fears.

'Has she wakened?' he asked. Lydia shook her head.

'What was she doing in the woods without shoes or cloak?' Bernadette asked, her voice rough with tears.

'I hope she can tell us,' Rees said.

Shedding the horse blanket as he walked, he went into the kitchen. It was by far the warmest room in the house with the fire blazing on the hearth. Rees stripped off his boots and wet stockings and put them on the stone to dry. He felt such longing for a cup of coffee he poured out the lukewarm liquid left over from breakfast and drank it down without sugar or cream. Although it was tepid, it warmed him going down and he finished the cup in one long draft. He poured out another cup and looked around at the children. He was surprised to see Jerusha and the other two eldest.

'Why aren't you in school?' he asked them.

'I fetched them early,' Lydia said, coming into the kitchen. She went directly to the kettle bubbling away over the fire. Rees had shot a deer a week ago and with the vegetables from the root cellar she had made a hearty stew. It had been simmering over the fire for days, a little different each time since she always added something new. 'Bernadette watched Sharon,' she added as she ladled a portion into a clean bowl. She turned to hand the bowl to Rees. 'Eat this. You must be hungry.'

'It's gotten very nasty outside,' he said as he took the bowl to the table and sat down. After a moment Lydia joined him.

'Where did you find Hortense?' she asked in a whisper.

Rees threw a look at the children and lowered his voice as well. 'She was running through the forest just south of the road up Gray Hill.' He lowered his voice still further, down to a whisper. 'She was abducted, Lydia. I found the tracks where she was taken.' Her eyes widened.

'Abducted? Here? In Durham? By whom?' She glanced involuntarily at Jerusha, kneeling on the floor beside Nancy and tickling her. Although still a child, both Rees and Lydia knew she would not remain one for too many years more.

'I don't know,' Rees said with a shake of his head. 'But she escaped.'

'She must have been desperate,' Lydia said, her voice cracking with sympathy. 'To run away without her shoes or her cloak.'

'I think her abductors took them so she wouldn't try to leave,' Rees said. 'She . . .' A soft sound at the door drew his attention. Bernadette, the empty stew bowl in her hands, stood paralyzed at the entry. Her white face rivaled the bloodless countenance of her unconscious daughter.

'Do you . . .' she stopped and started again. 'I do not believe she's been interfered with. But I saw bruises on her arms.'

'What do you know of Mr Bennett?' Rees asked.

Color began seeping into Bernadette's cheeks. 'You can't possibly believe Mr Bennett is at fault. Why, I've known him most of my life. And I delivered his last four babies.'

Rees grunted. He did not wish to comment since he had met Mr Bennett only once. But after twenty years of investigating all the reasons people harmed one another, he could not blindly agree to Bernadette's loyal assessment of the man.

'Do you know any of the other families living on Gray Hill?' he asked.

Biting her lip she shook her head. 'Only a few. There is another midwife who lives there. Well, she isn't really a midwife so much as a healer. Granny Rose. But I know she delivers a lot of babies as well as tends to broken bones and other things.'

Rees peered at Bernadette, hearing something in her voice. Not dislike exactly but wariness. 'You don't like her,' he said.

Bernadette shook her head. 'It isn't that I don't like her. But I don't trust her. She hasn't been properly trained. Why do you think Hortense went to deliver the Bennett's baby? And the Bennetts aren't the only family we've been called to.' She clasped her hands, her expression softening into hope. 'Maybe she went to one of the other families? For shelter, I mean?'

Rees guessed she was trying hard not to imagine the worst so he simply nodded. When the thud of heavy boots sounded on the wooden step outside he jumped to his feet and hurried to the door. Rouge and three men from town stepped into the kitchen. Snow-covered and red-faced with the cold, they stamped their feet, sending snow flying across the wooden floor.

'It's really coming down,' Rouge said. 'We didn't even make it halfway up the hill. We tried but the snow is turning into a blizzard.' He looked at his sister with ill-concealed worry. 'I hope Hortense . . .' He couldn't go on.

With a shaky smile, Bernadette stepped forward and put her hand on his sleeve.

'Rees found her, Simon. She's here; Hortense is here.' She gestured toward the front parlor and Rouge hurried to the door. Seeing his niece asleep under the layers of quilts, he smiled.

'Thank God,' he said. 'Thank God.' When he turned to look at Rees, Rouge's eyes were full of tears. His swiped his arm across his face. 'Where did you find this foolish girl?'

'In the woods,' Rees said, closing the door. As the constable's deputies shed their outer garments the earthy smell of unwashed bodies and clothing began to permeate the kitchen. With four men in the room, it felt small and cramped. Joseph began to wail and Lydia went to comfort him.

'Is Hortense all right?' Rouge said, returning to the front door. He discarded his coat and stepped out of his wet boots.

'Oh Simon,' Bernadette said, 'Hortense was out there in the snow without her boots or her cloak.'

Rouge turned to stare at his sister. 'What? Why? What happened?'

'We don't know. She hasn't awakened yet.'

The constable carried his coat and scarf to the hearth in front of the fire and dropped them on the floor. 'Let's see if we can bring her round,' he said. As he drew his sister through the door and into the parlor, Lydia, frowning, picked up the clothing and hung the coat on a hook. Catching sight of Rees's boots and stockings, she turned and eyed his bare legs and feet with disapproval.

'I'll go upstairs and put on shoes,' he said. He thought he would look at his loom as well. He'd begun receiving commissions for mostly simple weaving, and needed the money he would earn to support his family.

Pressing her lips together, Lydia nodded. Rees squeezed her shoulder. He knew she did not want to be left with all these people in her house. He too was finding the space crowded with strangers and all the noise and upset that came with them. One of the men was smoking a pipe and the smell of tobacco joined the musky odor surrounding the visitors. From where he stood, Rees could hear the rumble of the men's voices from one side and the conversation between Rouge and his sister on the other. He felt the walls closing in. He went into the much colder hallway and ran up the stairs.

Instead of his shoes, he slipped an old pair of moccasins over his feet. They were bloodstained but the deerskin lined with rabbit fur would keep his feet warm. Then he went into his weaving room.

He'd chosen the brightest room. Usually the sun streamed through the south window, even in winter. But today, the combination of the whirling snow outside and the frost spreading across the inside of the glass muted the light. It was curiously soothing.

Rees lit the kindling he'd arranged in the fireplace. When the flames caught he added a log. This small blaze did very little to beat back the cold. Wrapping himself in a heavy blanket, he put on the fingerless gloves he used here. His hands already felt stiff and he rubbed them together until they warmed.

The weaving pattern, a twill, was a simple design he'd selected for Jerusha. He intended to teach her to weave and at first the instruction had gone well. She displayed a natural aptitude. But lately . . . he sighed. Since Simon had elected to return to Dugard and stay with David, Jerusha had been a different, and far more difficult child. The lessons had not gone well. Shaking his head, he picked up the shuttle and threw it through the warp. With such a simple pattern he did not have to think about it at all. The cold room faded around him as his mind traveled to a different place.

Who, he asked himself, had spent so much effort capturing Hortense? And why? She was a young and pretty girl and he feared that might be the reason. Perhaps Mr Bennett had been attracted to her? Maybe the other midwife was jealous?

When the weather cleared Rees would insist on accompanying Rouge on a trip up Gray Hill and question Mr Bennett and Granny Rose himself.

FOUR

Once Rees caught his rhythm weaving, his mind drifted away completely. It seemed as though only a few moments had passed when Lydia spoke behind him. 'They want to leave now and take Hortense with them.'

'What?' Rees turned away from his loom. He had been so deeply engrossed he hadn't heard his wife come in. He felt now as though he were swimming up through some thick white light to consciousness. As he returned to himself, he realized his feet were numb and the fingers that protruded from his gloves were white with cold. The fire, small to begin with, had sunk down to a few glowing coals. His neck was stiff as well and he rubbed his hand over it to push out the kinks. 'What's happening?'

'The constable and his sister. They want to return home and take Hortense with them.' Lydia's tone was taut.

Rees glanced out the window. The snow still fell, so thickly he could barely see the barn. 'They can't leave,' he said. 'And they certainly can't take Hortense. She's unconscious. And Rouge has only a horse.'

'Bernadette drove over in her wagon,' Lydia said.

'But Hortense—'

'Yes, I know,' Lydia said, interrupting her husband. 'I wasn't suggesting Bernadette take her daughter home in that. Or in anything.' The sharpness in her tone caught Rees off guard and he looked at her more closely. She was clenching her hands together so tightly the knuckles were white. 'They won't listen to me,' she added. Her angry voice echoed in the empty room.

'I'll be down directly,' he said, stripping off his gloves and moving toward the fire. As Lydia turned to descend the stairs, he knelt to smother the few remaining glowing coals. Then he followed his wife to the first floor.

'We've trespassed upon your hospitality too long,' Bernadette was saying as Rees entered the kitchen. 'I'm so very grateful to you.'

'I think it is a mistake to take Hortense into the cold,' said Lydia.

'Indeed,' said Rees in agreement. 'She's still not awake.' The irony of his speech was not lost upon him; he had wanted these unexpected guests to leave and now that they were planning on it he was throwing out objections. 'I fear she will not survive another journey through the storm.'

'But I need to bathe and change clothes,' Bernadette said. 'And I think she will recover more quickly if she is in her own home.'

'Perhaps so,' Rees agreed with a nod. 'But she is not able. Who knows what will happen if you move her now, taking her out once again into the snow.'

Bernadette sighed and touched the unruly hair falling to her shoulders. 'I wish I didn't agree,' she said.

'Of course you may stay as well,' Lydia said, moving forward. 'Please, don't worry yourselves on that score.'

Rouge shuffled his feet and, although he did not speak, Rees knew the constable was anxious to return to his tavern.

'Or you may leave her here and return for her in the morning,' Rees said. 'No doubt she will have come to her senses by then.' Although he sounded certain, he was not. He knew there was no telling when Hortense might come to herself – if, indeed, she ever did.

Rouge cast Rees a quick look. 'You will of course take that opportunity to plague her with demands for answers.' It was not a question. He had now investigated murders twice with Rees and was quite familiar with the weaver's curiosity.

'Of course,' he said with a smile. 'It's important to find out exactly what happened.'

Rouge turned an inquiring glance upon his sister. She blew out a breath and then nodded. 'Very well,' she said. 'Thank you. I shall return tomorrow to claim my daughter.'

'I hope the snow allows you to return,' Lydia said, her brow puckering as she turned her gaze toward the kitchen window.

'I don't believe this weather will continue much longer,' Rouge said, gesturing as though to dismiss the snow as unimportant. 'And

I'll bring my sled. Warmly wrapped, Hortense should easily manage the journey into town.'

Bernadette extended her hand to Rees. 'And again I offer my thanks. Mere words cannot express the depth of my gratitude. What would I have done without your assistance?'

Rees, made awkward by the effusive thanks, stuttered helplessly for a moment until Lydia took pity on him. 'You delivered our wonderful Sharon,' she said to Bernadette. 'Of course we are happy to help you in any way we can.'

With much stamping and loud conversation the visitors went out into the cold and blowing snow. Rees, looking after his departing guests, did not think the snow would end as quickly as Rouge predicted; it fell in a white curtain of tiny flakes. The air was much colder than it had been earlier this morning. Shivering, he closed the door. He was already dreading the inevitable excursion into the cold for evening chores.

The house seemed very empty and quiet once Rouge and his deputies had departed. Lydia flapped her apron a few times to disperse the lingering odor of tobacco. 'At least no one was spitting,' she said to herself.

Rees, reluctant to return to his loom in the cold room upstairs, peeked into the front room. Jerusha had taken possession of the chair in which Bernadette had sat just a few minutes previously. 'Hortense is sleeping,' she said. With a nod, Rees entered the room and peered at the unconscious girl. Only her face could be seen above the coverings. But the chamber felt warmer and when he bent over Hortense he saw that the color had begun to return to her cheeks. With any luck, she would awaken tomorrow morning fully recovered.

'Shouldn't you be helping your mother?' he asked Jerusha. Scowling, she rose reluctantly and dragged herself unwillingly into the kitchen.

Ignoring his daughter's pique, Rees followed on her heels. He was eager to tell Lydia the good news.

He spent the remainder of the morning and most of the afternoon mending tack and tools. As Rouge had anticipated, the snow began to thin and by mid-afternoon had stopped. By three thirty the sun began its descent toward the horizon. When Rees, accompanied by Jerusha and Nancy, went outside to finish evening chores, long shadows stretched across the white ground. It was already too dark to see under the trees and around the barn. While Nancy collected eggs from the hens, Jerusha put the wooden yoke over her shoulders and trudged up the slope to the stream. In her old, faded, blue cloak, she soon disappeared into the shadows.

Fetching water had been Simon's job but now Jerusha was responsible. Rees knew she hated going: hated the wooden yoke, hated the walk even in the good weather. Now it would be a cold trip and she would have to break the ice in the stream besides. This sudden bitter cold would freeze the top of even the fast-moving water.

He went into the barn to throw down some hay for Daisy and her calf.

'Here, chick, chick,' Nancy called. Rees glanced through the barn door and saw her scattering grain and scraps upon the snow. Clucking, the chickens left their perches and ran outside. In a mass of bobbing heads, they pecked at the food. Nancy crawled inside the chicken coop to fetch the eggs.

He finished milking his cow and carried the full pail to the house. He looked around for Nancy. Her bright, recently dyed, blue cloak circled the yard as she hunted for eggs. He sometimes wondered if the more rebellious hens purposely hid their eggs just so she had to hunt for them. But every single one must be found. With winter, the number of eggs produced by the hens had dropped dramatically and every egg was valuable.

'Nancy?' Rees said. She held up the basket. Rees could see a few eggs inside, perhaps half a dozen. 'All right. Come inside.' He waited for her to climb the steps and go through the door before he followed her.

As he started up the steps he heard a scream.

'Father, Father!' It was Jerusha. He shoved the pail of milk at Lydia and ran back outside once again, sprinting up the slope and then down the other side to the stream. Jerusha was already inside the fence and running toward him. It was much darker than it had been and he could not see her expression until she was almost upon him.

'What's the matter?' he asked, peering down into her pale face. Her eyes were wide with fright.

'I saw something.' She turned and pointed at the screen of trees at the northern end of the property. 'Something moving.'

Rees tried to stare through the gloom but the line of trees was nothing more than a black shadow. Winter in the District of Maine meant early nightfall. 'Maybe wolves,' he said, although he did not hear howling. 'They won't get through the fence.' He was lying; he wasn't certain of that. The previous winter had been a hard one and he'd heard of wolves carrying off small children. He wasn't sure he believed that and anyway an eleven-year-old would be too big. But he knew several farmers hereabouts who'd lost livestock and Lydia had seen one of her precious chickens carried away – although that could have been by a fox.

Wondering if he should begin carrying his gun, Rees examined the dark line of pines, the tops sharp as spears against the gray sky. He saw nothing. But Jerusha, trembling, clutched at his coat in terror.

'We'll go to the stream together,' he said, lifting the wooden yoke from her shoulders. She had spilled most of the water from the buckets during her frantic run.

Since the wooden yoke was too small to fit over Rees's broad shoulders he carried the buckets in his hands. He and Jerusha walked quickly; with nightfall approaching the air was so cold it felt solid. His fingers ached even through the thick woolen gloves. And he had to re-break the layer of new ice over the stream. In the short time since Jerusha had raised the alarm a cloudy frozen skin had begun forming over the hole she'd cut.

Lydia looked at them in surprise when they entered the door together but did not comment as Rees poured the water into the barrel by the sink.

'Hortense is awake,' she said.

Rees hurriedly unwound his scarf and tossed it at the peg by the door. He sat down to unlace his boots and impatiently wrench them off before padding into the parlor in his stocking feet.

'Hortense,' he said as he stepped through the door. She was still on the couch, seated with her back to the door. He could see her dark brown braid lying across the quilt wrapped around her shoulders. 'I want to ask you about . . .'

As she tried to free herself from the quilt wrapped around her shoulders, thrashing like some caged bird desperate to escape, Hortense began to scream and scream and scream.

FIVE

'Hortense, Hortense.' Lydia ran into the room. She tried to put her arms around the girl but Hortense was beyond reason and flailing with ungovernable terror. She fetched Lydia a good blow on one cheek before the older woman managed to pin the girl's limbs to her sides. 'You'd better leave for now,' Lydia said to Rees. 'She was not like this when she woke; you are frightening her.'

So Rees, reluctantly, withdrew into the kitchen and stood out of sight behind the wall.

All of the children lined up in front of the door. 'What's wrong with her?' Jerusha asked.

'She's scared,' Lydia said. 'Something's frightened her.'

With Rees's departure, and Lydia's soothing voice, Hortense began to calm down. Her screams transformed into sobs and within a minute or two she was leaning against Lydia's shoulder and weeping without restraint.

'You're safe now,' Lydia murmured over and over. 'No one will hurt you here.'

Rees moved to stand behind his children. Lydia looked over Hortense's head to meet her husband's gaze. 'There'll be no opportunity to speak with her now,' she said, her tones still soft and soothing. 'Maybe after supper. Are you hungry, Hortense?' He saw the movement of the girl's head as she nodded. 'I'll bring you a bowl of hot soup. That will make you feel better, I promise.'

Hortense did not want to release her grip upon Lydia but clung even more tightly when Lydia sought to detach herself. After a bit of struggle, she looked at Jerusha. 'Would you please fill a bowl for Hortense and bring it in?' As the girl ran to fetch it, Lydia called after her, 'And mind you don't spill or burn yourself.'

'I won't,' Jerusha said.

Lydia leaned forward and took Hortense's hands in hers. 'What happened, child? Why were you out in the weather without shoes or a cloak?' She paused but Hortense did not speak. 'You're safe now, with us. Tell me, who frightened you?'

'There was blood,' Hortense said almost inaudibly. 'So much blood.'

'At the birth?' Lydia sounded confused. 'But your mother said Mr Bennett told her his wife and baby were doing fine.'

'You saw my mother?'

'Yes. She'll be returning tomorrow morning to bring you home.' Lydia paused while Jerusha, walking very carefully with the bowl held tightly in a towel, entered the room. 'Your uncle and my husband, and several others, searched for you. It was my husband who brought you here.' With a smile of thanks at Jerusha, Lydia took the bowl and began spooning stew into Hortense's mouth. As the girl swallowed, Lydia asked in a soft voice, 'Where were you, Hortense?'

'I don't know,' she said. Another spoonful.

'Were you on a farm?'

'Yes. No. I don't know.' Her voice rose.

'Shh, shh. It's all right.' Lydia's voice was soothing enough to put a man to sleep.

As silence reigned for the next few bites, the children drifted away to another part of the kitchen. Nancy was rocking her rag doll in a cradle while Judah galloped a wooden horse with a loud clopping around and around on the wooden floor.

'Were you on Gray Hill?' Lydia asked.

'Yes. Far up. It was so cold. But I don't know where.'

Since Hortense seemed about to begin crying again, Lydia delivered the next two spoonfuls without speaking. She might have continued questioning the girl, at least Rees hoped she would have, but Sharon chose that moment to break into a piercing wail. It was so sudden and so loud Lydia jumped. The stew slopped on her apron. Rees started as well. As Lydia rose to her feet, he held up a hand to stop her and turned. Sharon, screaming all the while, was trying to wrest the wooden horse from Judah.

'That's Judah's toy,' Rees said, taking possession of the horse and returning it to the little boy. Sharon let out a shriek that made her father's ears ring.

'Maybe she's hungry,' Jerusha suggested. Nodding, Rees smiled at her. Although he and Lydia had adopted Jerusha and her siblings only the past spring, he loved them as much as though they were his own. Until quite recently, Jerusha had been a comfort and a help to Lydia.

'Hortense wants to see Sharon,' Lydia said, stripping off her stained apron as she entered the kitchen.' Rees felt his eyebrows rise in surprise. 'I think Sharon's crying is calming her.' She reached out for Sharon's hand.

'I'll follow you,' Rees said as he swung his daughter up into his arms. 'I want Hortense to get used to me.' Sharon cried out and reached for her mother.

'Stop fussing,' Lydia said firmly, patting the toddler's cheek. 'Let's go.' Turning, she preceded her husband into the front room.

When Hortense saw him she began breathing quickly but, more alert than she had been, she did not scream. 'Oh, may I hold her?' she asked, staring at Sharon. 'Oh please.'

Rees put the toddler into Hortense's arms and stepped back. Sharon stiffened but as Hortense cooed and tickled the child under the chin she relaxed and began to giggle. Lydia pulled her chair nearer to the sofa until her knees almost touched Hortense's, her arms draped loosely in her lap, just in case her little girl needed her.

Rees withdrew to the doorway. Although he stared fixedly at his wife, trying to convey the importance of continuing the questioning, she ignored him, her entire focus upon her baby.

'Jerusha,' Lydia said without removing her attention from Hortense and Sharon, 'will you feed your brothers and sisters please.'

'Yes, Mother,' the girl said. She threw a look at Hortense and turned with a sigh.

Rees looked at the other children. Joseph was beginning to yawn and had stretched out on Sharon's blanket. He was just over three-and-a-half years old, at least that was what Rees and Lydia guessed. A foundling, Joseph had been assigned to Jerusha's mother for wet nursing. Upon her murder, Rees and Lydia had adopted the unwanted foundling as well as the victim's four children. His age was just a guess.

Missing eight-year-old Simon once again, Rees examined the

other three kids. Five-year-old Judah's eyes were heavy, and even six-year-old Nancy's – almost seven as she was quick to remind everyone – were beginning to droop. 'Supper and then bed,' Rees said, motioning his family to the table. Jerusha had already fetched bowls and ladled stew into them. She brought them to the table, stirring and blowing upon the hot soup to cool it.

When the children finished their suppers, Jerusha helped them clean their teeth and stood over them while they washed their faces and hands. Then she accompanied them upstairs. Jerusha put Nancy to bed in the room the girls shared, although the older sister would not go to bed yet for a little while. One of her chores was cleaning up the kitchen and washing the dishes. Rees followed Judah and Joseph into the boys' room. The sight of the empty space in the boys' bed where Simon used to sleep made Rees shake his head in regret.

He put both boys into their nightclothes. The dresses they'd worn throughout the day were filthy, although clean that morning, and Judah had ripped the pleat that went up the center. Again. Lydia had mended it so many times the cloth itself was worn thin. Rees shook his head. Judah was hard on his clothes, and Joseph wasn't much better. Rees sometimes felt he could spend all his time weaving just for his family and those boys.

He hurried downstairs to take up his position by the door, listening in the hopes Hortense would drop some piece of information.

Rees sat up in bed, gasping. Lydia slept on beside him, her breathing regular and even. Rees looked down at her, her body dimly seen in the faint moonlight leaking into the room. He did not want to risk waking her and he knew he wouldn't sleep again, not after the familiar nightmare that had left his heart pounding in his chest. Just when he thought he'd recovered from his experiences last year in Dugard – Lydia's almost hanging and Rees's own desperate flight for his life – his mind betrayed him. The memories flooded back as sharp and clear as though everything had happened yesterday. And sometimes he dreamed Lydia had been hung. Or he had been caught.

Closing his eyes, he sucked in a deep breath and forced himself to breathe slowly and evenly. These dreams were less frequent now than they had been but no less terrifying when they occurred. With another glance at his sleeping wife, he crept out of bed. He slid his feet into his shoes and wrapped a quilt around his shoulders. The cold seemed to bite through his very bones.

He went around the bed. Sharon, asleep in the cradle next to Lydia, sighed and rolled over. Rees paused and bent over, peering at his little daughter through the gloom. At fourteen – almost fifteen – months she was too large for the cradle but Lydia wasn't ready to release her. He touched her head, the knitted cap covering her silky hair warm to his touch, and continued out to the hall.

Everything was silent. He walked as quietly as he could to his weaving room. If possible, the air felt even colder in here. The moonlight shone sharp and white upon his loom and Rees considered sitting down and weaving a few rows. He could light a fire – but he'd left his tinderbox downstairs and it was so cold he was shivering underneath the padded covering wrapped around him. Not for the first time, he considered bringing the loom downstairs where it was warmer. The last time he had done so, however, Joseph had walked around and around touching everything including the finished cloth. Judah had taken the shuttle, Rees still wasn't sure why, and it had taken him almost an hour to find it. The thread around the bobbin had been unrolled and touched so often that, dirty and frayed, it had had to be discarded. As usual, Rees decided to leave the loom exactly where it was now.

He went downstairs and stirred up the banked fire. The flickering yellow light spread through the kitchen. Rees lit several candles and by their light began grinding coffee beans for coffee. As he measured out the grounds, a sudden thump outside made him jump and coffee went all over the table. Swearing, Rees went to the window and peered outside. He could see nothing. The barn was a big black shadow against the lightening sky. Rees saw nothing, no movement at all. The cow – Daisy – mooed and he knew he would soon have to go outside to the barn to milk her.

After spending several minutes peering through the window, and seeing nothing, he returned to the table and finished preparing the coffee. He put it over the fire to brew and returned to the window. Hortense's experience and the after-effects of Rees's dream had left him uneasy. But he saw nothing, no movement at all.

The fragrance of coffee spread through the kitchen.

'May I have a cup of that?'

Rees jumped and turned. Hortense stood in the doorway from the front room, clinging to the jamb for support. Although still pale and limping on her blistered feet, she regarded Rees with a cautious smile.

SIX

Hortense sat down at the table and wrapped the quilt tightly around her, despite the heat emanating from the fire blazing on the hearth. Rees leaned across the table to put the cup in front of her. She flinched away from him so violently the chair shuddered on the floor.

He stepped back. The girl was still terrified, that was clear, despite the tremulous smile she offered him. He pushed the milk and the sugar nippers toward her and sat down on the opposite side of the table. He regarded her in silence as she lifted the cup to her mouth, using both trembling hands to steady it. The rooster's sudden loud crow made her jump and coffee flew across the table in a brown arc. 'Sorry, sorry,' she gasped.

'Your mother will come for you today,' Rees said, his voice loud in the quiet room. 'Along with your uncle.'

'I'll go home?' she asked, sounding almost as though she couldn't believe it.

'Of course,' he said. 'You are not a prisoner here.' He saw the faint jerk of her body as she twitched in surprise. How could he tiptoe into the questions he wanted to ask her? 'You were free to leave yesterday but your mother—'

'I know. I had the good cart,' Hortense interjected with a nod. 'Did you find it?'

'I believe your uncle Simon recovered it,' Rees said. 'It looked as though you were driven off the road.' She nodded, tears glittering in her eyes. She put the cup down with exaggerated care and folded her hands, holding them tightly together. 'Two men. They took you captive?'

Although she did not agree she did not refute his guess either. 'You escaped,' he went on. 'That's why you were running through a snowstorm with no boots or cloak.'

'They took my boots so I wouldn't run,' Hortense said.

'Who? Who took your shoes?'

'I don't know.' Hortense's voice broke. 'I mean I don't know their names.' She gulped and closed her eyes as though she refused to see. 'There was so much blood.'

'Blood?' Rees repeated. 'What blood? What happened?' And when she did not respond, he repeated, 'What happened, Hortense?'

'He came after me.' She began to shake, a deep bone-shaking shudder that set the cup rattling on the table.

'Who came after you?' Rees leaned forward and put his hand over her clasped fist. She reared back like a skittish horse, her eyes rolling in her head, and uttered a breathless scream.

'It's all right,' he said, drawing back and quickly removing his hand from hers. 'It's all right. You're safe. I'm not going to hurt you.' He stared at her in frustration, wishing he knew how to penetrate Hortense's terror. 'I know you're frightened,' he said, softening his voice. 'I know about fear. More than a year ago I was accused of murder. Far away from here,' he added quickly when he saw her recoil. 'And it was a false accusation besides. I spent a week as a fugitive, running for my life, hiding in the woods . . .' Remembered terror roughened his voice and he stopped. But he had caught Hortense's attention.

'What happened then?' she asked, leaning forward slightly.

'I found the killer,' he said. Even now the shock and pain of that betrayal felt like a knife to the gut. Closing his eyes, he tried to shake off the memory. 'So I know about fear. But sometimes you have to look it in the face and beat it back.'

'You don't understand,' she said, folding her hands over her belly. Rees decided not to press her just yet about the event that was so terrifying her.

'Was there anyone else there?' he asked, keeping his voice soft and gentle. 'In the place where you were taken?'

'Jem and Jake.' Her voice changed slightly on the final name. Affection as well as guilt and shame if Rees was any judge. He knew all about guilt and shame as well as fear. He still blamed himself for the accusation of witchcraft against Lydia that had not only put her life, but the life of his as-then unborn daughter Sharon, in danger.

'Were Jem and Jake the ones who took you?'

She nodded, her clasped hands twitching. Her sudden movement sent the cup next to her flying off the table to the floor and the china cup shattered into pieces.

'What is going on here?' Lydia asked from the door. She held Sharon by the hand.

'Nothing, nothing,' Hortense said. She jumped to her feet and fled to the front room. Lydia turned a look of inquiry on Rees as she entered the kitchen. He rose and went to fetch the broom.

'Something terrible happened,' he said in a low voice as he approached Lydia. 'She saw it and she's terrified.' As well as ashamed and guilty. 'But she told me some names.'

'Maybe she'll eventually feel comfortable confiding the whole,' Lydia said, her brows drawing together. 'But there's no more time to press her. Not now. Here comes Jerusha. The others will be rising soon.'

'And it's past time to milk,' Rees said. He couldn't help the frustrated sigh that escaped his lips. Farm work frequently felt like a cage, confining him, not only to this property, but to a rigorous schedule of daily chores. Lydia looked at him in sympathy and stretched out her hand for the broom.

'I'll sweep up the broken cup,' she said. 'You have milking to do.'

So he put on his boots and his tattered old coat. As he moved toward the door, Jerusha ran into the kitchen. 'Wait,' she said. 'I have to fetch water. I'll go with you.' And Rees understood she was still apprehensive after her scare last night.

So he waited by the door while his daughter put on her boots and her old faded cloak. Then he held the door open so she could precede him into the darkness.

Dawn was creeping into the sky and he could see without a lantern. Although a light snow fell Rees thought it would end soon. The air felt warmer too and he hoped some of the snow already on the ground would melt.

As Jerusha disappeared up the slope he continued on to the barn. Daisy lowed plaintively. He patted her warm hide. 'It's all right, girl,' he told her. He brought up the stool and sat down, leaning his head against her flank. As his hands worked Daisy's teats, the milk began hissing into the pail.

David would have finished the milking an hour ago. He would probably have negotiated with Brother Jonathan for additional cattle too, Rees thought. David loved farm work and cows were his favorite. Although Rees had visited his oldest son only a month ago, he couldn't help wondering how David was faring. Their relationship had been a rocky one for many years. When Rees went on the road, weaving from farm to farm to earn the money necessary to support his son and the farm in Dugard, David viewed it as abandonment. But he had grown up and after Rees had been unjustly accused of murder, father and son had found a new closeness.

Rees missed David more than he had ever thought possible.

'Father. Father.' Jerusha's shrill scream broke into Rees's reverie. He quickly lifted the bucket out of the stall, moving it to safety, and ran through the barn door. Surely Jerusha could not imagine she'd seen wolves, not now. The sun was rising and the gray light of dawn was shot with gold.

But when Rees exited the barn and ran over the slope he saw she was not screaming because she was afraid of wolves. She was sprawled on the ground under a man. Another man, little more than a boy Rees thought now, was crouched over the two figures lying in the snow.

'Hey, hey,' Rees shouted, running forward. 'What are you doing?' Why had he forgotten his rifle? 'What do you think you're doing?'

The young man crouched over Jerusha scrambled to his feet. Rees had a brief but sharply clear view of an angular face under a coonskin cap. Eyes the color of black coffee, black hair and a shaggy unkempt beard faced Rees. Still, despite the beard, this fellow looked to be little more than a boy himself.

Both young men were dressed in buckskin and Rees saw with angry clarity the moccasins on their feet. The younger boy, still beardless, incongruously wore a knitted light-colored scarf tied around his neck.

The two lads turned and sprinted across the stream, their feet sliding on the icy surface. Once on the other side they fled toward the trees and soon disappeared within them.

Rees ran to Jerusha and dropped to his knees by her in the snow. He gathered the sobbing girl into his arms.

SEVEN

By the time he carried his daughter up the steps toward the kitchen door, Lydia had come out on the porch. She held the door open for Rees as he carried the girl inside. Trembling and white-faced, Jerusha clung to Rees when he tried to put her down.

'You're safe now,' he told her, speaking calmly although his heart was galloping in his chest. 'Go to your mother. I want to speak to Hortense.' Lydia held out her arms and after a moment's hesitation Jerusha allowed Rees to put her down. Lydia drew the child into her arms.

Still in his old cloak and the boots he wore in the farmyard, he stamped into the front room. Clutching the quilt to her chest, Hortense turned. Her eyes widened. 'Just now,' he said in a low fierce voice, 'two men came into the yard and attacked Jerusha. They wore coonskin caps and buckskin with moccasins on their feet. You had better start talking now and tell me who took you and why and what happened.'

'I-I can't.' Tears filled Hortense's eyes. 'Is Jerusha all right? I don't want anything to happen to her.'

'She's scared to death,' Rees said, approaching Hortense. 'What happened to you? What did you mean when you talked about the blood? Why were you so frightened you fled barefoot into the snow? Tell me. Now.' Rees did not realize he was shouting until Lydia came up behind him and grasped his shoulder.

'Will, Will. Calm down.'

'You don't understand,' he said, looking at his wife. 'The boys who attacked Jerusha were wearing moccasins, just like the tracks I saw in North Road.' He turned back to Hortense. 'Where the cart was driven off the road and you were taken. It takes no great stretch of imagination to guess these are the same individuals who abducted you. Are they still looking for you?'

Hortense gulped back a sob and stared up at Rees with watery eyes.

'If you know something,' Lydia said, 'tell us. I don't want to see Jerusha hurt and scared—'

'I don't know anything,' Hortense broke in. 'I don't. I don't know who took me. Or why anyone would come after Jerusha.' Despite her vehemence he did not believe her, not completely anyway.

'You said there was blood,' he said, trying to keep his voice level. 'Where did that blood come from? What happened?'

Hortense turned her face away, pressing her hands to her mouth. Frustration overcame Rees and, grabbing her shoulders, he began shaking her.

'Hortense. Tell me what happened.'

'I don't know, I don't know,' she screamed at him. 'Leave me alone.'

Lydia put her hand on Rees's right arm and pulled it back until he released his grip on Hortense's shoulder. Rees stepped back from her just as Bernadette ran into the room.

'Stop it. Stop it,' she shouted at him. 'How dare you attack my daughter.'

'I wasn't—' he began but she raised her voice even further.

'Leave her alone. She has already been through so much.'

'Jerusha was attacked,' Rees said, shouting in his turn. 'By young men who, I believe, were looking for her.' He pointed at Hortense. Bernadette frowned at him.

'That's not possible,' she said flatly in a voice that brooked no discussion. 'Come Hortense,' she said, holding out a shabby, pale-gray cloak and a pair of clogs. 'Uncle Simon brought around the sled; we'll go home now.'

Hortense nodded, her eyes downcast, and reached for the cloak. In less than a minute the clogs were on her feet and the cloak over her shoulders. Bernadette put her arm around her daughter and drew her from the room. As they crossed the kitchen and approached the door, she turned and said to Rees, 'You stay away from my daughter. Do you hear me?'

'You're making a mistake,' he said. 'She knows more than she is telling.'

'She doesn't,' interrupted Bernadette in a sharp angry voice.

'Those men who attacked Jerusha this morning will not give up. Hortense is still in danger.'

'No, she isn't. Except maybe from you. You stay away from my daughter from now on.' Bernadette bundled Hortense through the open door. Shaking with frustration, Rees watched the women climb into the sled.

The warm sun was softening yesterday's snow. Water dripped from the room. As Constable Rouge, who tipped his hat to Rees in a friendly fashion, turned the sled around, the runners left long grooves in the slushy snow. Rees closed the door with a sharp slam.

'Hortense knows more,' he said, turning to Lydia. 'A lot more.'

'I know,' Lydia said, nodding. 'But she is too terrified to speak about it.'

'I think there is more to her silence than that,' he said, recalling his impressions of her guilt and shame earlier this morning. 'And Bernadette is a fool if she thinks Hortense's silence will keep her safe.'

'Bernadette is no fool,' Lydia said as Jerusha left her seat by the table to join them. 'She knows her daughter is not telling all she knows. Bernadette is protecting her chick. As we wish to protect ours.' She smiled at Jerusha. 'Why don't you go upstairs and wake your brothers and sister. They have already overslept. And Nancy still has to collect the eggs.'

Jerusha nodded. Despite the marks of tears on her cheeks, she seemed to have recovered somewhat from her scare. 'There is something,' she said.

'What?' Lydia smiled at the girl.

'When . . . when those men grabbed me,' she swallowed, her voice beginning to tremble.

'You don't have to talk about this,' Lydia said.

'Yes, she does,' Rees said, turning to Jerusha. 'Did they speak to you?'

'Yes,' she said in relief. 'The one who pushed me down said, "This isn't her. I told you she was too short." And the other one said, "Let her go. She's just a kid." And the other one said, "Why don't we take her anyway." And then you came over the hill, shouting.' She smiled at Rees and leaned forward to hug him before leaving the kitchen.

He watched her as she went out the door into the hall. Both Jerusha and her brother Simon were resilient. Well, he guessed they'd had to be, living with their drunken mother in New York. Another thought struck him and he turned to Lydia. 'See?' he said. 'Those young men did come down here looking for Hortense.'

'But how did they know she was here?'

Rees thought of all the men who'd helped search and of Rouge who ran the local tavern as well as served as constable. 'There were a lot of people looking for her,' he said. 'Any one of them could have talked about it. And Rouge chats with people all day in the ordinary. I'd wager this house that the news of her disappearance, the wagon found by the side of the road, and my discovery of her unconscious body lying in the snow went through the town like a forest fire.' As he spoke Lydia's cheeks paled. She moistened her lips with her tongue.

'Will those wicked boys return?' she asked in a hushed voice.

'I don't believe so,' Rees said in a confident voice. 'They want Hortense and she isn't here anymore.' He sounded more certain than he felt. But if those young brutes did dare set foot on his property he would be waiting. From now on he planned to carry his rifle with him every time he stepped outside. After a short pause he continued, 'I just wish I knew what happened to Hortense. What was she involved in? It sounded almost as though she witnessed a murder. Or,' he added, thinking of the young men who were searching so determinedly for the girl, 'she committed one. And that's why she ran.'

'Oh, surely not,' Lydia said quickly. 'Not Hortense. She is not a murderer. But there is something . . .' Her words trailed away.

'I must talk to Hortense again,' Rees said. 'Despite her mother's wishes. Those lads don't seem willing to abandon their efforts to recapture her again.'

'Especially if she saw them murder someone,' Lydia said, an expression of horror crossing her face. 'Oh, how terrible.'

'I need to speak with her again,' he repeated. The determination of the young men to recapture her was easily explained if she had witnessed a murder. 'We need at least to discover what happened.'

'I doubt Bernadette will allow you to talk to her daughter now,' Lydia said. 'She warned you off, remember?' He nodded reluctantly.

'Do you think I should wait a day or two?' he asked. He did not want to suggest that Jerusha might still be in danger. The thought sent a shiver through him. He had done his best to comfort everyone. But there was no one who could reassure him.

'We will take extra care,' Lydia said. She leaned forward and put her hand over Rees's. 'I know you want to rush into town and pressure Hortense to speak. I want answers too. But I doubt Bernadette will even allow you to see her daughter, especially now when she is so protective.'

'I have chores anyway,' Rees said. He saw no reason to admit that once he had completed them, he would reward himself with a trip into town. Even if Bernadette would not permit him entry into his house, he would speak to Rouge. Although he was uncle to Hortense, he had never shown himself prone to the softer emotions. He was in fact, a suspicious cuss, and so would probably be able to listen to Rees's theories without anger. Rouge was, moreover, the constable and so would have a professional reason for wanting to capture Hortense's kidnappers.

As the children ate their breakfast, Rees went outside to harness Hannibal to the wagon. Usually the kids walked to school but after the attack on his daughter he couldn't risk it.

Jerusha and the others had attended school at Zion, the Shaker community, the previous year. But when Rees had moved his family to this farm, he and Lydia, after some discussion, had decided to put them in the dame school just outside of town. The Shakers separated boys and girls and Simon, a hard-working little boy for all he still didn't know his letters, had been humiliated. Rees hoped David had made arrangements for the boy to continue his lessons. For the hundredth time Rees wished Simon had not stayed with David.

The school was about five miles from the farm by road although the children had a shortcut through the woods that decreased the distance by a mile or so. Rees expected to finish his morning chores as the children ate breakfast. But Jerusha refused to go to school. She was still too frightened, she said.

Lydia threw a quick anxious glance at Rees. He had initially been reluctant to allow the girl to continue her schooling, even though she loved learning. In his opinion, Lydia had too much work and needed Jerusha's help around the house. Anyway, she would eventually get married and what purpose her education then? But Lydia had refused to yield, eventually wearing him down until he finally agreed.

And here was Jerusha, refusing to attend school.

'You will and that's that,' Rees said.

'I won't,' she said, her angry voice rising to a shriek.

Lydia grasped the girl's arm and drew her aside. He turned to the children grouped around the table. Although each had a bowl of samp – cornmeal porridge – before them not one was eating. Their eyes were focused intently on their older sister.

'Eat,' Rees said, moving so that he stood between Jerusha and the others. 'Eat now.' Nancy picked up her spoon and, after a slight hesitation, her brothers followed her.

He could not hear what Lydia said to Jerusha but, when he had gotten Hannibal hitched to the wagon and was ready to leave, the scowling and unhappy girl climbed in with her siblings.

After that excitement the children were almost late; the final vibrations of the big brass bell were just fading when they ran up the steps and disappeared inside. Rees waited outside for a few seconds, just in case he was needed. Then, reluctantly for he still felt a powerful urge to talk to Rouge, he drove home to finish his morning chores.

But he found himself too nervous to settle. Although he unhitched Hannibal and cooled him down he could not force himself to attend to anything else. Instead, driven by the need to identify Jerusha's attackers, he crossed the yard and went to the stream to examine the disturbed snow where his daughter had been tackled. That area, the snow scarred right down to dirt, told him nothing. But he could see the footprints on the other side of the stream leading into the woods.

Since the War for Independence, Rees had had many occasions to use the skills taught him by Indian guide Phillip. In this case no training was necessary. The two lads had made no attempt to disguise their presence and the trail was clearly visible. If the situation were not so serious Rees would have laughed.

The boys had paused just inside the line of pines. Behind that screen the snow was trampled, as though they'd lingered to watch the farm. One of the young men had relieved himself against a tree, the yellow at its base a clear marker of their time here. They had probably been waiting for Hortense to come out so they could capture her, Rees thought sourly.

The boys had paced back and forth, their repeated footsteps

digging a channel through the snow. From that trench, footsteps went deeper into the woods, curving over the hill in a shadowy blue line. One set, toes forward, came toward the farm. The other tracks went in the opposite direction. The two young men had run side by side, the steps widely spaced and deep. Those were the ones that interested Rees. He began to follow, carefully avoiding stepping into the trail left by his quarry.

Where had they come from? And where were they going now?

Although the sun was visible in the sky and gold streaked the edges of the woods, once he penetrated the thick trees the light faded to a dim grayish gloom. Without sun to melt it, the snow was deeper here. And it was much colder. The tracks, crusted with ice, remained clear although a little blurred.

Rees's farm lay in a valley – the same low point in which the town and the Shaker community rested. At the back of the property, the woods rose upward to the highlands of the mountains that stretched across the district. The tracks angled across these foothills, heading north-east.

He was already out of breath and he could see by the footprints that the boys were no longer running.

The ground rose for some time before dropping precipitately to a valley. He started descending the steep slope at a careful walk but slipped and fell and slid the rest of the way. The snow was much deeper at the bottom of the hill and a dead tree, lying on its side with its roots to the sky, barred his way. To his left an icy stream cut through the snow. He wondered if it was the same waterway that bisected his property and that he had crossed once already. Possibly not; many creeks and ponds wound through these hills.

When he looked east he saw a patch of blue sky through the leafless branches. If he somehow managed to make his way over the dead tree and continued in that direction he would probably reach the northern leg of Surry Road. But the tracks went north, uphill through the snow. He struggled through the knee-high drifts to the stream and crossed from rock to rock over it. He could see moving water under the ice here.

He followed the trail through a thick stand of evergreens to a bare slope of ice-spattered granite. There they ended. Panting, Rees stopped. Without the footprints to follow he could not continue. Paths and hidden shortcuts criss-crossed these hills and he knew better than to try and find his way. Most likely he would lose himself in the snowy forest and his body not be found again until spring. Anyway, the boys were too far ahead and he had no chance to catch them now, no chance to find out exactly what they were trying to accomplish. He turned around and began the long slog back to his farm.

EIGHT

By the time he reached the end of the woods, morning was well advanced. He guessed it was after nine; the sun penetrated the edge of the trees with golden fingers. He paused just inside the trees and surveyed his property.

Lydia's first husband, Charles Ellis, had left this farm to her and it had transferred to Rees upon their marriage. Living in Zion as a celibate Shaker Brother, Ellis should have given the farm to the community. Instead he had willed it to his wife. When Rees and his family had fled from Dugard, taking refuge in Zion, everyone understood that the Ellis property would go to the Shakers. Rees and his family were supposed to be living here only temporarily. But in truth he did not know what he was going to do over the long term.

The chicken coop had been built new this past fall by Brother Jonathan and already housed a flock, although there were not as many chickens as Lydia wished to own. Rees eyed the old barn. He could hear Daisy and her calf mooing, the beginning of what he hoped would one day be a herd. Attached to one side of the barn, the pigpen held a pregnant sow that grunted contentedly as she foraged for acorns. Next year Rees intended to purchase some sheep and Lydia had already begun planning for beehives. It appeared the family was settling in.

But as he gazed at the scene, he realized something was gnawing at him. What was it? He knew he had to fetch the pail of milk and bring it inside. But that wasn't it. He swept his eyes across the yard, the annoying itch increasing. The fields behind the chicken coop and the fence that protected it were in clear view of the piney woods.

Rees turned around and inspected his yard from another angle. The rutted lane that entered the property, looping behind the barn's back, was clearly visible. He backed up until he was pressed against his fence, realizing that the drive into the yard could easily be seen by anyone standing within the shadow of the trees across the stream.

Those buckskin-clad lads could have watched him bring Hortense into the house. And, if they'd remained hidden in the shadows, they would have seen Bernadette and her brother come for Hortense. Rees gulped. They would know she'd left the farm and exactly where she was going: into Durham to her mother's house.

Despite his worry, and his desperate hurry, Rees did not get on the road to town for another hour. First he pocketed the few eggs Nancy had missed as he hastened across the snowy yard. He fetched the milk, already showing a grainy crust of freezing cream, and brought it inside. He fed the cow and her heifer just a few forkfuls of hay and left with a promise to give them more soon.

But most of all it was Rees's attempt to explain to Lydia why he had to drive into town again that slowed him down. She seemed unaccountably reluctant to understand. 'You didn't see them, the boys I mean, did you?' she asked, laying one hand upon his arm. 'They may not have seen Hortense leave.'

'I have to warn her,' he said, staring intently into his wife's face. 'I don't believe Bernadette or Rouge understand the danger that girl is in.'

'But Mr Rouge is the constable,' Lydia objected. 'I'm certain they will not be so foolish as to approach his niece. Especially with him so close by – next door in fact.'

'They didn't hesitate to come on this property,' Rees said in a grim tone. 'I suspect they are too desperate to take the girl to hesitate.'

'You know Bernadette won't speak to you,' Lydia said, trying another tack. 'Not now. She is too afraid of you harming her child to listen to any warnings you might give.'

'I have to try,' he said. Grasping her upper arms, he drew her into his embrace. 'I will never forgive myself if I don't make the attempt to warn Bernadette and something happens to Hortense. Besides, those young ruffians need to be caught. What if they come after Jerusha again?' He felt Lydia nod against his cheek. When she drew away, her eyes were wide.

'You're right. And Jerusha is already frightened; more frightened than she is allowing herself to recognize. I will not be surprised if she experiences nightmares for a time.'

Rees swallowed. Sometimes he still had nightmares from that summer a year ago. It wasn't just that he'd been accused of murder or Lydia of witchcraft; that had been terrible enough. But the reactions of friends and others – the betrayals by people he'd known all his life had caused him to vow he would never return to his hometown. The betrayals still ached, an open wound that Rees feared would never heal. He would not fail his daughter.

'We have to insure Jerusha's safety,' he said. 'We can't allow those young men to threaten her again.'

Lydia nodded. 'Yes, I see. You must go,' she said.

Rees changed from his threadbare cloak to his greatcoat and from his old boots to his shoes. As he approached the door, Lydia said, 'Will you collect the children from school?'

He turned with a nod. 'Of course.' Neither he nor Lydia voiced their fears. Rees wished again that Simon had remained here, under his protection. Why, anything might happen with Rees too far away to help.

Rouge, planted in his usual position behind the bar, greeted Rees with a raised eyebrow. 'What do you want?'

'I need to warn your sister. Hortense is still in danger.'

'She won't talk to you.' Rouge put his hands flat on the wooden plank and leaned across it. 'She says you put your hands on the girl.'

'Listen,' Rees said. 'Your niece knows more about her abduction than she's willing to tell. Two young men accosted Jerusha while she was collecting eggs. They wore buckskin and moccasins, exactly like the tracks I found in North Road where Hortense was taken.' Rouge shrugged as though this was nothing important but he continued to hold himself still with total attention. 'I followed them through the forest, until I lost the trail. It went up the side of Gray

Hill. Rouge,' Rees said, leaning forward with the intensity of his emotion, 'I think they are trying to take Hortense back.'

'But she is not at your farm anymore,' Rouge objected.

'No. That's what I need to tell Bernadette,' Rees said. 'Those men waited under the trees; I know that. They could have watched you taking Hortense away. If so, they will know where she is. Bernadette needs to be alert; they may come after her daughter at *her* house.'

'You don't know that for sure,' Rouge said but his forehead puckered.

Rees said, 'Do you want to take that chance?' Rouge met Rees's gaze and then dropped his eyes.

'No. No I don't.' He took off his apron and dropped it on the floor. 'Therese,' he shouted over his shoulder. When the girl appeared in the kitchen door, Rees spared her only an initial glance. She wouldn't last here; Rouge was a difficult master and hired and fired barmaids more often than he changed his shirt. The skinny blond looked at Rouge, her face creased with alarm. Was the hand that she rested on the doorframe trembling? Rouge spoke quickly in French. To Rees's surprise, the constable's tone was softer than the one he usually employed with the girls. After listening for a few seconds, she disappeared behind the door.

'She is fetching her brother,' Rouge explained. And then, in case Rees might be wondering, he added, 'They are my cousins.'

'Are they French?' Rees asked. Since the XYZ Affair earlier this spring, especially the widely reported rudeness of the officials in France to American envoys and Tallyrand's demands for significant bribes, the French were roundly despised. Not that some of the Americans were any better, according to the newspaper. More French than American; their economic interests and dissipated morals were allied with the Directorie.

'No. From Quebec.' Rouge glanced at Rees. 'But too many people here don't know the difference.' Rees nodded silently. Like Rouge, his cousins would be Catholic and as foreigners besides they would be suspect. 'I would prefer Therese take the bar – she receives less nasty comment – but Thomas's English is better,' Rouge added.

Therese reappeared at the door. A young man, taller than the girl and with darker hair, appeared behind her. They nodded in agreement to Rouge's flood of instruction. Thomas came out to the bar and picked up Rouge's apron. He tied it on as Rouge came around and joined Rees at the front.

'Let's go,' he said, moving so fast through the front door that Rees had to take several long strides to catch up. He was very glad to know they would be walking around instead of scaling the fence as Rouge preferred. 'Emigrees,' Rouge explained.

'What?' Rees said.

'Emigrees.' Rouge gestured to the tavern behind them. 'My cousins. They've moved here.'

'Do they speak English?' Rees asked. Although he understood some French, as did many of the residents in this District of Maine, he was not fluent.

'Yes. Mostly. He does more than her.' Rouge shrugged. 'No one in town wants to work for me anymore. I had to search farther afield.'

Rees managed to keep silent but he couldn't help his mocking grin. Rouge's bad-tempered behavior with his help was a town scandal. Of course no one wanted to work for him, or allow his daughters and sons to work for him either. And Rees expected Rouge would learn nothing from this and would continue as before when Therese and her brother went on their way.

'What?' Rouge asked. But his lopsided grin told Rees the constable knew.

'Have you gone back to Gray Hill?' Rees inquired. 'Asked questions? So we can discover the men behind Hortense's abduction.'

'No. I've been busy. And tomorrow is Friday,' Rouge said. 'I doubt I'll have time until next week.'

'I think—' Rees began.

'No point,' Rouge interrupted. 'Hortense is home.'

'You're a fool if you think she's safe,' Rees said. He grabbed Rouge's arm and pulled him to a stop. 'What's to prevent those young brutes from trying to take Hortense out of Bernadette's house? Besides, as the constable, you should be thinking of the other young girls in this town. Do you want one of them to be abducted in Hortense's place? Let me assure you, if Jerusha is taken I will blame you.'

Rouge wrenched his arm away and leveled a furious glare at Rees. 'For one sou I'd leave you out here in the street,' he said.

He stamped up to Bernadette's scuffed porch. Despite Rouge's temper, Rees followed on his heels. 'Wait out here until I speak with my sister,' Rouge said in clipped tones. He pounded on the door. Bernadette opened it, saw Rees, and tried to slam the door in her brother's face. 'Wait,' Rouge said, 'hear me out.' Motioning with his forefinger, a gesture intended to caution Rees to keep his mouth shut and wait, Rouge went inside. Almost immediately raised voices penetrated the thin wood to the street outside. Rees did not speak French well enough to understand what they were saying but he heard his name several times. Deciding he did not want to hear whatever insults Bernadette chose to throw his way, he went down the steps and began walking up and down the street. Finally the door opened and Rouge whistled. When Rees turned Rouge waved at him and called, 'Rees. Come in.'

Rees hurried back to the dilapidated porch. Rouge, holding open the front door, gestured the other man inside.

Bernadette stood in front of the fire with her arms folded. 'My brother says I should listen to you,' she said. It sounded like the words hurt her as they passed through her tightly pinched lips.

'Where's Hortense?' Rees asked.

'In her bedchamber.' With fierce narrowed eyes, Bernadette stared at Rees.

He took in a deep breath and started talking, repeating what he had told Simon Rouge. Bernadette did not interrupt but her posture did not change either. When he finished, knowing he had not persuaded her, she said, 'So you don't know if they did see her.'

'True, I don't,' Rees said. 'But those young villains have shown they will not give up. I think we should plan for the worst.'

Although Bernadette's arms did not relax, she glanced at Rouge. He nodded. Turning to Rees, Rouge said, 'We will think of something to protect her. Just in case. Although I truly doubt anyone will come after her in my town.'

With that, Rees had to be satisfied.

NINE

The two men returned to the tavern in silence. As they neared the door, Rouge said with elaborate casualness, 'We can drive up to Gray Hill today, if you've a mind. And tomorrow, if you think it necessary.'

'I thought you would be too busy,' Rees said, realizing his fears for Hortense had had some effect.

'Thomas can tend the inn for me,' Rouge said. 'I daresay he is less likely to steal from me than most.'

'Hmmm.' Rees directed a mocking smile at the constable. 'I expect searching for these young villains will take longer than a few hours. We have so little information.' He stopped short of reminding Rouge that Hortense had offered almost nothing that would simplify the search. His black brows drew together.

'If required,' he said grudgingly, 'perhaps I can spare a few hours tomorrow. But the day following is Saturday – Market Day – and I *will* be too busy.'

Rees glanced at the sky. It was not quite noon; several hours remained before he must fetch the children home from school. 'Today then,' he said.

Without comment, Rouge increased his speed and soon pulled ahead. But Rees could hear the other man muttering about 'people wanting to prevent an honest man from earning a living'.

They took Rees's wagon although Rouge protested. 'I wonder if you're going to get that vehicle up the mountain. The road is steep and torturously curved. And now, at this time of year, covered with snow. When are you going to get a saddle horse?'

Rees shrugged and didn't answer. Saddle horses were expensive and Hannibal hadn't been broken to either a saddle or a man on his back. Although he might attempt riding astride in a desperate situation, with his wagon he usually had little need to do so. He needed mules for plowing but if he purchased another horse he would do so for Lydia's cart.

* * *

By the time the two men reached the Bennett home, first outpost of human habitation, the sun was hanging over the eastern peaks. Rees guessed it was now past mid-morning. Bennett's small house lay so close to the main road that he could see the weathered gray wood through the leafless trees. A thin plume of smoke drifted from the chimney into the sky, scenting the cold air with the fragrance of burning wood.

Rouge turned into the snowy drive. Ruts left by iron-bound wagon wheels and horse hooves scarred the snow right down to the dirt. The wagon jolted over the uneven surface. As they approached the cabin, Mr Bennett stepped out onto his porch. When he recognized his visitors he lifted a hand in greeting and motioned them to come inside.

They stepped into a small hall with stairs rising to the second floor at the back. Doors opened into rooms, one on each side. Most of the family seemed to be located in the room to the left but Mrs Bennett, wiping her hands on a rag, came to the door on the right.

Lines bracketed her mouth and dark circles shadowed her eyes but there was not a trace of gray in her blond hair. Rees thought she was probably not as old as she appeared. She looked up at them curiously.

'We wanted to ask you about Hortense?' Rouge said, sounding unexpectedly pugnacious. Mrs Bennett stepped back and Mr Bennett's eyebrows rose.

'We're trying to pin down her movements and identify the men who took her,' Rees said, trying to temper the constable's tone.

Mrs Bennett's tight mouth softened. 'Yes, we heard what happened. Did you find her?'

'Yes—' Rees began with a nod but Rouge cut in at once.

'He did. She was running through the woods barefoot.'

'Oh my,' Mrs Bennett gasped, one hand clutching at her chest.

'Rees here believes those villains who took her are still searching for my niece.'

'They attacked my daughter, I think because they thought she was Hortense,' he explained.

Both Mr and Mrs Bennett exclaimed in dismay and Mrs Bennett gestured to the kitchen. 'Come inside.' Her husband threw a quick look at the other room, where the sound of children's voices could be clearly heard, and nodded.

Rees took off his boots and padded after the Bennetts in his stocking feet. Even with thick wool socks the cold seeped through the floorboards and made his toes tingle. But a blazing fire burned in the massive fireplace. He guessed its twin warmed the main room where it could share the chimney.

'Is Hortense all right?' asked Mr Bennett.

'Frightened,' Rouge replied. 'And she may lose a few toes to frostbite.'

'When did she leave here?' Rees asked.

Mr Bennett looked at his wife.

'Let's see,' she said. 'Hiram is now almost three weeks old. So she left us almost that long ago. Maybe two weeks?'

Rouge uttered a guttural sound of protest.

'When did she first come to you?' Rees asked.

'The morning I went into labor—'

'No, I meant when did you contract for her services?'

'Oh. In late September.' Mrs Bennett looked up at Rees. 'I met Bernadette at market and asked her if she would be willing to deliver the baby. It was a trip up here but I didn't want Granny Rose.'

'You didn't want Granny Rose?' Rees repeated, wondering at the definite tone in Mrs Bennett's voice.

'She is a distance away . . .' But Mrs Bennett did not look at him when she answered him and he knew there was more to that tale.

'Yes, yes, and my sister agreed,' Rouge said impatiently, unable to keep still any longer. 'Let's return to the matter at hand.'

'So Hortense came to see you in October?' Rees said, darting a glance at the constable. Although curious about Granny Rose, Rees, who saw no connection to Hortense's abduction, allowed the matter to drop.

'Both Miss Bernadette and her daughter came to examine me in early October. I believe they worked together when they could. Then Hortense came alone several times during October and the first part of November. It was Hortense who came when the pains started. That was fine. Hiram arrived without difficulty and—'

'What happened when Hortense left after the birth?' Rouge interrupted, looking at Mr Bennett.

Rees exhaled, holding on to his temper with difficulty. Birthing and babies were in a woman's domain and it was Mrs Bennett who would have the answers.

Mr Bennett shrugged. 'She climbed into her cart and drove away.' Rees, his gaze focused on Mrs Bennett, saw the quick tightening of her mouth. She knew something. 'I didn't know Hortense hadn't gotten back to town,' Mr Bennett continued, 'until I went to town for supplies. And that was at least a week later.'

'Almost two,' said Mrs Bennett.

'You didn't leave the farm until then?' Rouge asked Mr Bennett. As he shook his head Rees turned to Mrs Bennett.

'Did Hortense leave? Maybe for a walk? And was she gone far longer than you expected?'

'Of course not, not in the snow.' Mrs Bennett flicked a glance at Rouge. 'Would you like some refreshment? Coffee or tea?'

'They want something stronger than that,' Mr Bennett said. He moved to the table on the opposite side of the kitchen and the whiskey jug sitting on the table.

'Thank you,' Rouge said, joining the smaller man with alacrity. But Rees shook his head.

'Coffee would be fine,' he said, following Mrs Bennett to the hearth. Under cover of the male conversation at the back, he said, 'Did Hortense take walks in October and November when she visited you?'

'No,' said Mrs Bennett as she handed him a cup of inky liquid. Rees took a sip and choked on the bitter liquid. 'But,' she continued, 'Hortense did not always turn toward town when she left us.'

'She didn't?'

'No. She turned left. I saw her once, accidentally – I was looking through the window – and then I watched. She often turned left.'

'Left?'

'Yes. And before you ask me, I don't know where she went afterward. Maybe she had another mother to examine . . .'

Rees dissected her sentence with its careful wording. 'But you can guess where she went?'

'No. I have no idea.' Rees wanted to shake the story from her but with a great effort of will kept silent. Mrs Bennett chewed her lower lip in indecision. 'It's just that,' she said finally, 'well, I got the impression when she arrived to deliver Hiram that she was excited about something. Happy but scared too. It was just an impression. I was otherwise occupied,' she added with the ghost of a grin.

'Do we have any cake or biscuits we can serve our guests?' Mr Bennett said loudly from the table.

'Of course. My sister baked just yesterday,' Mrs Bennett said, moving to the crock on the counter. As she placed doughnuts on a plate, the thin wail of a newborn baby sounded through the small house and a moment later a younger woman appeared at the door. Although her hair was darker, she looked enough like Mrs Bennett for Rees to guess this was the younger sister. She held out the blanket-wrapped squalling bundle.

'I think he's hungry,' she said. Mrs Bennett accepted the infant and with an apologetic look all around she left the kitchen. Rees heard her footsteps whispering up the stairs.

'We should go,' Rees said.

Rouge scowled. 'I'm just beginning to warm up,' he said. He picked up the jug and took another swig.

'Sit down and have a drink,' Mr Bennett said with a gesture of invitation.

'I'd like to,' Rees lied, 'but we are short of time now.' He'd already gained the information he'd come for and anyway, with Mrs Bennett's departure, Rees knew he wasn't likely to learn anything more.

Rouge rose to his feet and said with ill grace, 'Yes, I suppose we should go.' He helped himself to another drink and drained it before following Rees from the kitchen.

TEN

At the end of the Bennett drive, the deeply rutted track went up the hill at almost a ninety-degree angle. Although some traffic had passed this way, there had been too little to tramp down the snow and it caught at the wheels, pulling the wagon back as Hannibal struggled to keep his footing.

The road veered away from cliff edges or rock walls in switchbacks and hairpin turns, adding to the challenging climb.

As Hannibal strained against the weight of the wagon, Rouge jumped down to walk alongside and lighten the load. Rees wished he could do the same. He hated to see the gelding puffing and blowing with effort.

Finally they reached a small plateau – and a few buildings – before the road continued on its upward trajectory. This tiny settlement comprised a general store and a tavern perched at the edge of an overhang. As the two men had climbed up, clouds had swept across the sky and the air had grown significantly colder. The stream at the back of the tavern was frozen and there was a lot more snow here too, at least a foot. When Rees turned in toward the shop he had to follow the tracks of vehicles and horses that had come before them so his wagon would not catch fast in the deep drifts.

A cluster of empty barrels lined up on the porch identified the store. Rees threw the horse blanket over Hannibal, whose head was wreathed in fog from his panting, and followed Rouge inside.

The aisles were packed with merchandise and sacks as well as whittled hoops and stacks of jugs. Rouge and Rees picked their way around the clutter to the man standing at the counter. Smoke from the fireplace with its poor draw drifted through the air. Rees began coughing.

The storekeeper stared at Rouge for a few seconds and then ejected a stream of tobacco juice to one side. Brown stains already coated the floor around him. 'What do you want, Constable?' His tone made the title 'constable' an epithet.

'Mr Morton,' Rouge said, his tone as harsh as Rees had ever heard it. 'My niece was kidnapped by someone up here.' Rees glanced from one man to the other, interpreting their rigid stances, like the raised hackles of growling dogs, as a bad history between them. 'What do you know about it?'

The storekeeper stiffened. 'Nothing. And why'd you suspect one of our boys, Frenchman?' he demanded angrily.

'Because she said she was taken up the hill by two boys, Jem and Jake.'

The storekeeper spit again and laughed. 'Plenty of boys up here called Jake and Jem.' But his gaze shifted sideways.

'You're a liar,' Rouge said. The shopkeeper took a few steps forward, limping, his hand tightening around his cane.

'Hortense wasn't hurt and she is back home with her family,' Rees said quickly.

'So why come up here then?' Morton asked.

'Because they came down to the valley looking for her a few times. And it sounds like she witnessed something. Maybe a murder. At the very least a fight.'

'I ain't heard of anything,' said the storekeeper. 'Far's I know, nobody been killed up here.'

'Listen,' Rouge said, stepping forward until he was nose to nose with the shopkeeper, 'you better help me or I'll drag you down off this hill and—'

'Help you? You ain't given me anything to help you with. Not even proper names.'

Since he spoke only the truth, neither Rouge nor Rees could think of anything to say for several seconds. The silence continued until it became awkward. The storekeeper grinned, displaying his rotting brown teeth.

'She's a midwife,' Rees said in desperation. 'Bernadette's daughter Hortense. She was called out to help Mrs Bennett.'

'Yeah, I know who she is,' Morton said. 'Don't matter. No one is going to talk to you.' His gaze turned to Rouge.

'My sister didn't want to come up here, to this Godforsaken place,' Rouge said angrily. He took in a deep breath as Rees put a hand on his arm.

'Would Granny Rose speak to us?' he asked, clutching at the only other name he knew.

'And why would she talk to you?' the shopkeeper demanded.

Rees could feel Rouge trembling with fury and said sharply, 'When the boys came down to the valley they attacked my eleven-year-old daughter.'

Morton did not speak for several seconds. His jaws pulsed as he ruminated. 'I ain't heard nothing,' he said finally. 'Not one word. But there's a lot of families living higher up.' He paused and Rees could see him wrestling with himself. 'It's winter. Snow's getting bad. I don't see everyone like I might during the summer. A lot of the men work in the lumber camps and I don't even see them in the tavern.' He jerked his head left, toward the ordinary on the other side of the store's wall. 'They don't bring me barrel hoops or maple syrup and won't until spring. Hides once in a while, that's all. You're best off, I suppose, talking to Granny Rose. She and that old mule of hers gets everywhere. She mighta heard something.'

'And where does Granny Rose live?' Rouge said in resignation.

'Oh, an hour or so away. Straight up.' The shopkeeper grinned with malicious enjoyment. 'Follow the road outside. Take the second left.'

Rees recalled his visit to Western Pennsylvania in 1793. These directions reminded him powerfully of the settlers and the few roads in the mountains around Pittsburgh.

'Thank you,' Rouge said. He did not sound grateful. 'Let's go.' Rees preceded the constable from the store, almost running to the fresh clean air outside.

In their time inside, the clouds had thickened and the sky looked like curdled milk. A few fat white flakes spun lazily from the sky. Rees looked east. He could see only forest, ranks of trees marching up to the sky. But he knew behind this steep incline were other peaks.

'Looks like more snow is coming,' Rouge said. Rees turned around. A bank of black clouds hung over the mountains to the west. He could not see the town of Durham far below; thick evergreens interspersed with the gray leafless branches of maples and oaks seemed to continue forever and they completely occluded the valley underneath.

'It might not make it this far east,' Rees said. He did not sound hopeful.

'I don't want to be caught up here in a storm,' Rouge said, meeting Rees's gaze. 'I didn't want to spend tomorrow up here but it looks as though we may have to return come daylight. Besides, it is growing late. The sun will set in a few hours.'

Rees nodded reluctantly. The District of Maine, especially here, lay so far east the day seemed to last only six or so hours. Night would come soon. Still, it seemed foolish to turn around and go home when they were already on Gray Hill. He looked up at the sky. Without the sun, it was impossible to guess the time and he had left his pocket watch at home. But his belly was growling, telling him it was long past dinner time. And he had to be at the school in time to collect Jerusha and her siblings. He thought of his daughter, or any young girl, being kidnapped away from their home and family, brought up to this isolated place, and shuddered. This was a foreign country here in the hills. He was accustomed to feeling like an outsider but Rouge, despite growing up not ten miles away, had not been welcomed with any civility either.

'You're cold anyway,' Rouge said, mistaking the cause of Rees's shiver. 'We'll return tomorrow.'

'We should leave first thing,' Rees said. 'I'll meet you in town as soon as possible after daybreak.' Rouge nodded as he hauled himself into the wagon seat but he was frowning. Rees knew the constable was unhappy to spend another day on what he thought was a fool's errand. But Rees thought Rouge was too confident of his niece's safety in town.

They started down the steep incline. Both men rode in the wagon to give it some weight. Even so, it rolled too fast, the wheels in danger of outpacing Hannibal. The gelding wanted to run faster and faster to escape the rattling vehicle behind him and Rees spent a difficult hour trying to hold the alarmed gelding in check. Finally, in an effort to slow them down before they careened off the mountain, as well as to rest his sore arms, he fell into a pattern of stopping every ten yards or so. It made for a jerky descent but at least he felt he maintained some control. And they descended at a reasonable pace.

On one of the stops he looked back. Although the forest surrounded them and the hamlet where they'd stopped was invisible, Rees could see through a cleft to the row of highlands behind this one. Like pointed teeth, some shorter, some taller, the peaks rose to the sky. From this vantage the white snow-covered tops became one with the clouds.

ELEVEN

Rees finished his chores early and was just sitting down for breakfast before driving into town when he heard hoof beats outside. Throwing a 'what now?' look at Lydia, he rose to his feet and went to the door. He thrust it open just as Rouge raised his fist to knock. Behind him Rees saw Bernadette and

Hortense, the latter muffled to the eyebrows in her light-gray cloak. Had he mistaken his agreement with the constable and planned to meet here?

'I'm not ready,' he began.

But Rouge held up a hand to stop the flow of words. 'Can we come in?' he asked. 'I need to talk to you.'

Rees stepped back from the door and motioned the three people in.

'What happened?' Lydia asked, moving forward to take the wraps.

Bernadette looked at Rees. 'I owe you an apology,' she said. Her eyes were red and puffy from recent tears. He turned an inquiring look on Rouge.

'Bernadette's house was broken into last night,' he said.

'They came through the front door,' Bernadette said in a thick voice. 'Into *my* house.'

'Oh my dear,' Lydia said, stretching out a hand to take Bernadette's. The midwife's lips began to tremble. She did not speak for a few seconds.

'I sleep lightly. I must. I am always ready to leave my bed on a moment's notice to attend a woman in labor. So I heard them. I lit a candle and started downstairs. They were just coming up the stairs, the two young ruffians.'

'What happened?' Lydia asked in a hushed voice.

'I threw my candle at them,' Bernadette said. She forced a smile. 'Of course it didn't do anything. The flame guttered out when the candleholder fell to the floor. I suppose I was fortunate I didn't set my house on fire.' She turned to Rees. 'I'm sorry, I didn't believe you.'

'Don't worry about that now,' he said, brushing the apology aside. 'Hortense?'

'Safe, thanks to you,' Bernadette said, her eyes filling with tears.

'After you warned us, we moved her to a room above the tavern,' Rouge said. 'I spent the night outside her door.'

'You left your sister alone?' Lydia asked, her voice rising in dismay.

'I sent Thomas to her,' Rouge said. 'He spent the night in my sister's house.'

'In Hortense's room at the top of the stairs,' Bernadette said.

'When he heard me screaming he came flying down the stairs with a butcher knife.' Bernadette uttered a shaky laugh. 'Those two villains fled when they saw him.'

Rees nodded and looked around. His children were within earshot and Jerusha at least was listening intently. 'Let's remove to the front room,' he suggested.

'I'm sure you are all cold and probably hungry,' Lydia said. 'May I offer you tea or coffee?' Her forehead puckered. 'Oh dear, I have only yesterday's cake.'

Rouge accepted cake but asked for ale. Both Hortense and her mother requested tea. While Lydia put the kettle over the fire and brought the cake from the pantry, Rees escorted their visitors into the front room. The air was much colder in here than the warm kitchen so he brought in a brand from the cooking fire and lit the kindling. By the time Lydia had carried in the hot tea, cups and both milk and sugar as well as plates for the cake, he had a small fire blazing on the hearth. He stirred it with the poker, trying to restrain himself from jumping into his questions.

When the guests were settled and everyone had cake and something to drink Rees could wait no more. Turning, he fixed a stern gaze upon Hortense. 'All right,' he said, 'time to confess all. What exactly happened to you? And why are these young men so determined to recapture you?'

A flood of color surged into Hortense's cheeks and then drained away, leaving her skin dead white. She threw a quick glance at her mother but Bernadette said nothing. Realizing no help would come from that quarter, Hortense lowered her eyes to her hands. When she looked up once again Rees saw that the girl was ready to talk. But, he thought cynically, she had taken enough time to decide what parts of the story she would tell.

'I was on my way home from Mrs Bennett's delivery,' Hortense began in a soft voice, 'when these two men came up behind me.'

'Did you know they were following you?' Rees asked.

'I heard hoof beats.' She paused, her eyes shifting back and forth as she thought. 'They followed me all the way down Gray Hill. Then, when I was on North Road, they came up beside me, one on each side, and told me to pull over. I-I tried to outrun them but I couldn't. Not in the cart. They made me drive into the ditch. I jumped out and tried to run.'

Rees thought back to his examination of the tracks. They did not entirely support her story but he guessed it was close enough. 'What happened after that?' he asked. 'Where did they take you?'

'Somewhere into the hills,' Hortense said. 'As I said previously, I don't know exactly. I didn't recognize anything.' She stopped and took a sip of tea. Her hand was trembling. Bernadette leaned forward and clasped her daughter's other hand.

'It's all right,' Bernadette said soothingly. 'Take your time.'

'You must know something,' Rees said, not troubling to hide his impatience.

'Why did they want you?'

'They wanted me to care for their mother,' Hortense said. 'She was . . . is ill.' She turned a wide-eyed stare upon Rees. 'We went to a cabin. That's all I know.'

And that is a lie, he thought, holding his tongue with an effort.

'They didn't – I mean no one interfered with you?' Bernadette whispered.

Hortense shook her head. 'No. I didn't see very much of anyone else except Mother Sally.' The innocent gaze went to Bernadette. 'I spent most of my time with her.'

And that is the second falsehood, Rees thought, bursting into speech without thinking before he spoke. 'You told me there was a lot of blood. Where did that blood come from?'

Tears flooded Hortense's eyes and began pouring down her cheeks. 'Jake and his father got into a fight. A terrible fight. Screaming at one another so loudly even Mother Sally left her bed. We peeked through the door. They were fighting, Jake and his father. He, the father, got Jake on the floor and was punching him. Jem tried to pull his father away but couldn't. And Jake reached out and grabbed the poker and hit his father with all his strength. Oh, the blood! I thought Jake had killed him.'

A moment of shocked silence followed her account. This part of the tale, Rees thought, was probably mostly true.

'And that's when you ran?' Bernadette put her arms around Hortense's shoulders. 'Oh my dear.'

'Yes,' Hortense said, looking at her mother in eager relief. 'I knew I had to escape. They'd taken my shoes and my cloak to keep me there. But I knew I had no choice. I had to leave.'

'How soon after the fight did you flee?' Rees asked. He heard something off in her voice but didn't think everything she'd said was untrue. He just couldn't guess which part of her last few statements was false.

'Immediately, of course,' Hortense said.

And that, he decided, was the third lie.

'What does that matter now?' Bernadette said loudly. 'Those savages are coming after her. We must hide her. And stop them.' She glared at Rees as if he were to blame.

'She can't stay here,' Lydia said, moving forward. 'She can't. My daughter has already been attacked in Hortense's stead. I won't put Jerusha and my other children in danger. Not even for you, Bernadette, and your daughter.'

Bernadette met Lydia's gaze. Rees did not speak; he knew he did not have to. Lydia would not yield where the safety of her children was at stake. Finally Bernadette nodded. 'I understand,' she said, holding out her hands pleadingly. 'But it would be just for a little while. I thought I would send Hortense to my relatives in Quebec. They will make sure she marries someone more appropriate. She may return for a visit when you—' and she switched her gaze to Rees – 'discover the identity of those brutes behind this attack upon my daughter.'

Rees looked at Lydia. 'Let me speak to Brother Jonathan. Perhaps the Shakers will allow her to stay in Zion for a few days.'

'I'll go with you,' Rouge said, rising to his feet.

'No,' Rees said firmly, turning to frown at the constable. 'I want you to stay here and protect my family. Just in case those boys return.'

'You want me to stay with the women and children?' Rouge's voice rose in dismay.

'Unless you wish to speak to Brother Jonathan,' Rees said, turning to stare at the other man. Rouge lowered his eyes and shook his head. 'I don't want to see my wife and children put at risk,' Rees added. He did not say 'for Hortense' but that was what he meant.

'Very well,' Rouge muttered.

With the matter settled, Rees put on his greatcoat and went outside. It was colder today and yesterday's flurries had left a dusting of fresh snow on the ground. But it was still warmer than it would be; it would be far far colder in January and February.

He looked at the sky. Although it was overcast he did not think they would see more snow. He briefly considered walking to Zion, something he had done a few times in the fall, but decided against it. He did not want to be caught outside if the weather turned. So he hitched Hannibal to his wagon. Yes, if he and his family stayed here he should consider purchasing another horse. Not a saddle horse as Rouge suggested – that would be an expensive luxury – but a plow horse that Lydia could also use with another vehicle. Or a mule. As he led Hannibal from the barn, Rees paused and looked all around, paying particular attention to the snowy ravine beneath the trees. He saw nothing. Of course those boys could be hiding, far enough back so as to be invisible, but he felt cautiously optimistic that they had been finally scared away by Thomas and his butcher knife.

TWELVE

Rees found Brother Jonathan in the woodshop. Although the Shaker Brother was a talented carpenter, today he was sanding broom handles. A sheaf of finished poles, white and smooth, leaned against the wall. Jonathan looked bored; broom handles did not utilize his skills at all, but the sale of these Shaker brooms were a big part of Zion's income. Several young men, barely into their teens by the look of them, were attaching straw to the handles with a large wooden contrivance. Everyone worked in that total silence that Rees found so unnatural.

'May I have a word?' he asked the Elder. Jonathan looked at his unexpected visitor and stepped back from the lathe.

Rees had met Jonathan for the first time a year ago September. After the murders that had taken place in this community and the added responsibility that had come with Jonathan's promotion to Elder, he had grown gray. He looked much older now and careworn.

'In private,' Rees added.

Jonathan shook his head. 'Not another terrible crisis,' he said, sounding resigned and alarmed both.

'I hope not,' Rees said.

Jonathan looked at the lads. 'I know the Sisters in the kitchen will offer you something to eat. We'll begin again after our noon dinner.'

The young men, although they looked surprised, wasted no time hurrying from the shop. Jonathan turned his wary gaze upon Rees. 'What do you want?'

'The girl we were searching for in the woods? You know I found her. She needs a place to stay. Just for a short time.' Rees launched into the tale. At first he minimized the role played by the two young men and avoided mentioning the attack on Jerusha altogether. But when he paused and Jonathan began to nod, Rees felt guilty. This community had already seen its share of tragedy. The murders last year had left lasting scars. He didn't know if the Shakers here would ever recover. 'Before you answer,' he said, blurting into speech, 'there's something else you should know. The men who kidnapped Hortense are searching for her. They attacked Jerusha, mistaking my daughter for the midwife's girl. And when Bernadette took Hortense home, the villains followed her there and broke into Bernadette's house. Fortunately, the constable had already removed his niece to the tavern for safety.'

Jonathan picked up the broom handle and ran his hands over it. Frowning, he inspected it closely. The sanded finish did not meet his standards and after several seconds of disapproving examination he put it back down again. 'So,' he said, 'in the interest of keeping the midwife's daughter safe, you suggest endangering my Family.'

'I would not have described it in those terms,' Rees said, staring at the floor in shame. 'But put like that . . .' He supposed Jonathan was correct. 'I just thought that garbed as the Sisters are and traveling in a group, Hortense would be as safe as she could be. Certainly a stranger coming into Zion to search for her would be easily identifiable.'

'But if those ruffians entered Zion we would not be able to protect her,' Jonathan pointed out. 'We are not armed. We do not own weapons and we would not use them if we did.'

Rees bowed his head in silent agreement. For a moment they stood in silence, Rees cudgeling his brain for another place that might serve as a refuge for Hortense.

'How long would that young woman remain with us?' the Elder asked.

'Only a few days I believe,' Rees replied, a tiny flame of hope springing to life within him. 'Perhaps until Monday or Tuesday. Her mother is planning to remove the girl to relatives in Canada.' Jonathan stared unseeingly over Rees's head for several seconds.

'We know Hortense,' Jonathan said. 'Well, we met both her and her mother during Lydia's travail, when Sharon was born.'

'Do you have to ask the other Elders?' Rees asked, trying to keep the eagerness from his voice.

Jonathan offered Rees a sour smile. 'Both Esther and Daniel – you know that he moved from Deacon and caretaker of the boys to Elder? – would choose to do this for you. Both of them feel such gratitude for your assistance last year. Only the other Eldress, would hesitate.'

'I'm sorry,' Rees said, understanding that Jonathan felt he'd been put in an untenable position.

'All right, we'll do it,' he said. 'But you must bring her here as secretively as possible. I do not want to put my Family's safety at risk.'

'Of course,' Rees said. 'Maybe tonight, after nightfall?'

'It will be dark before suppertime. If you come when everyone is at their evening meal, the community will be in the Dining Hall and unaware of her arrival. By the following morning she will be seen simply as a new member.'

'That sounds like an excellent plan,' Rees agreed.

'I'll speak to Sister Esther,' Jonathan said. 'I'm certain she will wish to help. And of course she will assign work to the girl. While she remains here, Hortense must live as we do, no matter how few the days.'

'Thank you,' Rees said. 'Thank you. I'm certain Hortense will agree.' Turning, he hurried out of the shop. He knew Bernadette would wish to hear this news as soon as possible.

Rees pressed Rouge to follow the original plan and go back up Gray Hill, this time to question Granny Rose. But he would not hear of it. He was too frightened for Hortense's safety. It was all Rees could do to persuade the other man to return to town and

take up his post in the tavern. Rees had to promise he would
protect Hortense and insure her well-being.

He would have done so more readily if he'd been able to
question the girl again. But Bernadette stayed behind and watched
her daughter as closely as a mother bear with a cub. Every time
he even approached Hortense, Bernadette rose to her feet and put
her hands on her hips, prepared to do battle. If his children had
gone to school he might have confronted the midwife and her
daughter anyway. But Lydia, nervous about their safety, had chosen
to keep them home today. So Rees, reluctantly, withdrew from the
front room and tried to satisfy himself with regular circuits
around the farm.

Rouge arrived just as dusk began to creep over the farm. When
the darkness was absolute Bernadette hustled Hortense out to
Rees's wagon. She lay down on the wooden boards, out of sight
of anyone riding past. Rees covered her with a blanket before
driving through the gate to the lane. Although the full moon had
not risen yet, the silvery disc hanging just above the horizon
emitted enough light for him to see his way to Surry Road. He
turned right, toward Zion.

As he pulled into the road, Rees looked all around but saw no
lights. Unless those boys had eyes like cats, they would need at
least one lantern. He began to think this subterfuge might work
and Hortense would be safe within Zion.

Rouge and his sister followed in their cart.

Jonathan and Esther waited within the lighted doorway of the
Dining Hall. When Esther heard them she moved into the road
with her lantern held high. Rees stopped and, jumping down, went
to the back for the girl. She sat up, straw sticking out from her
hair, and turned a wide-eyed look upon him.

'You'll be safe here,' he said. Leaning forward he added in a
whisper, 'You might consider telling the truth, the whole truth,
not just the parts you wish to confess. Capturing those boys is the
only thing that will keep you safe.' Hortense glared at him and
scooted over the rough wood to the back. When she dropped to
the ground she hurled the blanket at him as though it was thick
with fleas.

Bernadette's sobbing sounded clearly through the gloom as they
came up behind the wagon. She climbed down and ran to her

daughter. Clutching Hortense tightly in her arms, Bernadette said, 'We will come for you in a few days, just as soon as we have set the arrangements for your journey.'

'Really, Bernie, what is the cause of these tears?' Rouge said with assumed impatience. 'She'll be scarcely fifteen miles from home.' But Rees saw the furtive swipe Rouge gave his eyes.

'What if something happens?' Bernadette said with a sniffle. 'I won't be here.'

'The more quickly you arrange to spirit her away to Quebec, the sooner she will be safe,' Jonathan said in an austere voice.

Bernadette turned. 'You can't possibly understand,' she said in shaky tearful voice. 'You are not a mother. And Hortense is all I have.'

'We'll make sure nothing happens to her,' Esther said, wrapping her arm around Bernadette's shoulders and urging her toward the Dwelling House. In the candlelight, Hortense's pale-gray cloak appeared white. As the two women disappeared up the steps and through the women's door, Bernadette uttered a sob.

Rees turned to Jonathan. 'Thank you. And please, extend my gratitude to Esther as well.'

Jonathan nodded without speaking and turned to the Dining Hall.

'I will let you know everything that happens,' Rouge said as he handed his sister into the buggy.

Bernadette turned a pale mournful face in Rees's direction. 'Thank you for all you did,' she said.

He nodded. 'I have daughters also,' he said. Having daughters changed a man; the world suddenly seemed a much scarier place. Children were so vulnerable and daughters even more so. Remembering how he felt when he saw the two men standing over Jerusha, he shivered.

'I hope they will be safe now and forever,' Bernadette said, nodding at him. 'I never thought something like this would happen.' Rouge climbed into the seat beside her.

'Good night,' Rees said, tipping his hat. He wondered if she remembered the September Sharon had arrived into the world, when Bernadette had told him that no one would interfere with her or her daughter. She'd been so certain. And, as it proved, so wrong.

Rouge flicked the whip over the horse's withers and the buggy began to turn. Rees walked back to his wagon. Jonathan had gone into the Dining Hall. Through the opened door the aroma of roast chicken seeped through the street. Rees's mouth began to water and he was suddenly very eager to go home to his own supper.

He did not light the lanterns that hung on each side of the wagon until he reached the turn-off to town. He climbed down and struggled for a minute or so with his tinderbox before he achieved a flame. Then he continued on his way home feeling that he'd accomplished a very good deed. But he could not help but hope he'd seen the last of Hortense.

THIRTEEN

When Rees took Lydia to market the following day, he visited the tavern and tried to persuade Rouge to join him on a journey up Gray Hill. But the tavern keeper, too busy to stand still, refused. 'Monday,' he said as Rees trailed after him through the crowded room. Frustrated, he left the ordinary and returned to market. Lydia was already finished although her basket was only half full. The scanty offerings from the local farmers had not appealed. But he saw some colorful ribbons and a few wooden toys in her basket. 'Christmas is coming,' she said in response to his inquiring look. 'I want something for the children.' She meant other than the mittens and scarves she had been knitting after the children had gone to bed. Rees nodded but sighed, thinking again of David and Simon. He was so afraid they would not make it here for Christmas.

He turned Hannibal toward home. Besides farm chores, which never seemed to end, he hoped he would have time to sit down at the loom with Jerusha today.

Sunday was Rees's least favorite day of the week. Church services took most of the day and Lydia insisted they attend, saying she did not want to see the children grow up as savages. But he knew she was remembering the events in Dugard where Lydia had been accused of witchcraft. One of the pieces of evidence against her was the failure of the family to attend regular Sunday services. Rees wasn't sure the effort would have helped in his hometown; the degree of malice was so great, but here in Durham he acceded to Lydia's wishes. He knew he wasn't the only one suffering from the after-effects – the terror and determination to prevent it ever happening again – from the final summer in Dugard.

Although Sunday was the Sabbath, it still began with chores. Rees carried his rifle outside when Nancy went to collect eggs and he stood and watched over Jerusha as she carried water into the house. Then he went to milk Daisy and throw down some hay into her stall. With this warm weather, warm for December anyway, Daisy and her little heifer could be released to graze but there was no time before church. Anyway, he preferred his few cattle safe within the barn. And he could not resist walking around the yard, paying particular attention to the area beneath the pines, just in case those young villains had returned.

He saw no sign the young men had come back to his farm. But when the family returned in late afternoon from services, an unfamiliar buggy was pulled up to the gate.

Heart thudding like a hammer, Rees scrambled out of the wagon seat, almost falling in his haste, and threw open the gate. It was Brothers Jonathan and Daniel. Rees's heart sank. Fearing the worst, Rees hurriedly unhitched Hannibal and released him into the paddock before following his family and their visitors into the kitchen.

Jonathan was frowning – well, that wasn't uncommon for him, but Daniel's mouth was tightened into a thin line. His reddened eyes sent Rees's stomach into a sickening spin.

'What happened?' he asked. 'Why are you here on a Sunday when you should be attending services?'

'Rees,' Jonathan said, turning, 'we've been waiting for you.'

Rees knew they brought bad news; he could feel it in his very bones. Staring at them in apprehension, he swallowed, unable even to speak.

'There's been a murder,' Daniel said, so pale even his lips were gray. Younger than Rees by a decade or more, he'd lived in Zion since boyhood. Apprenticed to the Shakers at the tender age of eight when his parents couldn't care for him, he'd grown up within their shelter. He'd signed the Covenant as soon as he could and never left.

'Water?' Lydia asked him, moving forward with a hand outstretched as though she would catch him if he fell. Daniel shook his head but when Lydia pulled over a chair he sank into it and put his face in his hands.

Rees turned his gaze to Jonathan who was staring at Rees with a mixture of anger and accusation. 'A Sister,' Jonathan said.

'Not Hortense,' Lydia said in a trembling voice.

'No.' Jonathan did not remove his wrathful gaze from Rees. 'But most likely in mistake for Hortense.'

'Oh God, I am sorry,' he said, his voice so hoarse and shaky he sounded like a different person. He tottered over to the table on weak legs and leaned upon it.

'Some Sisters saw the murderer,' Jonathan said. 'You must catch the man.' He did not say, "because this is all your fault", but Rees heard it just the same.

'And Hortense must be removed,' Daniel said. 'She is putting other lives, the lives of our Sisters, in danger.'

'Of course.' Rees half-nodded. 'I'll speak to Rouge. But I must see the body first.' He turned to look at Lydia. One hand was pressed to her mouth and the eyes that stared at her husband over it were big and dark with fear.

'Jerusha,' she said faintly. 'This could have been her.'

He nodded, feeling the gorge rise up into his throat. 'Let's go examine the body now,' he said. He needed to do something so he wouldn't fall into an agony of blame and self-recrimination. 'We need to go right now. And I want to talk to the Sisters who saw the attack.'

'They are all much distressed,' Jonathan said in a wintery voice. Rees knew that he was blamed for that as well. 'I don't know if they will be able to speak to you this evening. And anyway, you must do so with a chaperone.' His gaze moved to Lydia. She nodded without speaking.

If the situation had not been so terrible Rees would have smiled at her. They had met in exactly this way when he'd visited Zion the very first time. His son David had run away from his aunt and uncle. Rees, returning home from an extended weaving trip, had followed. He had been the first one accused of the murder of a young Sister. A farmer, in whose barn he had slept the night, spoke for him and as soon as he was released he'd begun searching for the real killer. Lydia had chaperoned him then as he questioned the Sisters. As she would now. Some of the tension went out of her shoulders and although she did not smile Rees knew she too recalled those first days.

'I'll go and examine the victim's body now,' he said. He did not want Lydia to see it; what if it was as horrifying as Mac's body had been last year in Dugard? Mac had been tortured and left hanging in the mill. Rees still had nightmares.

'It'll be dark soon,' she said, glancing through the small kitchen window.

Rees nodded, his forehead wrinkling. Dark came early in this district's winter. He would carry a lantern with him so he would have light on his way home. There would be no time to fetch Rouge today. 'Tomorrow, after I speak to the constable, I'll come home for you. We'll question the Sisters together in the morning.'

Lydia smiled. 'I'll bring the babies with me,' she said, throwing a quick glance behind her at Joseph and Sharon. 'But we must return before school ends. I don't want the children to walk home . . .' Her voice trailed away and she bit her lip.

Rees reached out to lay his hand upon her wrist. He understood; he too felt a quiver of fear at the thought of his vulnerable children and these villains on the loose.

'The murder may have nothing at all to do with Hortense,' he said. But not even he believed that.

Removed to the barn, the body lay on the hay-strewn floor, illuminated by two lanterns. The pale-gray cloak was indeed Hortense's and in the flickering candlelight from the lantern the cloth seemed to shiver and move. Rees closed his eyes and swallowed.

Once he'd calmed his rebellious stomach, he stared down at the body again. He could see nothing of the woman's face, someone had thrown a fold of the cloak across her so it was all too easy to imagine the body as belonging to the midwife's daughter. He saw the dark hair with some disquiet; it was close enough to Hortense's shade to be mistaken for the girl's hair. He knelt and gently pulled the cloak away from the victim's head, letting out his breath in a gust of relief. He had feared this would be a murder of a young girl, but the white face that stared blindly at the loft was of an older woman. Gaunt, her cheeks sunken in over missing teeth, she looked quite elderly. But her unwrinkled skin told another story, of a young woman no older than her thirties, and a rough life on the road.

The combination of the cloak and the dark hair was enough to persuade Rees that this woman had indeed been murdered in mistake for Hortense.

He pulled down the cloak a little further to reveal deep bruising around the woman's throat. By large hands too; he could easily see black finger marks from two hands meeting in the front of the woman's skinny throat. Over them was a thumb mark. When he lifted one of her eyelids he saw the red speckling that came from asphyxiation.

'You see?' said Jonathan. Although he spoke in a low voice, Rees could hear the quiver of anger underneath. 'This is my fault. This is what comes of allowing congress with the World.'

'But why – what I don't understand is this,' Rees said, turning his gaze back to the body. 'It looks as though the murderer stood behind her to strangle her. But then he moved around. For the coup de grace, I guess. So, he might not have seen her face at first. But when he went in front of her he would have seen her and known this was not Hortense. Why then, did he kill her?' Rees chewed his thumbnail as he thought. Had those two young villains both been involved? Or had the murderer known this woman and he was entirely mistaken about the reasons behind this woman's death?

'Does that matter? Our Sister is dead.' Jonathan's voice cracked.

'When did this happen?' Rees asked.

'Don't know exactly. A few hours ago. There was still enough light in the sky to see by,' Jonathan said. He rubbed his hand wearily over his eyes. 'The Sisters who witnessed this . . . this wickedness were on their way to the kitchen to prepare supper.'

'Did the murderer see them?' Rees asked, jumping to his feet in sudden agitation.

Jonathan, instantly understanding Rees's fear, licked his lips and nodded. 'Maybe,' he said. 'I hope not.' He threw a look behind him as though the Sisters were waiting there. 'We will have to ask them. I sincerely hope not; the consequences do not bear thinking of.'

Rees nodded in agreement. If the Sisters saw the murderer, then he most likely saw them as well and their lives would be in danger. He could only hope that in their identical dresses and square linen caps they appeared indistinguishable from all the other Sisters in Zion.

'You must take the girl.' Jonathan burst into speech. 'You must remove Hortense from our community now, before some other terrible deed occurs.' Turning, he gestured at one of the Brothers standing a few feet away. 'Ask Sister Esther to bring the girl here. Rees must take her with him when he goes.' He glanced at Rees and quickly looked away. 'You may leave our Sister—' and he gestured to the body on the barn floor – 'here. Although she was not a member of our Family for very long, she signed the Covenant when she joined. We will return her soul to Mother.'

'I'll speak to Constable Rouge,' Rees said. 'I'm sorry. I know you would prefer he not come here. But he'll want to view the body.'

Jonathan's lips stretched into a parody of a smile. 'I should think that, since Hortense is his niece, other concerns might absorb his attention. Surely the identification of the villain who murdered this poor woman must take precedence – especially if she was mistaken for Hortense. But, of course, if he arrives before we bury our Sister, he may look at her.'

He swiveled his head to look over his shoulder and Rees followed Jonathan's gaze. Esther and Hortense were approaching. The girl was now wrapped in a navy-blue cloak. She tried to remove her outerwear and hand it to the Sister. Esther shook her head.

'Keep it. You will not want your cloak returned to you,' she said.

Hortense nodded. Recent tears had left her eyes puffy and red and Rees could see that the white hands that clutched the edges of the cloak were trembling. The murder of the innocent Sister had frightened Hortense more than the other incidents and Rees thought she might be willing to answer his questions truthfully now.

He turned his gaze to the body lying on the ground, trying to fix the image in his mind. Then he looked up at Brother Jonathan.

'I'll return tomorrow with my wife to question the girls who found the body,' he said. The Elder nodded without speaking. Rees walked forward and, taking Hortense by the elbow, drew her toward his wagon. He could feel her shaking beneath the cloak's fabric. He pushed her into the wagon seat, as much from a determination to ensure she didn't run as from courtesy, and climbed up beside her.

'How did that woman come to have your cloak?' he asked as the wagon jerked into motion.

'I gave it to her. I felt sorry for her. Her life had been a hard one: widowed young and all her babies dead. When she admired it, I offered it to her.'

'I see,' Rees said. Hortense's generous impulse had saved her life. 'What happened to you on Gray Hill?' he asked in a much sterner voice.

'I told you already.'

'You confessed part of the tale. It is past time for you to tell the entire truth,' he said in a rough voice. 'That woman is dead, probably in mistake for you. I want to know everything, including the bits you've been keeping back.'

'I told you everything,' Hortense said in a shaky voice.

'No, you haven't,' Rees said. 'Those boys are determined to recapture you. I want to know why.' Hortense began to weep, her sobs clearly audible. He hardened his heart. 'Do you want the murder of another woman on your conscience?' he asked curtly.

'No. No, I don't,' she said, sniffling. 'But—'

'What is frightening you?' he asked. 'Did those boys threaten you?'

'Not them, no.'

'Then who?'

Hortense shook her head, twisting her hands together in her lap. 'You don't understand,' she said so softly Rees could scarcely hear her.

'Try me,' he said.

'Jake and I, we . . .' She bowed her head. 'He was kind to me.'

Although Rees wanted to jump in with his guesses, with a great effort of will he restrained himself.

'I understand,' he said. And he did. A young woman and a young man, the same age, thrown together under difficult circumstances, of course affection would bloom. Just imagining his innocent daughter in a similar situation made him shudder. 'So you and Jake formed an attachment?' Hortense nodded. 'And that is the reason he has been tracking you all over town?'

'Jake and I were going to run away together.' She looked at Rees and began speaking very fast and vehemently. 'He did not kill that woman. I promise you that. Jake would never ever hurt anyone. He is too kind and gentle.' Rees did not respond. It was clear to him that Hortense reciprocated Jake's feelings. Her opinion of the lad, therefore, could not be trusted. Somehow he would have to find Jake and question him.

'Does your mother know?' Of course she didn't. That explained Hortense's reluctance to answer questions.

'No.' Hortense tried to smile. 'She has higher aspirations for me than a boy like Jake. He is from the mountains and, besides, is neither French nor Catholic.' A wave of sympathy for Bernadette swept over Rees. He would not want an illiterate hill boy for his daughters either.

'I'm guessing,' he said, his thoughts moving forward, 'that Jake's father did not approve either and that was the reason for the fight.'

As color surged into the girl's cheeks, she dropped her eyes to her lap. 'Yes,' she said so faintly Rees could hardly hear her. He turned a glare upon her.

'Stop lying,' he said angrily. 'Stop it. The truth, now.'

Hortense began weeping harder. Shaking her head, she refused to speak again. Rees realized he still did not have the entire story and was so frustrated he wanted to shake the truth from her. But he understood that would not work; she would only resist more determinedly. So, instead, he tried to be content with the few morsels she had given him.

FOURTEEN

Since the evening was well advanced – supper was over – and it was far too dark to drive into town, Hortense spent the night in the front room. Rees's acute awareness of her presence and the danger it presented to his family made for a restless night. He finally gave up trying to sleep and crawled out of bed despite the early hour.

With dawn a few hours away, the house was very dark. He tiptoed down the stairs without a candle, hoping to keep from waking Lydia. But his efforts were in vain and she soon followed him to the kitchen. 'The sooner you bring that girl to her mother, the better,' she said. 'Leave as soon as you are able. I'll milk Daisy for you.'

'No need,' he said, putting his hand on her shoulder as he looked into her upturned face. 'I'll leave Hortense with Rouge and return home immediately. I want to be here to drive the children to school. Not that I believe anything will happen,' he added quickly, 'but just in case. Then you and I'll meet the Sisters who found the body and question them.' Lydia forced a smile but the worried line pleating her forehead remained.

As soon as the kitchen fire was blazing, she went into the front room to wake Hortense. While the girl washed her face and ate a piece of stale bread for breakfast, Rees went outside for the wagon. Although a gray light was beginning to seep through the trees he required the lighted lantern to harness Hannibal. But, by the time he drank a cup of coffee and put Hortense in the wagon, the first pink of sunrise colored the sky.

Lydia came outside in her nightgown with only a shawl thrown over her shoulders. 'Hurry back,' she said to him. He nodded with a smile and snapped the whip over the gelding.

When Rouge saw Hortense stepping into the tavern he dropped the flagon he was drying on the floor. Pewter, it did not break but it bounced with a dull thud that caused a momentary hush in the buzz of conversation. Although today was only Monday – and early in the morning besides – the ordinary was already crowded. 'What the Hell is she doing here?' he bellowed.

Rees led the girl up to the bar. 'She isn't safe in Zion,' he said, keeping his voice low. 'There was a murder.'

Rouge stared at Rees as though he didn't understand the words. 'What do you mean?'

'A woman wearing Hortense's cloak was strangled,' he said.

Rouge took several steps back. 'Hortense's cloak?' he repeated. 'I don't understand.'

Rees leaned across the bar and began speaking very slowly. 'Someone murdered a woman who, from a distance, resembled Hortense. She was wearing your niece's cloak. Even in Zion, your niece is not safe.'

Rouge shook his head. 'But where can she go?' He sound exasperated and frightened both.

'Perhaps you should have spent more time looking for her kidnappers,' Rees said. He didn't care that he sounded accusing. When Rouge did not respond, he continued speaking. 'Brother Jonathan demanded that I remove her from the Shaker community. I brought her home with me last night. But I will not keep her at my farm and risk the lives of my children.'

Rouge swallowed. Turning to the kitchen door, he shouted, 'Thomas. Thomas.' The young Frenchman opened the door from the kitchen and peered through the opening. 'Fetch my sister, please. And hurry.' With a nod, Thomas ran across the tavern and through the inn door. Since he had not paused to put on a cloak or even a scarf Rees hoped he was warm enough in his mad dash across the yard. Rouge returned his alarmed gaze to Rees. 'What should we do with Hortense to keep her safe?'

Rees shrugged. 'I don't know. I thought you and your sister were planning to send her to Quebec.'

'But it hasn't been all arranged.' Rouge reached up and tugged at his graying black hair. 'We need more time.'

'I doubt the men who are hunting Hortense will care that you are not prepared,' Rees pointed out in a dry tone. 'And you already know she isn't safe here in town.' He directed a quick glance at Hortense. She was very pale and one nervous hand plucked at her cloak.

'Jake would never hurt me,' she said in a low voice, so soft only Rees could hear her.

'Take her to my office,' Rouge said. 'The fewer people who see her, the better.'

So Rees guided Hortense down the hall to the office. As usual, it was cluttered and messy. Stacked ledgers covered every chair. He pushed one pile to the floor and gestured Hortense to the seat. He perched at first on a large barrel but the stink of brine and vinegar made his eyes sting and drove him away. He shifted the pile of papers from another chair and sat down.

'I don't want to go to Quebec,' Hortense said. 'I don't speak French very well and I don't know anyone there.'

'That is between you and your mother,' Rees replied. 'And, in this case, you should obey her without question.' Once she learned of Hortense's feelings for Jake, Bernadette was likely to keep her daughter in Quebec for months, if not years.

'I've met my cousins on only a handful of occasions,' Hortense said, her voice rising. 'I want to stay here and become a midwife like my mother. Please, Mr Rees—'

'It isn't safe,' Bernadette said from the door. Hortense jumped to her feet and, as her mother hurried to her, flung herself into Bernadette's arms.

'Eventually you may be able to return,' Rees said. When Hortense turned to him with an eager smile, he repeated, 'Eventually. When your uncle deems it safe.' By then, Hortense's feelings toward the mountain boy would surely have changed. 'But until that happens, you must be far away.'

'But I want—'

'Enough,' Bernadette said, her voice sharp. 'Don't argue, Hortense. None of us have been able to protect you. Rees's daughter was attacked in your stead. And now someone was murdered while wearing your cloak. We can't take any more chances. Besides, it is imperative we marry you off before you . . .' She stopped suddenly and cut her eyes toward Rees.

'When does the stage north leave?' he asked as Rouge entered the office, still clutching his drying cloth.

'Not until—' Rouge began.

Bernadette interrupted. 'I don't want to trust my daughter to the stage,' she said, her voice rising. 'Why, anything might happen. Those ruffians could stop the stage and take her from it. No, there must be another way.'

'Thomas will take her,' Rouge said. 'They'll leave tonight after dark.'

'Only Thomas?' Bernadette almost screamed.

'I can't leave the tavern,' Rouge said, his own tone sharpening. 'Especially if Thomas is gone. What would you have me do?'

'You would put my daughter into the hands of a young man? Without a chaperone?' She chewed her lip. 'I'll have to accompany them and pray none of the mothers go into labor until I return.'

Rouge responded with a flood of French, too rapid for Rees to follow.

'This decision does not concern me,' Rees said. Both Rouge and Bernadette turned to stare at him as though they'd forgotten he was there. He directed his gaze at the constable. 'I'll speak to the Shaker Sisters who found the body of that poor woman this morning. Then I will be going up Gray Hill to search for those boys, whether you can accompany me or no.' He nodded at Bernadette and withdrew from the room.

He climbed into his wagon and started home with a sense of relief. Maybe now he could concentrate upon finding the young criminals.

But when he pulled into the yard, only Nancy and Judah were waiting on the porch. 'Where's your sister?' Rees asked, jumping into a pile of mushy snow. 'Where's Jerusha?'

'Inside,' said Nancy. 'She doesn't want to go to school.'

'She must,' he said, stamping up the stairs. He flung the kitchen door open. Jerusha stood in the center of the kitchen, her face red and swollen with tears. 'What's the matter here?' Rees bellowed. 'I hear you don't want to go to school today.' Lydia turned a reproving look upon him and he passed a hand across his forehead. The restless night full of worry and the early trip into town had left him irritable. And now this. He didn't think he could cope with another crisis.

'Babette is mean to me,' Jerusha said, turning her face away. 'And the Widow Francine doesn't like me.' She spoke so softly Rees could scarcely hear her.

'I'm certain that isn't true,' Lydia said. Rees looked at her, noticing that although she was dressed in one of her best gowns – a deep indigo blue, one of his favorites – her hair still lay upon her shoulder in last night's braid. She had her hands clasped tightly together as though, for a farthing, she would strike her oldest daughter.

The devil take both Hortense and Jerusha, Rees thought.

'It is of no importance,' Lydia said in a tightly controlled voice. 'She may remain here today and watch Joseph and Sharon. But—' and she turned a fierce glare upon Jerusha – 'tomorrow there shall be no argument.'

Since Lydia still had to finish dressing, Rees drove Nancy and Judah to school.

Then he returned to the farm for Lydia. He keenly felt the passing of time. It was already past eight and he guessed that by the time he reached Zion he might have less than two hours before prayers. After the observances, a daily occurrence, the entire Zion community would go to the Dining Hall for noon dinner. If Rees and Lydia hadn't finished questioning the Sisters they would be forced to return to Zion that afternoon. And he wanted to spend the rest of the day on Gray Hill.

Lydia was waiting for him by the time he came back to the farm. Jerusha had Sharon held in her arms but Joseph wanted to go. He had wrapped an old cloak of Simon's around his shoulders. Before it was handed down to Simon, the cloak had belonged to Jerusha but she was not the cause of the numerous mended rips and patches. He was always hard on his clothing and besides had worn the cloak doing chores. A lump formed in Rees's throat when he saw the faded tattered article fastened around Joseph's neck and wondered if Simon, who had been glad to go live with David, missed his family here as much as they missed him.

'Simon will be here at Christmas,' Lydia said, as though she could read his mind. 'Simon *and* David.'

Rees nodded but was not comforted. 'I'm just a sentimental old fool,' he said.

'We all miss them,' Lydia said with a smile.

'I'm coming too,' Joseph said, running to Rees and throwing his arms around his father's legs.

'You can't,' he said, ruffling the boy's dark hair. 'Not today.' Jerusha came forward and pulled Joseph back. His face crumpled and he burst into loud wails. Rees looked at the boy and almost changed his mind. But what would they do with him while they spoke to the Sisters?

'We'll be home soon,' Lydia said, hugging Joseph.

'Stay here with your sisters,' Rees said. Joseph's sobbing followed him through the door. Rees felt guilt settle over his shoulders, heavy as a shroud.

'He'll be fine as soon as we leave,' Lydia said, correctly interpreting her husband's expression.

'Sometimes I feel as though I'm always leaving the children,' Rees said.

'The move here was hard on them,' Lydia said. 'They miss David too. I confess I don't feel the same connection to David you do. He came late to my life and I think of him as an adult.'

'He is an adult,' Rees said. At eighteen and married, David was old enough to serve in the militia. Rees had failed to care for David when he was a small boy and now regretted the years he'd lost. They were something he could never recapture and although he and David had navigated the anger and resentment caused by what the boy saw as abandonment and neglect, Rees knew he would never cease wishing he had lived his life differently. Unfortunately, he frequently felt he was doing no better this time.

FIFTEEN

When they drove into the village of Zion, Jonathan appeared so quickly from the stable that Rees knew the Shaker had been waiting for their arrival. Sister Esther, throwing a shawl about her shoulders, appeared only a few seconds later at the door of the Dwelling House. She ran down the steps, already speaking. 'Where is Sharon? You didn't bring the baby?'

Rees and his family had been living here in Zion when Lydia had delivered Sharon. As Rees climbed down from the wagon he realized he should have guessed that Esther, and some of the other Sisters, would want to see the children. When the family had fled to Zion for refuge, Lydia and the children had become part of this community for several months. Rees did not feel the same connection; Zion had never been home for him. But he had a long history with this Shaker community and Lydia, who had once been a Sister here, had an even longer one.

'Jerusha is watching the two youngest,' she said with a smile. 'And of course the two older ones are in school.'

'Please,' Jonathan said with a gesture.

Lydia nodded and allowed Rees to take her arm and draw her after Brother Jonathan.

They went into the Dwelling House, Rees and Lydia separating to enter through the appropriate doors. They went up the stairs and met at the top, in front of the door to the Elders' office. Jonathan had already entered the chamber and was taking chairs down from the pegs. Rees stepped inside, remembering his last visit to this room. He had identified the murderer of several members in the Zion community. It had been an emotional session and ended in fisticuffs, despite the Shaker's pacifist beliefs.

'How is Brother Aaron?' Rees asked, recalling the gangly Brother who had launched himself at the murderer.

'Sit,' Jonathan said with a gesture. 'We have a more important issue to discuss.' He shot a glance at Rees who saw that Jonathan did not want to speak of Aaron. Rees guessed that the Brother was continuing to go his own way, behaving in a manner that was just short of outright disobedience.

As Lydia and Rees chose seats across from one another, far enough apart so their knees were in no danger of touching, Jonathan left the room. Rees heard the Brother's footsteps descending the steps. The Sisters must have been just downstairs and waiting to be called; within a few minutes the footsteps of several people began to ascend the staircase.

Rees rose to his feet as the three Sisters entered the room.

They were all young and dressed identically in dark-colored dresses with berthas over their shoulders and square linen caps covering their hair. One of the girls was taller than the others, broad-shouldered and with large hands but it was the elfin fair-haired girl who stepped forward to speak. She looked up, directly at Rees. This is the leader of the group, he thought.

'Please, Sister Pearl, tell us what happened yesterday,' Jonathan said.

'We were going to the kitchen,' said the Sister. She spoke with unexpected self-possession and Rees wondered about her age. She could have been anywhere from twelve to twenty; her small frame was deceptive. 'We saw the body lying in the road.'

'Did you know what it was?' Rees asked.

Pearl shook her head, sudden tears filling her eyes. 'Not then.' She rubbed the back of her hand over her face. 'We saw the white cloak in the snow. I – we – thought someone had fallen or fainted.' The other two girls nodded in unison.

'What happened then?'

'Excuse me.' Esther appeared at the office door. 'I need one of the Sisters in the kitchen. Do you require all three?'

'I'll go,' said the third of the trio. She was a nondescript girl with sharp features and Rees thought she looked relieved as she followed Esther from the room.

'And then?' Rees prompted the two remaining Sisters.

'We ran over, didn't we, Glory?' Pearl looked at the tall, heavyset girl. She nodded her dark head. Glory's size and brunette coloring made Pearl seem even fairer and more diminutive.

'Glory,' Pearl said as she gestured at her companion, 'thought the woman was ill.' As Pearl spoke her acolyte kept nodding, her head bobbing up and down as though hinged.

'Did you look at the woman lying on the ground, Glory?' Lydia asked, startling Rees with her sudden question. The tall, heavyset girl jumped in surprise at being directly addressed. The quick glance she directed at the two adults revealed a broad face flushed with tears and puffy swollen eyes.

'Yes,' she said softly.

'We all did, didn't we, Glory?' Pearl asked. Throwing a quick glance at Pearl, Glory nodded.

'She was the first one there,' Pearl said. 'We all ran . . .'

'Were you walking with these Sisters, Glory?' Lydia asked, ignoring the fair-haired girl who so obviously wanted to be the center of attention. 'Or did you come upon the victim first?'

'We were together,' Pearl began.

'Please let Sister Glory speak for herself,' Lydia said, never removing her eyes from the taller, heavier girl.

'Yes, we were together,' Glory said. She did not raise her eyes to Lydia but kept them trained upon her clasped hands. Pearl smiled, a slight triumphant smile.

'We ran to help,' Pearl said. 'Didn't we, Glory?'

'You looked at her face?' Rees asked. Glory nodded.

'I saw . . . I saw . . .' She broke down into sobs. Lydia took a few steps forward and put a hand on the girl's arm. Glory stiffened and then half-turned, leaning toward Lydia for comfort. Lydia moved her hand to the girl's shoulder and patted her. Rees shifted from foot to foot with impatience until Lydia narrowed her eyes warningly at him.

'We saw a man running away,' Pearl announced. Glory and Lydia both turned to look at the girl.

'You saw the murderer?' Lydia asked in surprise.

'We did, didn't we?' Pearl applied to Glory for corroboration. Glory nodded. 'We did.'

'A young man?' Rees asked, stepping forward in his eagerness. 'Dark haired? In buckskin?'

Glory lifted her face. 'No. No,' she said. Wiping her wet face with her sleeve, she repeated, 'No. It was an old man. He carried a gun.'

'That's right,' Pearl said in agreement, her voice rising with excitement. 'An old man carrying a gun.'

Rees and Lydia exchanged a glance of mingled astonishment and mystification. Who could that old man be?

'What I don't understand,' said Rees for perhaps the third time, 'is why, if he had a rifle, he did not shoot her. He could have done so from a distance with no one seeing him.'

Lydia nodded. 'I know. He must have known he hadn't killed Hortense as soon as he saw her face.'

'Why strangle her? It doesn't make sense.'

'Maybe his powder was wet,' Lydia suggested.

'And who is this old man Glory saw?' Rees flicked the ribbons over Hannibal's withers. They were on their way to Gray Hill hoping to speak with Granny Rose. Both Sharon and Joseph had been napping when Lydia and Rees had returned home. Seizing this opportunity, he proposed a journey to Gray Hill. Lydia agreed with such eagerness that he realized with a twinge of shame that his wife also found a life lived at the farm and bounded by relentless chores tedious.

He turned to smile at her. The cold had whipped color into her cheeks and teased a tendril of hair from her cap. She was frowning with thought but, despite the line between her brows, a smile curved her lips.

'What I want to know,' she said now, 'is how anyone knew Hortense was staying in Zion. You had just moved her there.'

'Unless the murderer's intended target was the victim,' Rees said. 'That would explain that unknown old man. He may have no connection to Hortense or her abduction whatsoever.'

'But there was Hortense's cloak,' Lydia argued. Rees nodded. For a moment they drove in silence and then she added, 'I did not like Sister Pearl. One would have expected her to feel more shocked by their experience. Instead she seemed excited, rather than horrified, by the violent murder of her fellow Sister.'

Rees nodded without comment. After spending significant time with the Shaker community he thought that life in Zion must be boring – especially after a few months. It would be for him. And he suspected that young Shaker Sister was trying to enjoy this bit of excitement while she could and hadn't stopped to consider the death in all its horror.

SIXTEEN

R ees paused in the small clearing with the general store to rest Hannibal. Both he and Lydia climbed down and walked around for a few minutes before returning to the wagon. The sun was high in the sky, almost directly overhead, and shining brightly. The air was cold; otherwise today would feel almost like spring.

The shopkeeper stepped outside. Smoke from a pipe wreathed Mr Morton's head and a brown tobacco stain in the snow betrayed his regular position there. He eyed both people walking around his yard and, recognizing Rees, nodded. It was an acknowledgement, no more, and barely polite.

After the short rest, Rees and Lydia resumed their journey. The track was snow-covered but grooved by wheels and pocked by both hooves and footprints. Rees peered at the white surface wondering if he could spot tracks left by moccasins, but far too much traffic had been this way. And, most people would choose to use the road, no matter how mean, Rees thought as he glanced from side to side at the thick snowy woods hugging the path. The trees grew closely together and snow filled the spaces. Breaking through would be a battle. The terrain itself with its sudden ravines and steep hills would be difficult to traverse even in the best of weathers.

Rees handed the reins to Lydia and climbed down to walk alongside Hannibal's head. The footing was difficult on the scarred snow – treacherous and slippery. The gelding struggled to pull the wagon.

Rees soon began panting as his leather-soled boots slipped in the icy slope. Almost at the crest of this hill, he spotted the left-hand turn that the shopkeeper had mentioned to him and the constable previously. Taking Hannibal's bridle, Rees guided the horse into the lane.

The snow cover was even deeper here and the trees lining the road grew so thickly he began to wonder if they had taken the wrong turn. The woods looked like virgin forest, untouched by any human hand.

But a curve revealed a sun-filled opening ahead and the grade began to flatten out. As they rounded the final bend a small cabin with a ramshackle barn behind it came into view. A large fire blazed in the yard and, as Rees pulled the wagon up to the split-rail fence, the old woman stopped tossing branches into the flames and turned to stare. She wore a heavy cloak and a pair of men's boots on her feet.

'Granny Rose?' Rees asked as he pulled Hannibal to a stop. The woman nodded, her gaze going to Lydia.

'You don't look like you're increasing,' the midwife said.

'No,' Lydia said.

'How old is your baby?'

'About fifteen months.' Lydia sounded astonished. Granny Rose nodded as though satisfied.

'We wanted to ask you a few questions,' Rees said. Granny Rose looked up at him. Her skin was grooved into deep wrinkles from spending a lifetime outside in all weathers. Although a skinny woman she looked strong with ropy muscles revealed by her turned up sleeves. Sinews corded her hands.

''Bout what?'

'The midwife's daughter was abducted,' Rees said.

'Ah. The young woman that birthed Mr Bennett's latest,' said Granny Rose.

Rees nodded. 'Hortense.'

'Why do you care? You're not the constable,' the midwife said.

'Rouge has some family problems,' Rees said.

'That's partly why we're here,' Lydia said, climbing carefully down from the wagon seat.

Granny Rose looked from one to the other. 'Very well. Bring your nag and wagon inside the fence. The fire keeps the wolves away.'

Lydia unhooked the leather strap holding the gate close and swung it back. Rees drove into the yard. The mule contained in a small paddock to the right turned to look at them. He rolled his eyes at the wagon and continued nibbling on the withered leaves springing from one of the deadfalls that formed the posts.

Granny Rose opened the door to her cabin and stood back to allow them entry.

Although primitive, just logs chinked with mud, the one-room cabin boasted a wooden floor and a stone fireplace. 'Coffee?' she asked, moving to the coffee pot sitting on the hearth. Both Lydia and Rees accepted and Granny Rose busied herself fetching cups, pouring the inky brew and putting out sugar. Rees guessed the pottery cups were probably her best; no doubt she ate and drank from woodenware.

He almost spit out his first sip; the liquid could barely be called coffee. Although some coffee beans had been ground for this drink, the dominant flavor was of chicory.

'It's a long trip for a few questions,' said Granny Rose. 'What happened?'

Rees looked into the old woman's wrinkled countenance. The hair pulled back into a bun was an unusual bright white, so white even her cap looked dingy. Rees wondered how old this woman was. She might be in her fifties, or even older, a great age especially in the mountains, but her blue eyes were sharp and piercing. She was no fool and Rees opted to tell the bare truth. After explaining what had happened to Hortense, he said, 'The constable has decided to remove the girl to Canada. And now, with a murder, we are trying to find these boys.'

Granny Rose nodded, but not as though she was prepared to tell him anything quite yet. 'Lot of boys named Jacob and Jeremiah here in the hills,' she said. 'I don't want to direct you to some family with innocent young men.'

'We don't believe they murdered the Shaker Sister,' Rees said quickly.

'Women living celibate, without home and family,' the midwife said. 'Ain't natural.'

Rees recalled the worn face of the dead woman. He thought she, whatever her past, had found a refuge among the Shakers but elected, for once, not to argue.

'Are there any women here on Gray Hill who have had babies recently?' Lydia asked suddenly. Granny Rose smiled. Although an old woman, she still had most of her teeth.

'Many women,' she said.

'I think this would have been someone you didn't assist,' Lydia said. When Rees turned to look at his wife in surprise, she said, 'Hortense went to help Mr Bennett's wife. Maybe she was called to another lying in, not necessarily this time but before.' Throwing a quick look at her husband, she added, 'Her kidnapper had to have seen her, wouldn't you agree?'

Granny Rose eyed Lydia and then, chewing her lip, stared at the floor in thought. 'I don't know the Bennetts. Well, they live so far down I'd guess not many of us Hill people would know them.'

Rees shrugged. 'Perhaps my wife is correct,' he said. 'Someone might still have seen Hortense.'

Granny Rose glanced at him and then down at the floor once again. 'So the girl, Hortense, could have been called to a birth any time within the last four to five months?' she said.

'Possibly,' Lydia said cautiously.

'Up to the last few weeks,' Rees said. He wasn't sure where his wife's thoughts were leading. But then, he knew little about midwives and birthing babies so Lydia most likely recognized some detail he did not.

'There was a birth I didn't get called to. A couple of months ago. Not recently.'

Rees and Lydia exchanged a glance. 'Perhaps these young men saw Hortense when she attended that birth,' Lydia suggested.

The midwife inclined her head, reluctance in every line of her body.

'Perhaps. Probably.' She chewed her lower lip as she ruminated and Rees knew there was more. Leaning forward, he opened his mouth. Lydia put her hand on his wrist and shook her head at him.

So they sat in silence, waiting for Granny Rose to come to her own decision. The quiet went on and on until it achieved a weight of its own. The midwife shifted uncomfortably and said at last, 'The Woottens are a large family. The two youngest boys are called Jake and Jem.'

Rees, who could barely contain his excitement, could feel Lydia trembling.

'And where does this family live?' he asked.

Granny Rose sighed. 'Go back to the main road and follow it all the way up to the top. When you reach the stream – it'll be on your left – follow it. Turn left at the waterfall.'

Rees nodded and stood up. But Lydia remained seated. 'Why would Hortense be called to a birth that high in the mountains when you are so much closer?' she asked.

Granny Rose shrugged. 'I don't know. I'm sure the family had its reasons.' Rees was tempted to break in and ask the midwife what she thought those reasons were. 'I heard tell both mother and babe died,' the midwife continued after a brief silence. 'A mercy really although I doubt that would have happened if I'd been present at the birth.' She shook her head and Rees felt a chill sweep over him. Did she really believe that God had punished that poor woman for not calling on Granny Rose? 'But then who knows what happened there?' she went on. Rees held the old woman's gaze. He was certain she knew more than she had said. Or was willing to say. But the dark-blue eyes that met his were unyielding and he knew she would tell him nothing more. Not today anyway.

He held out his hand to Lydia. 'We should go. I know Mrs Rose must have much to do.'

'Just call me Granny Rose, everyone does,' said the midwife. She preceded them to the cabin door and threw it open. She stood there, in the cold, watching Rees and Lydia climb into the wagon and begin the journey down from this side of the mountain. When Rees turned to look back, just before they went around the curve and the cabin disappeared from sight, Granny Rose was still standing in her doorway watching them.

SEVENTEEN

'She knows something more,' Rees said.

Lydia smiled knowingly. 'Something shameful I'll be bound,' she said.

Rees nodded in agreement. People always held back information, evaded questions, or told out and out lies. The trick lay in discovering which secrets were private sins and shames and which were important to the resolution of the mystery.

'What do you think?' Rees asked Lydia. He respected her ability to decode the nuances of female conversation.

'Perhaps an out-of-wedlock baby?' Lydia said. 'But suggesting the deaths of both mother and child was a mercy seems – I don't know – a peculiar response to such a tragedy.'

'We have to speak to the Woottens,' Rees said with a definitive jerk of his head.

'I believe we still have time before the children are released from school,' Lydia said. Rees turned to look at her. Although she seemed calm, he saw the excitement in her sparkling eyes.

'Very well,' he said. 'Let's see if we can find the Woottens.'

Once they reached the fork in the road they turned left. The narrow track began climbing once more. They had not gone very far before they reached the stream, frozen into rough ice. A short distance away they passed the waterfall. Although ice coated the rocks, the fall itself was not frozen and the water rushed over with a tremendous roar. They crossed over a bridge, the rough-hewn boards worn gray with weather and splintering from heavy traffic. Now the water went rushing down a deep gully on the right. Visible on the other side of the cleft were the signs of logging, open patches where both hardwoods and tall pines had been chopped down. The forest was silent now, save for the sound of Hannibal's hooves and the creak of the wagon wheels. The lumber camps had moved to the other side of the hill.

They ate the dry pone from Lydia's bag. Rees longed for coffee but they had only a jug of stale tasting water. A series of grunts sounded from the woods to their left and two fat bears ran across the road twenty feet in front of the wagon. Although the animals did not pause, or even glance at the wagon, Rees began wishing he'd brought his rifle. What were they doing awake? Shouldn't they be hibernating? When Hannibal caught the bears' scent he snorted and stopped short, dancing at the end of the reins. As soon as the bears disappeared into the brown, frost-stiffened underbrush on the other side, the gelding pulled forward, eager to be gone from this place.

As they ascended the mountain, the hardwoods thinned, leaving primarily evergreens. Tracts of open land filled with low bush blueberries, crusted with frost, scrub and sometimes bodies of water began to appear. Ice coated the shallower tarns but the larger, deeper ponds were only partially frozen. As Rees and Lydia trundled past one such lake, a moose, up to his belly in the water, turned his dripping snout to stare at them.

Rees began to see open sky ahead. The road, which was little more than a narrow lane, dead-ended in front of a small shabby cabin. Hannibal stopped, head hung low, and panted. Rees climbed down into the snow and looked around.

To the left of the cabin was a small barn. Through the missing boards on the door Rees could see the wall of an empty stall. He wondered if this was where the horse stolen from Hortense lived but without going into the barn he couldn't be sure. He saw no sign of cattle or even goats. If the family who lived here owned pigs, and it would be uncommon if they did not, the swine must live wild. There was no sty, not even for the sows and the piglets.

But a tall stack of firewood piled against the cabin wall and the plume of wood smoke coming from the chimney betrayed human habitation. Rees started walking toward the cabin door. He had taken no more than a few steps when the door opened and a woman cradling a musket stepped outside. She was the largest woman Rees had ever seen, round as a ball of butter but nowhere near as appealing. Her feet were bare, the flesh rolling over her ankles in pendulous folds. He could barely see her eyes over her round cheeks. An untidy black braid snaked down her back.

'Git off my property,' she said, her words slurred. She had lost her teeth so long ago her cheeks fell, in deep creases, over her empty mouth. Rees held up his hands to show they were empty.

'We're just looking for two boys, a Jem and a Jake,' Lydia said.

'They ain't here.' Her tongue pushed out of her mouth in a vaguely reptilian motion. 'No one's here. Git going now.' As she spoke, she hobbled down the steps and stood in the snow in her bare feet. Rees stared at the woman's grimy toes, the long yellow nails chipped and broken and wondered why she didn't feel the cold. 'I said git.' She attempted to fire over Rees's head but, although a muffled pop sounded, the ball did not eject. He guessed the powder was wet, a common problem.

Still he backed up in a hurry. She might reload and next time, with the gun's notorious inaccuracy and the woman's apparent drunkenness, she might hit Lydia.

'Now Mother,' said a man coming around the back of the cabin and climbing the slope. 'Go back to bed.' Gray sprinkled his black hair and a healing crimson scar branded the left side of his face, running from eye to mouth. Recalling Hortense's description of the fight, Rees stared at the wound. This then must be Mr Wootten.

Although dressed in several layers of ragged homespun shirts and a battered straw hat, he wore buckskin boots upon his feet and carried a rifle in his left hand. 'What are you doing here, pulling a sick woman from her bed?' he added, turning on Rees as Mrs Wootten retreated to the porch.

'We were looking for someone,' Rees said. 'Two boys, Jem and Jake.'

'No one here by that name,' said Mr Wootten. 'You're in the wrong place.'

But Mrs Wootten had already admitted the boys lived in this cabin, although they were not here now. Rees eyed the other man thoughtfully, wondering why he lied.

Wootten was just a little shorter than Rees and the arms protruding from his sleeves were solid and sinewy with muscle. He smiled but his eyes were watchful and Rees, who'd been something of a fighter in his younger days, recognized a fellow brawler. He suspected Wootten was the kind, though, who would beat an unconscious partner to death just because he could. 'We're sorry to trouble you,' he said, turning back to the wagon. He would return, of that he was certain, but next time he would come with Rouge instead of Lydia.

It took a minute or two to turn the wagon and start down the slope once again. All the while Rees was conscious of Mr and Mrs Wootten watching him.

He did not speak until they were a distance away. 'He was lying of course.'

'They both were, I fancy,' Lydia agreed. She sighed. 'But while the Woottens may be guilty of abducting Hortense, Mr Wootten cannot be the man the Shaker Sisters saw standing over the dead body.'

'Why not?' Rees asked. 'He might have strangled that poor Shaker Sister because his musket would not fire.'

Lydia shook her head. 'Pearl would not have missed the wound on Mr Wootten's face. It is too obvious and would have been visible from a good distance away. And she wouldn't be able to help commenting upon it.'

'Maybe it just happened?' Rees asked hopefully. He had taken against Mr Wootten, although he couldn't have explained his violent antipathy even to himself, and he wanted the other man to be guilty.

Lydia shook her head again. 'No. That wound occurred four, maybe five days ago.'

'About the time Hortense fled,' Rees said, turning to look at his wife.

She returned his gaze, her eyes widening. 'Yes,' she said. 'That's true.'

'There was blood, Hortense said,' he murmured. 'That cut would explain the blood.'

'Indeed. The wound is healing, although I believe Mr Wootten will carry a scar for the remainder of his days.'

'It looks as though it was made by a shovel or a poker,' Rees said, recalling Hortense's story. The part about the fight and Jem striking his father was true. But Rees had known something was off about the tale and now he knew what it was. Although he could believe one of Wootten's sons had struck out with a handy weapon, he did not believe Hortense's explanation for the reason behind the fight. Wootten was tough, a fighter, and a man used to getting his own way; that Rees had seen. Would his sons have engaged in a physical brawl with their father over something trivial? Rees doubted it. So what, he wondered, had Hortense kept back?

'I'll have to question Hortense again,' he said aloud. 'That girl has told so many lies I don't know what to believe anymore.'

Lydia sighed. 'I feel for her mother,' she said. After a moment of silence she continued, 'I want to speak with Granny Rose again. Why did she tell us anything? Loyalty runs deep here in the mountains.' She flicked a glance at her husband. 'I don't believe Granny broke her own code – allegiance to her community – because of our charm.'

'Maybe she told us because it was the right thing to do,' Rees suggested.

Lydia shook her head. 'It wouldn't have been the right thing for her. Or if it was I suspect she would have tried to protect her own, even if it meant lying or evading our questions.'

'Then why?'

'I don't know. Because she doesn't like the Woottens.' Lydia considered the statement she'd just made and nodded. 'Yes, I believe that's it. In fact, I would guess that Granny Rose doesn't just dislike them, she detests them. The question is why?'

Rees studied his wife for a moment. 'After meeting Mr and Mrs Wootten,' he said with feeling, 'I not only understand Granny Rose's feelings, I fully concur. Especially with Mr Wootten. He's dangerous. The next time I come up here, I'll dragoon Rouge into accompanying me. And I'll bring my own rifle.'

EIGHTEEN

Descending the mountain took a long time, almost two hours by Rees's estimation. And reaching the foothills, with North Road almost in sight, felt like reaching civilization. Hannibal, although he was panting with fatigue, broke into a ragged trot as they drove toward town. 'I guess he's glad to be home too,' Rees said to Lydia.

They drove immediately to Rouge's tavern. Lydia hesitated, worried about going inside, but Rees assured her the stagecoach passengers, including women, always stopped for a meal here. 'Anyway,' he added, 'I'm famished.' Breakfast seemed very far away. So Lydia allowed herself to be persuaded, probably because she too was peckish, and they went inside.

Therese was behind the bar. 'Where's Rouge?' Rees asked.

'Gone.' Seeing Rees's expression Therese clarified her reply. 'He went with Madame Bernadette and Mademoiselle Hortense to Quebec.'

Only Therese's presence prevented the epithet on Rees's lips from springing into speech. 'Well. I daresay this is the end of my plan to question Hortense once again,' he said, turning to Lydia.

She nodded, grimacing. 'You know Bernadette will not ask anything either,' Lydia said as they turned toward the tables. 'She'll be afraid of the answers.'

Therese hurried out from behind the bar and scrubbed down a table not too distant from the fireplace. 'What do you have today?' Rees asked her. She looked at him with her pale-blue eyes and he wondered for a moment if she understood him. Then she went to the back and spoke in a flood of French to her brother. When she returned to the table, she offered them a ragout, a dish that turned out to be a kind of stew made with venison and carrots. But it was surprisingly flavorful and the bread served with it was hot from the oven.

Although Rees felt disloyal for even judging, he thought the brother and sister were far better cooks than Rouge or any of his other employees.

Rees and Lydia ate quickly. She had begun to worry about Sharon and Joseph, still in Jerusha's care.

They stopped by Widow Francine's school to collect Nancy and Judah even though she had not yet dismissed school for the day. As the children put on their cloaks and mittens, the Widow said, 'Today was a very pleasant day. Nancy and Judah worked hard. And there were no upsets.'

It was only when they climbed into the wagon and began driving home that Rees began wondering what the dame had actually meant by those statements. Was she implying that Jerusha was a difficult child to have? He glanced at Lydia. She was chewing her lower lip in thought. When she felt him looking at her she offered him a faint smile but did not share her thoughts.

On Tuesday morning Rees drove his children to school, even Jerusha, albeit reluctantly. He had begun wondering if it was safe enough for them to walk once again, especially now that Hortense had left the area. The constant trips were beginning to wear on him and he knew Hannibal was tired, especially after the long journey up Gray Hill the previous day. Besides, Rees had farm chores to catch up on. They were low on water – Jerusha had been afraid to fetch it the previous day – and he wanted to walk around his fence. Neither the split rail nor the stone wall would prevent wolves – or men – from crossing it if they were determined, but he hoped to discourage them.

But when he drove through the gate he saw a wagon tied up in front of the house. He thought it might be the Shakers. With his heart sinking, Rees unhitched Hannibal, loosed him into the paddock, and went inside.

Jonathan was standing uncomfortably by the door. He turned when Rees entered and said in a gust of relief, 'You're home.' It sounded as though he would follow up his exclamation with the word 'finally', but he didn't.

'What happened?' Rees said in resignation.

'Some man has been creeping around Zion,' Jonathan said. He sounded accusatory and Rees couldn't blame him. 'Pearl saw him.'

Rees's initial concern faded a little. That girl would always try to keep herself in the center of attention. 'Are you certain she actually saw something?' he said.

'No. But she was alarmed. I think you should come and speak with her.'

Rees glanced at his wife and she nodded. 'I think you should go,' she said. 'After all, one of the Sisters was murdered.'

'I'll hitch Hannibal to the wagon again,' he said, heaving a sigh.

'Join me in my cart,' Jonathan suggested. Rees hesitated, reluctant to tie his transportation to the other man, but finally nodded.

'Very well,' he agreed and followed the Elder from the house.

Jonathan maintained his silence for the entire journey and Rees was, for once, glad of the Shaker prohibition on unnecessary speech. He needed to think. He was convinced the answer to Hortense's abduction and the murder of the Shaker Sister lay on Gray Hill. But was the Wootten family involved? Rees thought so but he knew he was basing his suspicion on the slimmest of evidence – Granny Rose's statement – and his own dislike of Wootten senior. He needed to go up the mountain once again. Somehow he had to press the Wootten family for information.

Rees exhaled in frustration. That meant waiting for Rouge's return and how long would that take?

But maybe Pearl was lying, Rees thought hopefully, trying to find a silver lining. Perhaps she was telling stories? He wished Lydia and her skill at reading people were with him.

When Jonathan pulled up at the Children's Dwelling he spoke for the first time. 'Esther is inside. She'll remain with you while you speak to Sister Pearl.'

Rees nodded and jumped down. As he started up the steps Esther opened the door and motioned him inside.

Rees followed Esther into the large room on the right. Usually this chamber was crowded with the youngest of the children but right now only Pearl was inside. She jumped to her feet. Rees stared at her, realizing he might have to revise his opinion. Her cap was twisted on her fair hair and her apron was crumpled from nervous twisting of the linen.

'What happened?' he asked, more gently than he'd planned.

'I saw the man,' she said. She swallowed and licked her lips. 'I think he was the one who murdered Sister . . . Sister . . .' She broke down into sobs.

Esther moved quickly to the girl's side. 'I daresay he was not,' she said soothingly. 'Tell Mr Rees what happened.'

When the girl continued weeping, Rees said, 'Did he approach you?' Pearl shook her head. 'But you saw him?' She nodded. 'What was he doing?'

'R-running.'

'Running where?' Rees heard the increasing sharpness in his voice and took a deep breath. Despite Pearl's tendency toward drama, she was genuinely trembling.

'Toward the Meetinghouse.'

'Could he have been leaving the village?'

'M-maybe.' Putting her hands over her face, Pearl began weeping wildly. Rees struggled to maintain his patience.

'You weren't hurt,' Esther said, her voice taking on an impatient crispness. 'He didn't speak to you or even, as far as I believe, notice you in the slightest. I don't understand these foolish vapors. Cease your crying before I shake some sense into you.' Rees turned a look of admiration on Esther. He guessed she had realized what he had: Pearl had recovered from her initial terror and was beginning to playact, hungry for the attention. Esther offered him a slight smile.

Pearl gulped twice more but when Esther offered her a handkerchief the girl took it and wiped her face. 'But he might have seen me,' she offered in a trembling voice. 'And he might have killed me as he did the other Sister—'

'He didn't,' Esther said. She shook her head at the girl. 'Now you are just putting on your own little tragedy.'

'How did you come to be among the Shakers?' Rees asked. He thought a neutral remark might calm her.

'How did I come to be among Shakers?' Pearl repeated, her voice rising in surprise. Esther threw Rees a look but she did not speak. Pearl took a deep breath. 'My father said I would never marry,' she replied. 'That I had a face like the ass of a mule and no man would ever want me. I should be grateful I had a home and food on the table.' As she spoke she straightened up and the quivering that had shook her delicate frame ceased.

Now it was Rees's turn to be surprised. He could not imagine anyone saying something so hurtful to this beautiful young girl. 'That must have been very difficult for you,' he said. Pearl nodded and wiped her eyes with a flourish of her handkerchief.

'Answer Mr Rees's questions now,' Esther said. 'Was the man leaving?'

Pearl frowned at the floor. 'Yes, he was probably leaving the village,' she said in a distinctly sullen tone.

Rees stared hard at the girl. 'How do you know he was the same individual who murdered your Sister?' he asked.

'He wore buckskin.'

'Did he carry a rifle?' Rees asked.

'No.' Pearl's gaze shifted to the ceiling. 'I didn't see one anyway.'

'Was he tall or short?' Rees asked a little desperately. 'Young or old?'

'Tall. Very tall,' Pearl said. Rees thought that that answer was not helpful. Most likely everyone looked tall to the diminutive Pearl. Then the girl continued. 'He wasn't old, though. He was young. Probably just a few years older than me.' Then her lips curved into a smile. 'He was handsome.'

'Young?' Esther repeated, directing an astonished gaze at Rees.

He shook his head at her, ever so subtly, and she closed her lips over the words she'd intended to say.

Rees repeated a few more of his questions, using different words, but Pearl's story did not change and finally he indicated he was finished. Esther told the young girl she could return to her chores.

'Are there *two* strange men roaming the streets of Zion?' Esther asked when Pearl had disappeared through the door.

'It seems so,' Rees replied.

'I'd sooner believe that child was embellishing,' Esther said, shaking her head. 'No good can come of strange men running through the streets of our little village.' She chewed her lip. 'I am puzzled about one thing.' Her voice trailed away.

'Yes?' Rees said.

'As far as I know, she never met her father,' Esther said. 'Her mother brought her here about five years ago and dropped her off. Her mother . . .' She stopped short but Rees could interpret the silence.

'Was no better than she should be.' He finished the phrase.

Esther nodded. 'I believe Pearl is waiting for her mother to return.' she sighed. 'Although if she did it would not be to collect her child but to recover her valuables.'

'So where did Pearl hear that scene that she described so movingly?' he asked.

'I don't know,' Esther said.

'From one of the other girls maybe?'

'Maybe,' Esther agreed, her forehead wrinkling. 'Maybe not. Pearl makes up stories. And she likes the boys. Handsome indeed.' She sniffed disapprovingly. 'She has to be prevented from hanging out the window and waving at the boys when their caretaker leads them past.'

Rees wondered if any of the girls had a clearer picture of Pearl. Did he trust any of the young Sisters to tell him the unvarnished truth? Of course he did. Annie, the girl he'd rescued from a bawdy house, still lived here. She believed – falsely Rees thought – that Billy, the young boy she'd loved in Salem would come for her when he finished his time at sea. 'Do you know where Annie is now?' he asked.

'In the laundry, I believe,' Esther said. 'I'll come with you.'

'I suspect she will speak more freely to me alone,' Rees said.

Esther paused, looking disappointed Rees thought, and then nodded. 'Very well. One of the other Sisters will be present.'

Rees made his way to the stone building at the extreme southern end of the village. He could smell it before he saw it; an odor of wet wool and hot irons. The Sister in charge of the laundry this week seemed disposed to forbid him entrance until he threatened to leave and return with Esther. Then the Sister, reluctance in every still line of her body, allowed him to enter.

Annie was folding freshly ironed shirts and napkins and other linens but she stopped when she saw him. 'Father!' she exclaimed in delight. Rees wondered if Billy would recognize Annie now. She'd grown into a full-fleshed young woman and was already taller than most adult women.

'Annie,' he said as she threw herself into his arms. The Sister coughed forbiddingly. 'Walk with me a minute,' Rees said. Annie fetched her cloak from the hook and followed him outside into the cold and windy day.

Annie peppered Rees with questions about Sharon and Joseph and the other children until he lost patience. 'They are all fine,' he said, cutting through her eager chatter. 'I will ask Brother Jonathan if he'll allow you to visit someday. But for now, I need your help.'

'With the murder?' she asked in excitement.

'In a way,' Rees agreed and watched her eyes begin to shine. 'I need to know what you think about Pearl.'

'Pearl?' All the pleasure disappeared from Annie's face. 'She's a liar, that's what I think. Why?'

'She claims she saw someone in the village.'

'I wouldn't believe her if she told me the sky was blue,' Annie said. 'Pearl always has to be the focus of every eye.'

Rees thought back to Pearl. She had seemed genuinely frightened. This time she might be telling the truth. But Annie was correct about one thing; Pearl placed herself at the center of everything.

'There's something else,' Annie went on. 'If she finds out you have a secret – like a letter from your sweetheart that you aren't supposed to have – why, she'll make you do half her chores for a week so she won't tell.' The color rising into her face told Rees that she was speaking about herself.

'Does she have any special friends?' Rees asked.

Annie shook her head. 'We aren't supposed to. And anyway nobody likes her.'

'What about Glory?' Rees asked. 'Or the other girl that was with them when they found the Sister?'

'You mean Louisa. I don't know about her. But Glory likes Pearl least of all. I've seen her hide—'

'I hope you are not gossiping,' said the laundry Sister, striding toward them.

'Not at all,' Rees lied.

'I'd better go,' Annie said. 'But don't forget about the visit.' With a final look at Rees, she followed the Sister back into the laundry.

Feeling that he understood less now than he had before, Rees walked down the path and across the bridge into the village. Esther was walking slowly toward him and he had the distinct impression she'd been loitering there, waiting for him to appear so that she might discover what he'd learned.

'Did Annie know anything about Pearl?' Esther asked.

'Pearl is a teller of tales,' Rees said. 'And none of the girls like her.'

Esther sighed. 'Oh dear. But I confess I am not surprised. I expect several of our girls – both Louisa and Glory among them – will sign the Covenant as soon as they are old enough. They will make Shakers. But Pearl?' Esther shook her head.

'But what if this time she's told the truth?' Rees said, chewing his lip. 'Two men have entered Zion. What do they want?'

'Hortense?' Esther suggested uncertainly.

'But Hortense is gone. And then there's the murdered Sister. Are there two men working at cross purposes?' Esther could only shake her head.

NINETEEN

'Maybe the two men don't know Hortense has left our community,' Jonathan suggested reasonably for the third time as he drove Rees home. Rees grunted, unsatisfied.

He considered once again the possibility that there were two men searching for the midwife's daughter. He tried to imagine a situation in which that possibility would make sense. He already knew the two young boys, Jake and Jem, were searching for Hortense. Could their father, Mr Wootten, be hunting for the girl as well?

Rees felt certain of only one thing: everything, from Hortense's abduction to the most recent sighting of the boy, centered on Gray Hill. Although Rees had known he must return and ask more questions, the journey into the mountains now seemed more urgent than ever. He wondered if Rouge had returned from Quebec.

'Maybe I should put up a sign,' Jonathan said, interrupting Rees's thoughts. 'To let everyone know Hortense is gone.' When Rees turned a startled glance upon the Shaker Elder Jonathan smiled faintly.

'A joke, as I live and breathe,' Rees said in surprise. Jonathan was such a serious fellow.

'I wish something like that would work,' Jonathan said, his smile fading. 'But I'd guess neither of those men can read.'

'Surely they – at least the lad anyway – now knows that Hortense is not in Zion,' Rees said. 'There will be no further trouble or upset in your community.'

Jonathan threw a quick look at his companion. 'I hope that's true but I won't count on it. For one thing, you still live ten miles distant and trouble seems to follow you like fleas on a dog.'

To that Rees, uttering an awkward chuckle, had no reply.

Once home, he went inside, but only to tell Lydia he planned to drive into town. 'I want to see if Rouge has returned,' he said.

'I doubt he has,' Lydia said. 'He and his sister have only been gone a few days and Quebec is a great distance.' When Rees said nothing, she added, 'Hannibal is tired. As you must be. Don't you think you should wait at least another day or two?'

'No.' He shook his head. 'Although Hortense has been taken to Canada, the danger from the lads hunting her and the old man who strangled the Shaker Sister remains. Maybe greater than ever. Who knows what they will do if they can't find her.'

'Does this have something to do with the Woottens?' Lydia asked.

'I believe it might,' Rees said with a jerk of his head. 'Father and son. Jake wants Hortense and I suspect his father is trying to prevent that.'

She sighed, her lips tightening. 'But Will, Mr Wootten threatened us off his property with a rifle. Even if Rouge joins you, traveling to the top of Gray Hill is dangerous.' Rees nodded. He knew Lydia was right. 'And look at the sky,' she went on. 'It looks as though it might snow.' He agreed; he could smell it on the air. When he said nothing, Lydia continued. 'Promise me you won't go back to the mountain without the constable.'

Rees hesitated. He wanted to promise but he couldn't lie. He thought of Pearl, white and shaking from her sight of the man she thought might be the murderer of her fellow Sister. He thought of the break-in at the midwife's house and the attack on Jerusha.

Although he didn't speak, his silence was enough. Lydia stepped back, pressing her lips together. 'I know you, husband,' she said. 'You are mastered by impatience.'

'That's not what this is,' he said, stung. 'I wish to prevent future crimes. And I want to see justice for those who've been murdered or otherwise harmed.'

She exhaled in exasperation and nodded. 'May I at least ask you to be careful?'

'I promise I will be careful,' he said, turning to leave.

'And please, take care of Hannibal,' Lydia added. 'Yesterday was hard on him.'

When Rees reached the inn, he found the yard more crowded than he would have expected on a Tuesday. He left Hannibal and the wagon with the ostler and went quickly into the tavern's main room. Almost all the tables were full and everyone was eating. He stepped up to the bar where Therese stood. 'You're busy today,' he said.

'Snow is coming,' she said, adding proudly, 'and my brother is a good cook.'

He looked around at the people, all eating with gusto, and nodded. 'So I see.' He turned back to the young woman. 'Any word from Rouge? When is your cousin coming back?' She shrugged. Rees chewed his lower lip as he ruminated. It was unlikely Therese had received a letter. There wasn't time – mail service was even slower than riding from place to place – and anyway, he didn't know if Therese could read. And if she had been taught by the nuns it would probably only be in French. 'Merci.'

Rees left the tavern but he paused on the steps outside. From the landing he could see Hannibal, standing on the other side of the yard with his head drooping. Recalling the difficulty of driving the wagon to the upper elevations of the mountains, he went back inside the tavern. 'Do you know where I can rent a horse?' he asked Therese.

She pointed west. 'Near the fairgrounds,' she said.

After handing Rouge's ostler a few pence for Hannibal's care, Rees started walking.

It was already much colder than before and gray clouds covered the sky. He briefly considered postponing his journey up the mountain until tomorrow but the thought of Pearl's frightened white face spurred him on. What if that had been Jerusha?

The livery was behind the jail, now empty. Rees spared a thought for the former Shakers' hired men. Suspected of the murders that had occurred in Zion, the youngest boy had been imprisoned here. Last Rees had heard he had gone south. But he was now reminded that he should question the hired men currently employed by the Shakers.

The owner of the livery stables, a gentleman who smelled worse than the animals he owned, showed Rees the three horses he had to let. 'Broken to the saddle,' said the livery owner, moving the toothpick from one side of his mouth to the other. Rees looked at the aristocratic mounts and shook his head. Why, one of the horses looked like a lady's ride. That mare would not be able to carry Rees's bulk for any distance at all.

'You don't have anything else?' he asked. The stable owner gestured behind him at a mule tied to one of the posts. He stared at the animal. Although his coat was rough and shaggy the mule appeared strong. He raised his head and with a flick of his ear and turned a belligerent glare upon Rees. 'Will he allow me to ride him?' Rees asked uncertainly.

'Certainly,' the stableman said. 'And he'll cost you less too.'

Rees considered the few coins in his pocket and nodded. 'I'll take him.' He rented a saddle as well and transferred the rifle he'd brought, just in case. Then he mounted and started off.

Imagining curious and mocking eyes staring at him, he felt uncomfortable riding a mule out of town. Usually horse owners rode mules only when the horses had to be sold during financial reverses. But as Rees began to climb into the hills he was grateful for this mount. The mule proved to be more surefooted on the snow-covered slopes as well as on the rocky terrain lower down. Also, because the mule was slightly smaller than a horse, riding him astride was easier on Rees's unprepared thigh muscles. He did not ride often, preferring his wagon.

He passed the small store in just over an hour. Although it had seemed high up on Gray Hill the first time Rees had accompanied Rouge into these highlands, now the shop seemed almost to sit in the valley below.

Rees continued up. As he passed the turn off to Granny Rose's cabin, snowflakes began to fall from the sky, fat lazy flakes from clouds that reclined indolently across the sky. But when he turned and looked to the west he saw a darker gray wall racing toward him. He paused, considered returning to town but he was already so far up that the storm would hit him before he could make it down. Swallowing, and realizing that Lydia had been right – this journey had not been the wisest course – he turned and urged the mule forward.

The snow thickened quickly. The fat flakes fell faster and faster and the winds began picking up. Despite the thick forest on either side that protected Rees from the worst of the increasing storm, he and his mount were soon quickly wrapped in cold white whirling snow. Rees could feel the mule trembling beneath him and the wind went right through his greatcoat. When he looked down at himself he saw only white. The blown snow pasted itself to him so he resembled a walking snowman.

Rees could no longer tell how much snow was falling from the sky and how much was whipping up from the ground. With the thick white curtain surrounding him he could no longer see the narrow track ahead. Now he must rely on the mule to find his way.

The wind began to take down branches; the air was filled with the sounds of snapping and cracking wood. He heard something big go down in the woods to his right but the thick snow prevented him from seeing what it was. It was close enough though that the thud reverberated through the forest. Both the mule and rider jumped and Rees almost fell off.

Realizing that the snow was deepening around the mule's legs, Rees slid off and began to walk. The snow was well over his

ankles and rapidly approaching his knees. His leather boots were
already wet and soon the damp would seep through to his feet.
How he missed his wagon now although he knew that the snow
would catch at the wheels and make movement difficult.

He did not know where he was. He could feel the rise and fall
of the track but otherwise had no sense of location. Even the thick
woods that pressed in on both sides had almost completely
disappeared into the flying snow.

Then he caught the scent of wood smoke. Although he could
not identify the direction from which it emanated or even estimate
the distance, at least he knew a human habitation lay nearby.

The mule knew it too. He plunged forward, almost pulling the
reins from Rees's grasp. He hurried after his mount, terrified that
if he lost hold of the leathers he would be alone out here. His
boots slipped and skidded in the snow and if it were not for the
mule, who kept pressing forward, he would have landed face-first
several times. Besides keeping Rees on his feet, the mule's forward
momentum carried the man forward as well. Presently, Rees sensed
the ground leveling out. From the white wall ahead the shadowy
form of a porch, steps, and a cabin behind them solidified into
view.

TWENTY

B reathing a prayer of relief, Rees looped the reins around the
porch rail. He had arrived at the Wootten cabin. They might
greet him with a rifle but right now Rees didn't care. He
stumbled up the steps and to the door. He needed to get inside,
he and the mule both lest they freeze to death. He pounded on the
door with one gloved, but still very cold, fist. After only a few
anxious moments, the door opened. The young man in the opening
looked at Rees and motioned him inside, saying as he did so,
'What are you doing up here?'

'I have a mule outside,' Rees said.

The air within the cabin smelled of damp soil, of wood smoke
and bacon, and of unwashed people. He looked at the two boys,

recognizing the young man who had opened the door as Jem. Jake was seated in front of the fire, whittling an ornately carved bowl. He looked up and Rees saw the flare of recognition in the boy's eyes. He knew who Rees was.

He looked at the beaten earth floor and decided not to remove his boots. As he unwound his scarf a shower of snow fell to the ground. His hat and coat followed, adding more moisture to the wet patch by the door. Jem took each article of clothing as Rees removed it and slung it over a peg on the wall. Jake put the bowl by the hearth and stood up.

'I'll put the mule in the barn,' he said, brushing by Rees as he went to the pegs. Rees saw the yellowish fading bruises on Jake's face before he shrouded himself in a hooded cape and disappeared outside into the whirling snow.

'Warm yourself by the fire,' Jem invited.

'Where are your parents?' Rees asked. He was not eager to meet Mr Wootten, not after their first encounter had ended so badly.

'My father left early this morning,' Jem said. Although his expression was illuminated only by the firelight, Rees sensed that the boy was as reluctant to see his father as Rees was himself. And he knew by the bruises he'd seen on Jake's face that Mr Wootten was as violent with his boys as he was with others.

'And your mother?'

'My mother is sleeping.' Jem gestured to a door in the wall next to the fireplace. A door had been cut into the wall. Rees guessed that at some point the Woottens had built another room onto the cabin.

He looked around at this small, one-roomed cabin. A table made of planks, the bark just barely scraped away, sat a few feet from the fireplace. There was a bench on either side. Some wooden bowls, carefully carved with incised decorations around the rims, still sat on the table, left over from the most recent meal, Rees guessed.

In one corner, positioned so that the light from the nearest window fell upon it, was a hoop maker. Barrel hoops of all sizes, all expertly scraped white, leaned against the wall. Rees wondered which of the men in this family made the hoops. He couldn't imagine Wootten Senior spending long hours on the bench leaning over the scraper, patiently working the wooden splints into hoops. He guessed it was Jake who made the hoops. With spring, these hoops would be brought down the hill and sold, most likely providing the majority of cash this family received.

Rees squatted by the hearth and extended his hands toward the flames. He did not want to kneel in the cold dirt and the hearth was grimy with soot and grease.

'What are you doing here?' Jem asked. 'We don't get many visitors.'

'When do you think your father might return?' Rees asked, his teeth still chattering from the cold. Right now he felt as though he might never feel warm again.

Jem shrugged. 'Don't know.'

'But you better be gone when he comes home,' Jake said, coming through the door. 'My father don't like trespassers.'

Jem turned a look of surprise on his brother. 'He's company,' he said in a reproving tone. 'Mother says—'

'He's a spy for the constable,' Jake said. Raising his eyes, he added challengingly, 'That's right, isn't it? You come up from town?'

'I saw you, you know, when you attacked my daughter,' Rees said, rising to his feet. He didn't think the boys would jump him but he wanted to be ready, just in case.

Jake's eyes shifted away from Rees's and he mumbled, 'I didn't attack her. I thought she was Hortense. We didn't mean no harm to you or your daughter.'

'Hortense has been taken away by her mother,' Rees said. 'To Quebec.'

'I know that now,' Jake said, his mouth quivering. He looked away but not before Rees, to his surprise, saw the tears forming in those dark eyes.

'She said if her mother knew—' Jem began.

'Hush,' Jake ordered his brother, turning on him.

'Hortense said her mother wouldn't approve,' Rees said. 'She told me that.'

'She told you that?' Jake repeated, his voice rising into a question.

'Yes. She said that the two of you developed tender feelings for one another,' Rees said, examining the young man standing before him. Jake's shaggy black hair hung lank and uncombed over the collar of his buckskin jacket and a dark beard shadowed his chin. Rees guessed the boy was illiterate and knew nothing outside of the mountains in which he'd grown up. No wonder then that Bernadette would not want to see her daughter married to this young man.

But Jake's eyes were fringed with thick dark lashes and despite the bruises on his face he seemed gentle. 'Hortense must have been very frightened when you abducted her from the cart,' Rees said.

'No—' Jake began.

'How long did it take before she began to respond to you?'

'She wasn't scared of me.'

'But you took her,' Rees said. 'And you stole her horse.'

Jake looked down. 'Yes, we did do that. But I already know'd her. I saw her one time when she was visiting the Bennetts.'

'You already knew her?' Rees repeated, recalling Mrs Bennett's description of Hortense and the unexpected turn she'd made to the left.

Jake nodded. 'Yes. I told you. I saw her once when she visited the Bennetts. So I kept an eye out for her. Next time I saw her I spoke to her.'

'She knew you,' Rees said. Jake nodded again. 'You were meeting?' Hortense had kept that fact to herself.

'When my father wanted us to get help to look after Mother,' Jem said, speaking for the first time, 'Jake thought Hortense would—'

Jake hissed at him to be quiet.

'Did she know you were going to take her?' Rees asked.

'Well.' Jake's gaze shifted to the floor. 'I kept watch for her. I knew that when Mrs Bennett started birthing her baby, Hortense would come. And she did.' Jake's response did not answer Rees's question. But he knew it already. Hortense and Jake had arranged the false kidnapping between them.

'I see,' Rees said. His tone sent the blood into Jake's face and he burst into speech.

'She told me her mother wouldn't approve of me. So I thought, well, if Hortense really got to know me that wouldn't matter . . . and when she did she liked me.' Jake's voice lifted with pride.

'But she fled from this house, barefoot and without a cloak, in the middle of a snowstorm,' Rees said. 'If she liked you so much what happened?'

'That was because Father—' Jem began, stopping when Jake told him to shut his mouth.

Rees nodded in understanding. No doubt both parents objected to this connection. He himself could not imagine a more mismatched pair.

'Hortense does love me,' Jake said. 'She does. We were planning to run away together. But I couldn't find her once she returned to the flatlands. I kept searching for her.' Jake looked up to meet Rees's eyes. 'I'm sorry if I scared your daughter. I just thought – I hoped it was Hortense.'

'All right,' Rees said. He believed the boy. Desperate to find the girl he loved, Jake had not been thinking clearly.

The thud of footsteps on the porch sent Jake to his feet. 'Father,' gasped Jem. Even in the dim and flickering firelight Rees could see Jem's cheeks go pale. 'He can't find Mr Rees here.'

'The loft,' Jake said, grabbing Rees by the elbow and jerking him toward the ladder.

Once Rees would have stood and fought, despite standing in the other man's house. But the events in Dugard had burned some of that combativeness out of him and he allowed Jem to hurry him to the ladder. He paused only to point and say, 'My coat.'

Jem fetched coat, hat and scarf and hurled it at Rees. He quickly climbed the ladder into the loft. As soon as he pulled his leg up into the opening Jem pulled away the ladder.

Rees realized he would have to remain on his hands and knees. He could not stand upright in this space. The ridgepole that held up the roof was no higher than shoulder height and anyway the smoked meats – ham and bacon mostly – occupied almost all the center of the attic. The eaves pitched down at a steep angle. Cracks between the wooden shingles permitted snow to sift into the loft; the floor was dusted with the white powder. At either end of the pole, two windows filled with greased paper let in a faint light. Very faint. He realized the sun was going down and soon even the dim illumination coming through the thick clouds would be gone.

Although smoke from the fireplace below penetrated the loft, the air was bitterly cold. The only heat coming into this room emanated from the fireplace chimney and it was barely noticeable. Rees put on his coat and huddled as close to the stones and daub as he could.

Not more than a few seconds passed before Mr Wootten, stamping and blowing, came through the cabin door. 'How is Mother?' he asked.

'She's sleeping,' Jake said. Rees wondered if Mr Wootten could hear the slight tremor in the boy's voice.

'Good. Where'd that mule in the barn come from?'

Rees could imagine the terrified expressions on the boys' faces as the silence went on and on. 'Answer me.' Wootten's voice rose. 'Did that girl come back, Jake?'

'N-no.'

'Don't lie to me, boy.' The meaty sound of a fist striking flesh was clearly audible even in the loft. Rees looked around frantically. He had to get out of here.

'Someone came up from below.' Jem's voice rose and broke with a squeak.

'Who? Who came up?'

'Just a traveler. Someone lost.' Even at this point, Jake tried to lie and protect Rees. But Wootten didn't accept the explanation.

'Who is it?' The sounds of slaps and punches punctuated the words. 'Who are you hiding?'

'Mr Rees,' screamed Jem. Rees didn't blame the boy, understanding that Jem was trying to protect his brother.

'Where's the ladder. Git me that ladder.' Another slap. 'Don't ever lie to me again, boy.'

By then Rees had kicked out one of the windows and was squeezing his big body through the opening. A thicket of evergreens edged the back of the cabin but were too far away for him to jump to. He lowered himself from the window ledge and hung by his hands for a few minutes before he dropped to the ground. Although he twisted his weak ankle, the snow cushioned his fall and he was able to walk. At a hobbling run, he headed right. He could barely see the shed through the thickly falling snow. But he needed that mule. Rees knew he wouldn't make it very far at all on foot in the snowy and rapidly darkening woods.

TWENTY-ONE

Only two horses, an old cob and the mare stolen from the midwife's buggy, shared the barn with the mule. Rees looked around. His rifle, the shot bag and powder horn were neatly hung upon a nail, but in the rapidly darkening shadows he could not immediately see the saddle he'd rented from the livery. He did not dare take the time necessary to search for it. Wootten would be on him as soon as he realized Rees had escaped through the window. Although he could not be sure the other man would shoot him, he did not want to take the chance. Wootten clearly did not like visitors. So Rees put an old rope bridle on the mule – the first one he found – and threw the saddle blanket over the shaggy back. Then he took his rifle, his shot bag and the powder horn from the nail and mounted.

Without the saddle, the rifle had to be carried and was awkward in Rees's grasp. But he was afraid to leave it behind – and leave himself weaponless if Wootten threatened him. He kicked the mule in the side and they went out into the snow. The cold wind bit through Rees's greatcoat.

He headed in the direction in which he believed the path lay. As he crossed the yard, Wootten barreled out of the door. At least Rees assumed the shadowy figure moving from the cabin was Wootten. The combination of twilight and the thick whirling snow made objects just a few feet away invisible. He saw only the motion.

'Hey. Hey you!' Wootten shouted, his baritone distorted and muffled by the snow. 'Stop.'

Rees kicked the mule's side once again and the mule obediently broke into a bouncy trot. As they started down the track, a gunshot sounded from behind them. Rees could not tell where the bullet had gone but he did not believe it had come anywhere near him. Wootten had fired blindly. The mule, however, jumped forward into a ragged trot.

Traveling through the spinning curtains of snow felt like being enclosed in a white cocoon: silent, private and safe, especially after the mule settled into a fast walk. Rees, however, knew the sensation of security was an illusion but he didn't dare travel any faster than they were already going. He could occasionally see the woods on either side when the white lacy shroud gyrating around him parted but otherwise he was relying entirely on the senses of his mount.

The howl of a wolf, taken up and repeated by others in the pack, sounded nearby. Rees felt the hairs on the back of his neck prickle and stand straight up.

Now the mule began flat out running, his legs thrashing through the snow. The clots of cold white flung up by his hooves smacked into Rees with muted pops. He hung on with all his strength. But his rifle, clutched to his chest with one arm, shifted and as he struggled to adjust his grip the mule shied. Rees slid off and found himself spread-eagled on his back in the snow. And the mule, relieved of his burden, shot off at top speed and disappeared into the white maelstrom.

Rees heard Mr Wootten shouting. Clutching his rifle, he stumbled into the pines edging the track. Oh, how his ankle, the one injured a year ago, ached. He hesitated. He did not know where he was and could barely see a foot in front of his face. Rather than haring off into the woods, lost in a storm and hunted by the wolves, it would be better for him to stay close to the road and follow it to civilization. But for now, he had to hide from the man pursuing him.

The howls of the wolves rang through the forest, much, much closer. It wasn't common for a wolf pack to attack a grown man, especially if he carried a gun. But the past few years with their bad winters had seen a surge in wolf attacks. And Rees knew that if he were on foot and lost he would be easy prey. Another howl shivered through the trees, this one sounding barely yards from where he stood. Terror decided him. He crept under the largest of the pines and began to climb. His left ankle was a blaze of pain. Rees found himself climbing with his right and dragging the re-injured limb behind him.

The lower branches were bare but as he climbed he found himself pushing through thick green boughs. Most of them bent away but some of them broke and the snap sounded like a cannon

shot to his ears. He paused, breathless. He didn't want Wootten
to hear him climbing clumsily into the upper branches. Besides,
as the tree limbs grew narrower they began bending under Rees's
weight.

His hands were so cold he couldn't feel the tips of his fingers.

He parted the green screen and peered down at the road. He
could see very little through the falling snow. But he thought the
flakes were not coming down so thickly now; he hoped the snow
would stop soon.

The creak of leather and jingle of a harness alerted Rees to
the Woottens' arrival. The golden glimmer of a lantern penetrated
the blowing snow, twinkling like stars, as Wootten rode around the
curve. He was speaking, although blowing snow muffled his words
and Rees couldn't understand what the other man was saying.
Rees guessed at least Jake, but probably both boys, accompanied
their father. A gunshot suddenly reverberated through the woods.
Rees jumped and almost fell off his branch.

'Did you get 'em?' Jem's voice rose high and excited. 'Did you
get the wolf?'

'Think so. You boys drag the carcass to the edge of the road
and cover it with branches. We'll get it on our way back. The pelt
will fetch a good bit of cash money.'

Through the screen of needles, Rees peered down at the track.
He caught glimpses of movement as the boys obeyed their father.
A gust of wind caught the snow and pulled it back, just as though
a giant hand drew back a curtain, and he had a clear view of the
men and horses beneath him. At that moment Jake looked up and
for a long few seconds he and Rees stared at one another. He
wondered how quickly he could load his gun, but before he moved
Jake looked away. The snow fell back across the scene, obscuring
the people below. Had Jake not seen him, Rees wondered. Or had
Jake chosen to say nothing?

The faint tinny clatter of bridle rings began to move away.
Without the reflection of the lantern, the road and the forest went
dark. Breathing a sigh of relief, Rees leaned his forehead against
the bark of the trunk.

He couldn't rest for very long, not in this cold. After only a
few seconds he lifted his head and prepared to descend. But he
paused. Was that a light shining in the distance? Although the

snow was no longer falling as heavily, the flakes still occluded Rees's field of vision. He focused upon the illumination and stared, blinking his eyes as he tried to see through the falling snow. It *was* a light, a faint orange spark that spoke of a warm fireplace burning on a hearth. Or was he just imagining it? Rees gazed upon the glow until his eyes began to water. This beacon didn't move. Could it be Granny Rose's bonfire? He closed his eyes and tried to orient himself. He knew Wootten's cabin was out of view and much higher in the mountains. Rees's eyes popped open. That blaze must be the fire burning outside Granny Rose's cabin. And that was where he must go.

During his sojourn in the tree, his ankle had stiffened and both feet had become solid lumps of cold flesh. Rees climbed clumsily down to the ground and made his way to the track. He would follow it as long as he was able rather than attempting to cut through this dark and unfamiliar forest. He might have enough warning besides to load his rifle before the wolves caught his scent and began hunting him.

When he came out upon the road, he saw the disturbance in the snow left by the horses. On the other side, almost invisible under the fir trees, was a lump covered by branches. A dark stain – blood – from the wolf shot by Wootten, had seeped out from underneath the pine boughs.

Rees started walking.

The road was easy to follow. Despite the snow that had fallen over the tracks left by Wootten and his party, the agitated snow was clearly visible. Rees walked in the hoof prints as much as he could, it was less difficult than trying to flounder through the deep untouched snow at the sides.

A wolf howled nearby. Rees lurched into an awkward run, fumbling for his shot bag as he did so.

A chorus of yipping and barking responded to the initial howl. He gulped. The wolves were all around him. Despite the cold, he began to sweat.

He had to remove his gloves to load the rifle and his cold hands were stiff but he managed to get the ball down the muzzle. He poured in the black powder, tamped it, and began to jog again. A shaggy gray wolf leaped out upon the road, its yellow eyes fixed upon Rees.

He hesitated only a second before raising the rifle and firing.
He knew Wootten would hear the shot and return but right now
Rees feared the wolves more than he did the other man. The wolf
jumped and squealed in pain. Although the animal dropped to the
snow he did not think he had killed it.

He took the few seconds necessary to reload and started running
again. Although the gunshot had scared away the pack for now
he knew they would return and very quickly too. He gave the
wounded wolf a wide berth. As he had suspected, he had not killed
the large male. The movement of the furry chest was clearly visible.
Rees began to run as fast as he could, an ungainly loping gait that
kept his weight from landing on his left ankle.

He made it as far as the hairpin curve, when the track took a
sudden and very sharp turn to the left. Rees could hear the wolves
behind him. He whirled and fired off another shot. His hands were
trembling as much from fear as from the cold and this shot went
wide. Nonetheless, the pack pulled back. But they were gaunt from
hunger. Rees knew they would keep coming until he found shelter
or they brought him down.

He left the track then, heading into the woods at an angle,
moving in a rapid limping run toward what he thought was the
location of Granny Rose's cabin. He could not see the firelight,
not yet anyway, and he prayed that soon he would be close enough
to see it shining through the trees. At least, as white snow reflected
the diffuse gray light from the cloudy sky, Rees could pick his
way through the black trunks.

He knew the pack ran behind him. He turned again, dropping
to one knee so he could more easily load his rifle. He fired from
this position but this time nothing happened. Rees swallowed and
his belly went hollow with terror. His powder must be damp. His
gun was useless.

Rees began looking around him for a likely tree to climb. He
wanted to live; he wanted to see Lydia and his children again. Oh
God, he thought, please don't let me die today.

The lead wolf, fangs shining in the dim light, began to creep
forward. Rees pushed himself upright, using his rifle as a support.
His legs trembled. He shifted his weapon in his hands so he gripped
the barrel. The stock would be effective as a club.

A shot rang out from behind Rees, missing the wolf but sending up a puff of snow just in front of him. The wolves fell back. Another shot, even closer, and the pack melted into the shadows under the trees. He knew they hadn't gone far. He tried to turn around but his legs would not move.

'Come on,' snapped a woman's voice. 'We don't got long. They'll be back.'

'Granny Rose,' Rees said, his voice so weak even he could barely hear it.

'C'mon.' Granny Rose grabbed his arm and pulled at him. 'Wootten came to my cabin looking for you. When I heard the gunshots I knew you was in trouble. And he'll be back.'

Shamed by his weakness – he should not need the help of this old woman – Rees pulled his arm from her grasp. But, although he knew they had to hurry, fear and relief had drained all his strength. It took the sudden defiant yipping of a wolf to send him scrambling into a clumsy run.

TWENTY-TWO

'Wolves were real bad last year,' Granny Rose said as she hurried through the snow. Her men's boots were too large for her feet and each step pressed into the snow with a peculiar thudding sound. 'We all lost livestock and even a couple of old men out hunting. So far this year they've taken a couple of children, sent out to gather firewood. And it's early yet. No one travels without a musket.'

'My powder is wet,' Rees said, realizing as soon as he'd spoken that he sounded as though offering excuses.

Granny Rose said nothing as she threw a quick glance over her shoulder but she increased her speed. Rees couldn't help himself. He had to look. He saw the shadows slinking furtively in his wake. Re-energized by fear, he broke into a ragged trot.

'Almost there,' Granny Rose panted after a few minutes of rapid running. Rees nodded. He could see the orange light coming from the fire burning in Granny's yard.

She stopped abruptly and, turning quickly, she loaded her old

musket and fired off another shot. A sharp cry told them she had
hit one of the pack. By accident, Rees guessed, since she hadn't
aimed and muskets were unreliable anyway.

'Dang,' Granny Rose said, sounding regretful. 'I didn't mean
to do that. Just meant to scare 'em off.' She reached out and tugged
at Rees's arm. 'Let's go.'

She had fixed a lantern to one of the posts of her rail fence.
She untied the rope holding it and motioned Rees through the
gate. He did not think he had ever been so happy to see a house,
small and shabby though it was, in his life.

Once inside, Granny put the lantern on the table. She stirred
up the fire and as the flames took hold and the heat seeped into
the room Rees finally began to feel warm. Not warm enough to
remove his greatcoat however. He dropped into a chair, finally
realizing how very tired he was. Now that he was safe he began
to feel every one of his hurts. His ankle ached, oh, with such a
grinding pain he groaned. And as sensation returned to his fingers,
they tingled and then stung as though a hive of bees were at them.

'What's the matter?' Granny Rose asked as she slopped stew
into a bowl and put it before him. It smelled far better than the
slimy pottage offered him by the Wootten boys and Rees reached
for the wooden spoon. His fingers couldn't pick it up. Granny Rose
took his hand and looked at the fingers. 'You were lucky I found
you when I did,' she said. 'You're starting a case of frostbite.'

Rees stared at her in horror. 'I can't lose my hands,' he said,
his voice rising. 'I'm a weaver.' The midwife offered him a thin
smile as she put her warm hands around his white fingers and held
on for a moment.

'You won't lose your fingers but they'll be sore for a little
while.' She gestured at his foot. 'What's wrong with it? I saw you
limping.'

'I sprained my ankle,' Rees admitted. 'It's weak. I injured it
last year . . .'

'Off with the boot. Let me look.' As she knelt before him he
struggled to remove his footwear. Every movement hurt. Granny
Rose finally took the boot by the sole and pulled. He could not
prevent the scream that broke through his lips when the leather
scraped over his ankle. Nauseous and trembling, he held on to the
table as she ran her fingers over his leg and foot.

'Nothing broke, as far as I can tell,' she said. 'But I wager it hurts.'

Rees, who hadn't the strength to speak, nodded.

'Finish up your stew now,' she told him. 'You'll need your strength when we go down the mountain. We don't have much time; I know Mr Wootten will be here soon. He's bound to have heard the shots.'

'What's wrong with him?' Rees asked, aggrieved. 'I've done nothing to him.'

'You asked questions.' Granny Rose hesitated. Rees could see the thoughts flashing behind her eyes as she tried to decide what to say. 'No one up here likes people interfering, him most of all. Why, what he done to Mr Morton . . .' She stopped suddenly.

'What'd he do?' Rees asked curiously.

'I shouldn't say nothing. It was gossip, that's all it was.'

'I often find gossip has a basis in truth,' he replied. 'What was it? You started this.'

'Some say he pushed Mr Morton off a log during a drive.' And when Rees did not immediately react, Granny added impatiently, 'Morton was on a log, spinning it for all he was worth, as he guided it down the river. When he fell off – or was pushed – his leg got caught. Broke his ankle and leg in so many places he'll limp the rest of his life.' Rees thought of the shopkeeper, walking with the aid of a stick.

'I know Wootten is dangerous,' he said.

'You'd best steer clear of him,' Granny Rose said.

'You mean I should pretend those boys, Jake and Jem, didn't jump my daughter? Granted, they thought she was Hortense but they still attacked her. Or that one of that family, probably Mr Wootten himself, killed a Shaker Sister at Zion? I can't let it go.'

'You'd best steer clear, that's all I'm saying. Now, you eat up. We'll talk but later, when we're safe. I'll wrap your ankle. Not sure how well you're going to be able to walk on it.'

As she gathered linen rags and began tearing them into strips, Rees tried to eat his stew. But he could barely choke down even a few bites; the combination of panic and pain had left his stomach in knots and he had no appetite at all. He did better with the chicory coffee offered by the old woman. He downed the hot liquid – with a liberal helping of sugar – in a few mouthfuls. His belly protested but he refused to yield to the rumblings and after a few seconds it settled.

Rees tried again to swallow a spoonful of stew but although the broth went down he finally spit the masticated chunk of meat back into the bowl. 'Sorry.' He shook his head at Granny Rose.

'Fright has a funny way of changing the body,' she said. 'Don't—'

The jingle of harness and the whinny of a horse penetrated the cabin. Granny Rose, a sudden nervous flush tinting her cheeks, turned a glance at the window. 'Wootten and his boys are here,' she said. 'You've got to hide.'

'I don't want to hide,' Rees said.

'He won't do nothing to me. But you?' Granny Rose shook her head at him.

'You're frightened too,' Rees said.

'Josiah Wootten is a man of quick temper and he's very protective of his family. Right now he's a cornered animal and dangerous. If you want to make it back to your family you better do as I say.'

Footsteps crunched through the snow outside. Rees exhaled unwillingly but he knew there was no more time to argue.

'Hide where?' he asked, looking around at the one room cabin.

Granny Rose twitched away the rag rug covering a trap door. 'Down here. My father dug out a room and a tunnel leading to the barns when there were regular Indian attacks. Down you go.'

Rees, with one boot on and one boot off, hobbled to the square cut into the floor and climbed down. The basement was not tall enough for him to stand upright but enough firelight penetrated through the cracks between the floorboards above to produce a dim light. At a painful crouch, he hobbled forward into the chilly gloom. Granny Rose hurled his boot in after him, almost striking him in the head, before she closed the trap door. He could hear the thuds of a fist on the door and Granny Rose's quick footsteps across the floor.

Rees sat down on the cold dirt floor behind a wall of hemp sacks with his back against the stone wall. Carrots and turnips spilled from the sacks. There were apples too. Although he couldn't see them he knew there must be apples; he could smell them, the sweet winey smell of overripe fruit.

'What do you want?' Granny Rose's voice easily penetrated the cellar.

'Where is he? Where is Rees?'

'Not here.'

'I heard gunshots.'

'I shot at a wolf pack that came too close. Chased them off too.'

Heavy steps crossed the cabin floor. After a pause Wootten said, 'You fired this musket recently.'

'I told you, I fired at a pack of wolves.' Granny Rose sounded irritated and Rees tensed, expecting Wootten to strike the old woman.

'You need to clean this weapon,' Wootten said, the sound of metal striking stone. Rees guessed Wootten had put the gun back above the fireplace. 'Jake, Jem, look around for him. Check the barn too.'

The door slammed. Wooten's weighty tread circled the cabin and Rees could hear the sound of opening doors and shifted furniture. 'I told you, he ain't here,' Granny Rose said. 'He's probably down off the mountain by now. You told me he had a mule.'

'He don't know the hill like we do,' Wootten said.

'Don't take much knowledge to follow the road down,' she said, sounding as though she were trying not to laugh.

'We followed the tracks most of the way,' Wootten said. 'Didn't find him. But it looked like the wolves mighta took down the mule.'

'Oh no,' Granny Rose said, sounding genuinely grieved.

Rees was grieved too – at the thought of paying for the beast.

The door slammed and the lighter quick steps of the boys tapped across the floor. 'No sign of him,' Jake said.

'Only mule in the barn is that old, broken-down animal she rides,' Jem said.

'You leave Job alone, you hear?' Granny Rose said sharply. 'I got a birthing to attend to.'

'If that farmer is lost in the woods he'll meet up with the wolves sooner or later,' Wootten said, crossing to the door. The floor squeaked as he turned. 'If he comes by, you send word.'

'How am I supposed to do that,' Granny Rose said. 'He'll be suspicious if I leave suddenly.'

'Shoot three times in a row. That'll tell me. And you better clean your musket before it blows up in your face. That musket is older than I am.'

As the three men stamped from the cabin, Rees tried to fit his boot over his swollen ankle. He could not stay here, that much was clear. He knew the hill man would return, over and over until he was satisfied Rees wasn't there. The leather of his boot had begun to dry stiff and hard and it seemed to have gotten smaller. Although the boot went over his foot and partially over his calf, the leather would not stretch over his swollen ankle.

The trap door suddenly swung open. 'Come up,' Granny Rose said. 'We've got to get you back to your family.'

'I know,' Rees said. 'Wootten will be back.' He stood up, barely suppressing a groan, and limped to the fire-lit opening in the floor. When he stood upright his head and the tops of his shoulders were above the floor. He swung his arms out and pushed himself up until he could put his knee on the floor. Climbing the rest of the way out took some twisting but he finally managed to crawl on to the floor. Granny Rose closed the trapdoor with a bang and re-covered it with the rug.

'I know another way off the mountain,' Granny Rose said. 'We'll go that way.'

'You don't need to come,' Rees said.

'You'll never make it without me,' she said. 'You can't hardly walk. And you don't know that way. Through the woods you'll run into wolves. And you go down by the main road you'll walk straight into Josiah Wootten's arms.'

Rees could not dispute the truth of that but he didn't like it. 'This isn't your fight,' he said.

Granny Rose shook her head at him. 'You'll have to ride my mule Job. I'll walk beside him and bring him back after.'

'Absolutely not,' he said, staring at the skinny, gray-haired woman.

'You're injured,' she replied implacably. 'You won't make it ten yards walking.' As she spoke she banked the fire and blew out the candle in one of the lanterns. 'Is your powder dry yet? We'll need both guns.'

Rees opened the powder horn and sniffed. He did not smell the characteristic odor of damp. 'I think it's all right now,' he said.

'Good. It's stopped snowing. That'll help.'

Rees put his gloves back on his hands and hung the scarf around his neck. He picked up his gun and shuffled after Granny Rose as she opened the cabin door and went out. Although he didn't want to admit it, he thought she might be right. The pain in his ankle was so severe he didn't know if he could make it to the dilapidated barn barely twenty feet away.

By the time he reached the shed – he moved far more slowly than Granny Rose – she had already finished saddling the mule. Rees stared at the silvery gray beast. Job was a smaller animal than the mule he had rented and for a moment he considered making a stand against riding. 'I don't want to hear any foolishness about your pride,' Granny Rose said, turning to stare at him. 'You can't walk down and that's a fact. You just climb up on Job's back. No argument, hear?'

Rees met Granny Rose's fierce gaze. Although this small, wiry woman bore no resemblance at all to his grandmother, a tall, fiery-headed Irish woman, he was reminded of her all the same. She'd ruled her family, including her husband, with an iron fist. Arguing with her achieved the same result as quarreling with a stone: no surrender at all, except the stone didn't turn around and give a little boy a clip on his ear. Rees suspected fighting with Granny Rose would end in the same way. Meekly he mounted the mule.

Granny Rose looked around her little farm and sighed, almost as though she never expected to see it again. Then she shuttered the lantern. 'I'll light it when we're safe,' she said. Rees thought of Wootten's loud and angry voice and nodded. The old woman took a firm hold on the mule's bridle and they started forward.

TWENTY-THREE

At first the ground sloped downward only slightly but once they entered the trees the incline became much steeper. Rees could not see a path but Granny Rose walked with confidence, her hand resting lightly on the neck of her mule. They threaded their way through the trees, the tall evergreens, their needles frosted with white snow, and the bare gray trunks of the hardwoods. Rees wondered how many times she had taken this route. She, and her mule, seemed to know instinctively where to step and which way to turn even when the direction was not obvious. At one fork, he would have gone right, where the trees grew less thickly, but Granny Rose went left, down a very steep hill into a ravine.

Although snow lay on the ground, the cliff on the left and the high wall on the right had shielded this space some and the white only dusted the stony surface. The high walls also blocked the dim light from the cloudy sky and so it was much darker here. Granny Rose pulled Job to a stop. She drew a small clay jar from her cloak pocket and used the ember within to light the lantern. The surroundings sprang into view. Rees gasped. Huge waterfalls of thick white ice coated the surface of the rock wall on the right. The ice dropped to the floor and through the narrow crevice. Shattered ice, sparkling in the lantern light, fringed that side of the rocky path. He shivered. Just knowing those huge sheets of ice coated the cliff just feet away made him feel even colder than it had above.

'What do you know of Wootten and his family?' Rees asked idly, trying to take his mind off the cold and the pain in his ankle.

She turned on him with a finger pressed across her lips and shook her head. 'Sound echoes,' she whispered, tugging the mule into a walk after her.

They followed the rocky cleft for what seemed like hours but was probably barely one. Rees took his scarf from his neck and wrapped it around his hands to form a huge wooly ball clutched upon the reins. Since the lantern illuminated a circle barely six feet in diameter, he could not see how far they had to go. When he glanced back over his shoulder he saw deep shadow broken only by a few flashes of orange where the candlelight reflected from the icy wall. The howl of a wolf penetrated the still cold air. Although, to Rees's ears, the baleful call sounded far away Granny Rose threw a nervous glance behind her and increased her pace.

The snow underfoot began to grow deeper. He lost the sense of walls pressing in upon him and suddenly he saw a silvery light ahead. The moon had risen and as the clouds parted it shone upon the snow with a bright white glow. Granny turned back and said,

'We are almost at the end of this part.' Her voice sounded hoarse, rusty with disuse.

The cleft ended on a bare hillside that dropped into forest. Under the moonlight the shadow of Granny Rose's small frame and Rees astride the mule floated across the white surface. His upper body appeared impossibly tall and his knees stuck out like jug handles. The stirrups, even adjusted to the longest length possible, were still too short for him. He stared at the shadow. It looked like some grotesque parody of the Holy Family on their way to Bethlehem. Rees knew he should be the one leading the mule but he also knew he couldn't. His ankle felt swollen, the skin stretched over the bone as tightly as a tourniquet. Anyway Granny Rose, although an old woman, did not seem tired by the journey. She was not even breathing hard. She pulled on the mule's bridle.

'Come on now,' she said. She cleared her throat. 'I've known him since he was born.'

'What? Who?' Rees asked in confusion.

She glanced back at him. 'Your question about Josiah Wootten. I've known him since he was born.'

'It's safe to speak now?'

'He won't be on this side of the mountain,' Granny Rose replied. 'Not yet anyway. He might know of the cleft, although I doubt he does, but by the time he reaches it you should be home.' She paused and then added, 'We still have to fear the wolves. They don't usually come down this far but last winter they hunted even in town. We'll have to see how this winter goes.' She paused. 'What were you doing at Wootten's cabin anyway?'

'I wanted to ask him some questions,' Rees said. 'I didn't have a chance before.' Since talking about the kidnapping and the murder would be so much better than focusing upon his physical misery, he decided to take this opportunity to question Granny Rose. He recalled Lydia saying she was sure the midwife hadn't told all she knew. But he didn't know what Lydia had intended to ask so he thought he would tiptoe into the subject by returning to the question of Josiah Wootten. Rees said. 'We have witnesses who say they saw him strangling the Shaker Sister. But how can I know if he's guilty if I don't speak to him?' He hesitated for a few seconds and then said, 'Do you think Wootten would travel down to Zion?'

'And strangle a Sister?' Granny Rose glanced back at him, her head tilted. Although Rees couldn't see her face, he sensed a certain puzzlement in her posture. 'He might go into that little village and threaten a man. But I can't see him harming a woman. He beats those boys, to keep 'em in line, he says, but I don't know that he ever laid a finger on his wife. I know he would never hurt me. He has a code, you see. He feels he must protect his kin – or anything that belongs to him. A fight with a man? That I can believe. But going into town and strangling an unprotected woman?' She shook her head.

'So, what happened with the shopkeeper? I mean why did Wootten attack him?'

Granny shook her head. 'No one really knows but gossip says that Morton was sweet on Wootten's daughter Bathsheba. Wootten didn't like it. Tried to warn Morton off. When he didn't listen . . .' She shrugged.

'Hmmm.' Rees thought that was interesting, especially since Morton had tried to shield the Wootten boys. 'Would you take his protection?' he asked.

'Me?' A gust of breathy laughter shook Granny's frame. 'Not me. I go wherever I please. Josiah's protection is too suffocating for me. And, to give the devil his due, he don't try to control me.'

Rees mulled over her description in silence. He thought Granny Rose might be a little too kind to Wootten. Rees had heard the man slapping his boys around. Of course most parents believed that to spare the rod was to spoil the child.

'He wouldn't hesitate to brawl with you,' Granny added warningly.

In his younger days Rees would have taken that challenge but he had other priorities now. 'The more he reacts by threatening me the more I wonder if he is trying to hide a murder.' he said.

'Iffen he thinks you're trying to hurt a member of his family he'll come after you.'

'But I'm not threatening his family,' he replied, sounding confused.

'You're not threatening Jake and Jem?' Granny Rose asked.

Rees hesitated. 'Well,' he said at last, 'it doesn't look good for them. They admitted kidnapping Hortense. But,' he added more strongly, 'I swear I am not persuaded either boy had a hand in the murder.' He saw the movement of Granny Rose's head as she looked back at him.

'I believe kidnapping may be too strong a term,' she said. 'I saw that girl with Jake, oh . . . weeks ago. Lower down on the mountain. She seemed as interested in him as he was in her.'

Rees could think of no response to that. He knew Granny's comment was essentially true – both Hortense and Jake had admitted as much.

'All right,' he said. 'Still, Wootten's reaction seems too strong.'

'His wife, Sally, is very sick,' Granny Rose said. 'And there are other things.' Her voice trailed away as they exited the forest into a clearing. Bright moonlight pierced the ragged clouds.

Rees looked around. 'Where are we exactly?' he asked. He heard Granny's chuckle.

'Off the mountain. You'll see.' She clucked at her mule and he moved forward reluctantly. Granny Rose might not seem tired but her mule definitely was.

They picked their way down the slope. Since the snow was deeper here the going was much slower. But, in a short time, they arrived upon a bank of a stream. The white ice surrounding the large stones protruding over the surface looked like lace. Rees heard a faint gurgling so he guessed the water was not entirely frozen.

He stared around, his gaze finally settling on the other side of the channel. An enormous downed tree reposed upon the ground. He stared at it, trying to pin down the elusive sense of familiarity. 'I know where we are,' he said suddenly. He had come this way a few days ago in his pursuit of Jake and Jem.

'Yes,' Granny Rose said with a nod. 'We are behind your farm.'

'I want to walk in,' he said, hating the thought of Lydia seeing him riding while a woman – an old woman – walked ahead. He would be unmanned in his wife's eyes.

'No,' she said. 'We may still meet a wolf pack. They always attack the weak and injured first and right now that's you.' She tugged at the mule's bridle and they walked alongside the stream for a short distance, until she deemed it possible to cross. Rees recognized the series of fairly flat rocks that formed an icy path over the stream. Granny Rose picked her way carefully across the rime-crusted stones and easily made it to the other bank. But Job, her mule, had a more difficult time. Halfway over one of his hind feet slipped from the stepping stone. As soon as his hoof touched the thin ice over the stream, he broke through. Both Rees's feet went ankle deep into the stream. The water underneath the thin film was running very fast. Although his booted right foot remained dry, his swollen left foot, with the boot only partially covering his foot and leg, took on water. His entire foot went numb. It was the first time since the morning that the ankle did not hurt.

Granny clucked at Job from the bank. He pulled his foot out of the water, lurched up to the next flat stone and scrambled, half-in and half-out of the stream until he reached the bank. While he panted, Granny ran her hands over his hind leg, 'You're all right,' she said at last.

'Maybe I should get off,' Rees said. Granny shook her head and took hold of the bridle once again.

They began the climb up the snowy slope. The mule was tiring. The journey had already been a long one and now they were climbing with Rees's heavy weight dragging the animal back. Job kept pausing to rest, blowing hard.

Rees, who knew they were close to his farm, couldn't wait to reach home. They were not traveling fast enough to suit him. Had Lydia waited up for him? He had been gone since early this morning and now it was approaching midnight. For the first time he wondered how she might feel. She would be frantic with worry. He pondered that for a moment and then decided, somewhat nervously, that Lydia would understand when he explained all that had happened. Surely then she would not blame him, he thought. But he didn't believe it. His mouth went dry at the prospect of her wholly justified anger and he licked his lips. In the cold air they began to sting.

Wrenching his thoughts away from the inevitable explosion waiting for him at home, he said to Granny Rose, 'Tell me more about Mrs Wootten. Is she a drinker?'

'Not really,' Granny Rose said. 'She drinks weak tea constantly. Allus has a cup in her hand. Her feet pain her and she is going blind. It is puzzling.' She paused and then added in a lower tone, 'I feel for her husband. She can't work and now he has the burden of her care.'

Rees nodded, his thoughts flying in another direction.

Mrs Wootten was a dead end. 'The boys, Jake and Jem. They must help.'

'Keep up with women's work, you mean?' Granny Rose laughed mockingly. 'They do no more than they must. They won't be staying home much longer, I'll be bound. I'm surprised they remained with their parents this long.' Rees nodded, trying to formulate another question.

But before he could think of one, Granny Rose said, 'We are almost there. Do you see the light?'

As his heart began to jump in his chest, he squinted through the trees. Both of the doors into the house faced west, on the opposite side from him. But he could see candlelight shining through a window; a beacon guiding him home through the trees.

TWENTY-FOUR

When Rees opened the door he found Lydia sitting at the table in the light of a fat white candle. She had dressed for bed, a blue shawl wrapped the shoulders of her voluminous white nightgown, and her braided hair lay over her shoulder. The candlelight struck flashes of gold from the thick auburn plait.

She had in fact lit many candles; candleholders sat on every windowsill.

She started when he limped through the door and rose to her feet with a grim expression. 'Where have you been?' she said, her voice rising as she moved forward. 'You've been gone since yesterday morning.' Before he could answer, Lydia burst into tears. Rees, who knew his wife scorned weeping, pulled her into his arms. She pounded on his chest for a moment before collapsing against him. He felt guiltier than ever.

'I'll see to my mule,' Granny Rose said from behind him.

He turned his head. 'You must stay the night,' he said to the old woman. 'Please. It isn't safe in the woods. No one knows that better than I do.'

She did not reply as she slipped out. The door slammed shut behind her.

'I'm sorry,' Rees said. 'So, so sorry. I couldn't get word to you. I went up Gray Hill—'

'I know.' Lydia looked up into his face. 'I mean, I guessed when you didn't return home for noon dinner. You could have been killed.'

Rees held her tightly. 'I wasn't. And after I reached Granny Rose, I was perfectly safe.' Rees hated lying to her but it was only a little lie. He felt Lydia begin to relax. They stood in silence for a few seconds before she spoke again.

'Are you hungry?'

'Ravenous,' Rees said, realizing it was true.

Lydia pulled away and went to the hearth to stir up the fire. 'Rouge came here looking for you.'

'The constable is back from Quebec?' Rees asked, momentarily diverted.

'Yes. Apparently, he changed horses twice. And he is quite annoyed with you for questioning the Woottens without him.' She pushed a kettle over the flames.

'I talked to the boys,' he said. 'Not to Mr Wootten.' The memory of his wild flight down the mountain suddenly hit him and he shuddered. At this moment, he did not think he ever wanted to climb that hill again.

'What happened?' Lydia asked. She put down the coffee grinder and crossed the floor to put a hand on his arm.

'I fell off the damn mule and twisted my ankle,' he said. 'And there were wolves.' She inhaled sharply.

'The wolves are bad this year,' said Granny Rose as, with a soft tap, she came through the kitchen door.

'I'm heating stew for my husband,' Lydia said to the older woman. 'Would you like some?'

'No. But a cup of coffee wouldn't go amiss.'

With a nod, Lydia recovered the coffee grinder. As she began turning the handle and the chopping sound filled the kitchen, Rees turned to Granny Rose. 'Do the Woottens know of that path we took down from the mountain?'

'Through the cleft, you mean?' she asked, cocking her head at him. He nodded. 'No, I don't think so. Possibly the boys. But that cleft is on my land. I found it one time when I was looking for another, quicker way, to the other side of the hill.'

Lydia brought Rees a bowl of steaming stew and put a loaf of freshly baked bread on the board. Rees cut a huge slab and slathered it with a thick layer of butter.

'I have 't eaten baked bread since I can't remember,' said Granny Rose, eyeing the loaf hungrily. Smiling, Lydia brought over another plate and put it in front of the old woman. She took out her dinner knife and sawed at the bread, cutting a piece that was almost as large as the one Rees had taken.

'What happened?' Lydia asked.

Rees shrugged. 'You heard most of it,' he said. She shook her head and he knew she would not be satisfied with that reply for long. 'What happened here?' he asked. He took such a big bite his mouth was too full to answer any more questions.

'You know Jerusha has been reluctant to go to school lately?' Lydia said.

Rees nodded, recalling his daughter's tears and her claim the other girls were mean to her.

'Apparently she quarreled with some of the other girls. That Babette . . . It became physical – I'm not sure why or how – and one of the others pushed Jerusha down.'

'A tempest in a teapot,' Rees said. 'Is that coffee ready?' Lydia nodded and rose to her feet to fetch the pot from the fire. But the frown between her brows did not disappear.

She brought a cup for both Rees and Granny Rose as well as the sugar bowl, full to the brim with jagged chunks nipped from the cone, and a pitcher of cream. He noticed with some amusement that Granny Rose lightened her coffee to a shade even paler than his own. An expression of utter delight crossed her face with the first sip.

'Not often you drink real coffee?' he asked.

'No,' she said. 'This is a real treat, I don't mind telling you.'

Lydia returned to the table and sat down. 'I'm curious about the Wootten family,' she said, smiling at Granny Rose. Although she sounded as though she were preparing for nothing more than a good gossip, Rees knew better to make the mistake of underestimating her purpose. And, from the sudden tension in Granny Rose's shoulder, he could see she understood Lydia's intentions as well.

'What do you want to know?'

'There are other children besides Jake and Jem?' Lydia cut herself a piece of bread and buttered it with careful deliberation.

'Oh yes. Six or seven in total. Let's see. The two oldest girls are married with babes of their own. Jake is the oldest boy. Now. His older brother cut his hand on an axe and died. Then Jem is next. Two more girls after him.'

'What happened to them?' Lydia asked.

Now we are getting to it, Rees thought, watching Granny Rose freeze.

'The older one run off, some say to get married.'

'And the youngest girl?'

'She died.' Granny Rose took in a deep breath. 'I told you about her. She was with child. No husband of course. That Hortense come up the mountain to deliver the baby.'

'And both mother and baby died?' Lydia said.

Granny nodded. 'It was a mercy really. You see, she were simple. Why, she couldn't hardly take care of herself. The Woottens kept her close to home.'

Both Rees and Lydia nodded in understanding. Many families bore children who were touched. It was always a shame the family bore in private.

'And what happened to her older sister?' Rees asked.

Granny shrugged. 'Don't know. She ain't around. Can't really blame her for running away. Couldn't have been much of a life, could it? Taking care of her mother and her sister.'

'Are you certain the girl and her baby died?' Lydia asked, following her own train of thought. 'I mean, did you see the bodies?'

'There was a nice service at the church.' Granny Rose drew out her reply. 'Memorial service.'

'Did you see the bodies?' Lydia persisted.

Granny blinked. 'No. The ground was already froze. Couldn't bury them.'

'What are you thinking?' Rees asked his wife.

'That perhaps both girls left,' she said with a shrug.

'But how would they live?' Granny Rose asked, her voice sharp with skepticism.

'Relatives?'

'I would've heard.' Her certainty brooked no dispute. Lydia hesitated, her gaze fixed blindly over the midwife's head.

'So, we should find the man the older daughter ran off with,' she said at last.

Granny Rose uttered a bark of laughter. 'Won't be hard to find him,' she said. 'He's old Morton the shopkeeper.'

'Morton?' Rees repeated in surprise, recalling the dour fellow he'd met on his first visit to Gray Hill.

Granny Rose nodded. 'That's him.'

'Not exactly a young woman's dream,' Rees said.

The old woman chuckled. 'No indeed.' Her smiled faded. 'Mr Morton was widowed a few years ago. He wanted to marry, no surprise about that, and was sweet on Bathsheba. But her father, didn't like it.' She paused and Rees remembered her story.

'That's when Wootten is reputed to have thrown Morton from the log?'

'Yes. He set up the store after that. Well, it was clear to everyone Morton wouldn't join a drive down to Falmouth ever again. Anyway, Bathsheba was never allowed out. Too busy taking care of everyone. I suppose she were sent to the store – for sugar and the like – and they started seeing each other on the sly.'

'So, what happened?' Rees asked. 'I didn't see a young woman in the cabin—'

'No. She's not there. Someone saw her with Morton and told her father and he dragged her back home. Of course she run off again. This time her father couldn't find her.' Granny Rose added with a shake of her head, 'He tore around in the devil's own temper. I'm glad he didn't find that child; he was threatening to beat her within an inch of her life. I don't know that he would've but I am certain she would never have gotten out of that cabin again.'

'When was this?' Lydia asked.

'Fall. I think. No, October. Late October or early November?'

Lydia and Rees exchanged a glance. 'She's probably far away by now,' he said.

'I would be,' Lydia agreed.

'I'll talk to Mr Morton tomorrow,' he said. 'See what he knows.'

'Be careful,' Granny Rose warned. 'Wootten is on watch for you now.'

'This time you better ask Rouge to accompany you,' Lydia said. When Rees glanced at her she added sternly, 'And maybe some deputies. Just in case.'

'She's right,' Granny Rose said. 'Just in case.'

'Very well,' he promised. It wasn't that he was frightened of Wootten – not exactly anyway. But his threats were a distraction. Rees could not imagine a reason so strong it would compel him to travel to Gray Hill alone.

'But I wonder . . .' Lydia paused, her brows pleated together. 'If the younger girl was always kept inside, who fathered the baby?'

Granny Rose shook her head. But Rees, staring at her, sensed the old woman knew something more.

'Who is it?' he said. 'You must have heard something.'

Throwing a quick look at her husband, Lydia added, 'Gossip maybe?'

Granny Rose sighed. 'Some say it was the girl's own father, Josiah Wootten, that fathered her babe.' And, seeing Rees and Lydia's shocked expressions, Granny Rose added, 'But it may not be true. Josiah ain't well-liked even on the hill. Some say it was Mr Morton. Likeliest, it was some stranger passing through. I told you it was a mercy the simple girl and her child died.'

TWENTY-FIVE

Granny Rose and her mule were already gone by the time Rees limped downstairs for breakfast later that morning. He'd overslept after his late night and dawn pink flushed the sky. The sound of Daisy's plaintive mooing clearly penetrated the kitchen.

Rees's ankle ached and his new boots were still too wet to wear. He dragged out his old worn boots and put them on. One of the soles flapped loosely but, after many years of wear, the leather was soft and stretched and he was able to pull even the left boot on over his sore ankle. Not pausing for breakfast, he limped out to the yard to milk the cow. Then he went back for his musket.

He wasn't sure if it would fire after the journey down the mountain earlier that morning. But he worried that Wootten might still be on the trail and would appear outside the farm.

Although the sun was rising and it looked as though today would be fair, the air was very cold. The snow that had fallen the day before would not melt away soon. He looked around carefully but did not see anything moving in the woods.

Usually, after milking Daisy, Rees threw down hay for cow and calf. But he did not dare climb the ladder to the hayloft. Fortunately Lydia had sent down a small hill of hay the previous morning and the cattle hadn't eaten all of it. Rees tossed some hay into the stalls and, leaving Daisy and her calf to their breakfast, carried the brimming pail of milk inside the house to his own meal.

He walked into a household drama. Lydia held Sharon's morning dish of porridge with one hand while she patted Jerusha's shoulder with the other. Sharon was screaming. Lydia threw Rees a desperate glance. Without pausing a beat, he put down the milk and took the dish from Lydia. He sat Sharon down in a seat and placed the cereal in front of her. She pushed it away. He made a show of blowing on it and poured some of the fresh milk over it. He stirred it and once again pushed the dish at his daughter. She picked up the spoon.

'Apron,' Lydia said, directing a sharp nod at the child. Rees looked at the little girl. Although she had a spoon in her hand, most of the cereal had dribbled down her chin and onto her dress. Recoiling in disgust, he tied a cloth around her. He knew David had probably gone through this stage but he had been away too often and had never seen it.

'I miss Simon,' Jerusha sobbed.

Rees turned to look at his wife. He thought she might scold Jerusha but instead Lydia sighed. 'I do too,' she said. 'We all do.' She turned a quick glance over her shoulder at Jerusha's four other siblings. They were playing on the other side of the kitchen. 'But it was Simon's decision to remain with David.'

'You should never have allowed him to stay there. Why couldn't we stay at Zion? Why did we have to come here?' Jerusha lifted her head and Rees saw for the first time the bruising around her left eye.

'Were you in a fight?' he asked.

His wife motioned him to silence. 'That's not the problem here, is it, Jerusha?' she asked. And when the girl did not answer, Lydia said again, 'Is it?'

Rees realized suddenly that he was missing at least one conversation. What had happened with his daughter?

'We'll be leaving for school shortly,' Lydia said. Although she looked at her husband, he guessed her comment was actually meant for Jerusha.

'You're mean to me,' the girl wept. 'My real mother wouldn't have been so cruel.' Turning, she fled into the front room, her feet stamping a rhythm to her sobs. Lydia closed her eyes briefly and exhaled.

'I'll speak to her,' Rees said, rising to his feet.

'No, don't. Please.' Lydia turned to him and forced a smile. 'She misses Simon.'

'And what happened to her eye?' he asked.

'There was some problem at school. I don't know all the details.' She paused and then added very quietly, 'Jerusha is in danger of being expelled.'

'What?' Although he'd had reservations about Jerusha's attendance, hearing that she might be expelled inspired an entirely different emotion in him. Now he was prepared to fight for her right to remain in school.

'This morning Jerusha and I are meeting with the mother of that girl Jerusha has been spatting with, as well as with the Widow Francine,' Lydia said.

'I'll drive you to school,' he said, wishing this girlish storm had not come to a head just now.

Lydia nodded. 'I'll walk back home with Joseph and Sharon.' She directed a weary smile at her husband. 'It is not a far distance. You can go on into town. I know you want to meet with Constable Rouge.'

'I don't want to go to school,' Jerusha said from the door of the front hall. 'No one likes me. Why can't I go back to the school in Zion?'

Rees thought of the murdered Sister and shook his head. 'It isn't safe there now,' he said. Watching Jerusha's face fall, he added, 'Maybe in the spring.' Lydia shook her head at him but did not contradict him.

'Help your brothers and sisters dress, please,' she told Jerusha.

Rees ate a square of yesterday's bread and gulped down the dregs of his lukewarm coffee before hurrying to the barn to hitch Hannibal to the wagon. Although the air was cold, even in the barn, he enjoyed the quiet and the calm.

Climbing up into the driver's seat felt like greeting an old friend. Rees's thighs still ached from the previous day's adventures so he was not sure he could ride astride even if he owned a saddle horse. He was also able to rest his sore ankle on the front board. All of the children scrambled into the back.

Driving to the school took almost as long as walking – because the wagon couldn't cut through the woods. Besides, even though it had not snowed as hard here as it had on Gray Hill, the snow on the road was deeper by several inches; not quite deep enough for a sleigh but enough to slow down a wagon.

When he pulled up to the dame school he saw a buggy with red-painted wheels there already. Lydia climbed down. As she and Jerusha went up the steps to the main door, Rees gathered the other children and brought them to the small room the widow used as her school. The door separating the schoolroom from the rest of the house stood open and through it he could see his wife and another woman nodding stiffly at one another. He glanced back at his other children. While Joseph and Sharon ran around and around the benches, Nancy and Judah played quietly some game involving Nancy's doll and Judah's horse. Since all of them were occupied he ambled down the hall to the small sitting room beyond.

The other mother had dressed in her best for this occasion. With the removal of her gray cloak, a dress of pale green was revealed. She wore white gloves as well and Rees understood this mother had aspirations of gentility. But, although she might employ several women as help, her cheeks bore a light brown color from days spent outdoors, so Rees knew she was still required to work outside. The school fees were probably a struggle. A flaxen-haired girl, a few years older than Jerusha if Rees was any judge, stood beside the woman. That must be Jerusha's enemy, Babette.

'Please sit down, ladies,' Widow Francine said with a desperate smile. 'May I offer you tea? Or coffee?'

'No, thank you,' Lydia said politely.

'This is not a social call,' the other mother said with a nasty snap to her voice.

The widow, hands fluttering anxiously, circled the two other women like someone trying to work up the courage to separate two fighting dogs.

'Your daughter struck my Babette,' said the aggrieved mother, staring at Lydia accusingly.

'As did yours strike mine,' Lydia said, turning Jerusha so that the light fell upon her bruised eye.

'That was her brother, trying to protect his sister,' said Babette's mother. 'After your daughter slapped mine. Several times each week this past few months,' she added with a sniff.

From the shelter of the shadowed hall, Rees examined Babette. She had her hands folded and was looking down, striving hard to appear innocent. But the glance she shot at Jerusha was full of malicious glee.

Jerusha was staring at the floor as well but her face was contorted with the effort of holding back her tears.

'My daughter tells me your daughter says mean things to her and pinches and slaps her when no one is looking,' Lydia said in a low controlled voice.

Rees wondered why his wife was not defending Jerusha more strongly.

'Well then, she is a liar,' said Babette's mother. 'My Babette would never ever be cruel to another. She is a sweet girl. A proper feminine girl, not a hoyden like your daughter who will run around throwing a ball with the boys.' She smoothed her skirts over her pregnant belly.

Two spots of color flamed into existence on Lydia's cheeks and she took in a deep breath. Rees could see her clenched hands. But she brought her anger under control. 'I'm told the girls will not play with her. Under the instruction of their leader.' She flicked a glance at Babette.

'Then you must look to the behavior of your own daughter,' Babette's mother said in a sharp voice. 'She is a hoydenish unfeminine girl.'

'Ladies, ladies,' said the widow in a wispy voice. 'I'm certain that, excepting this unfortunate quarrel, both girls are lovely, well-brought-up children.' Under the combined stares of both mothers she wilted into silence.

Babette stuck her tongue out at Jerusha and mouthed, 'Teacher's pet.'

Rees, furious on behalf of Jerusha, and seeing moreover that if he left this discussion to his wife they would be here another hour and more, walked to the end of the short hall.

'I daresay Babette was the favorite, the best pupil and the one chosen for all the desired tasks,' he said. Babette's mother jumped and everyone turned to stare. Rees bowed his head when he stepped through the doorway. He was so tall his head almost touched the ceiling. With him inside, the sitting room seemed to shrink and become both tiny and cramped. In this feminized atmosphere, his masculinity was both strange and intimidating. The widow sat down in her rocking chair and began fanning herself.

'Of course she was,' Babette's mother said, lifting her chin. 'And why shouldn't she be? She is sweet, well-behaved and clever.'

'What are you . . .?' Lydia, staring at her husband in annoyance, stopped and bit her lip.

'Babette didn't like the competition with someone cleverer, I suppose.' He turned his gaze upon the girl. She shot a glance at him and he saw the anger and defiance sparkling in her eyes. Then she looked down at her clasped hands, the expression of sweet-natured compliance that she used with adults sliding down to mask her true feelings.

'I don't know what you mean,' she said in a soft voice.

Rees would almost have believed it if he had not already seen her anger. He looked at the widow. 'Why are we here?' he asked. 'I am certain you do not usually call in the parents for a childish quarrel.'

'Well, she—' and the widow's eyes darted to Babette's mother – 'asked for a meeting. She was disturbed—'

'By the tales of physical altercations and other improper behavior,' Babette's mother interjected.

'It sounds like Babette already has support,' Rees said, reaching out to turn Jerusha's face so that the bruised eye was again clearly visible in the light. 'Babette's brother did this?'

'But she was hitting me. And she tore my dress,' Babette said.

Rees nodded, now understanding why Jerusha kept wishing Simon was here. 'And how old is your brother?'

'He's fourteen,' Babette's mother said. 'But I don't see what that has to do with it.'

'I see,' Rees said. 'Your daughter, who is older than Jerusha, and her fourteen-year-old brother have joined forces to attack my daughter. So, not only bullying but cowardice as well.' Babette's mother's mouth opened but no words came out. 'I will make it my business to drive my children to school and pick them up every day,' he continued 'And I'd better not see your son striking Jerusha. Otherwise he will have me to deal with.' He met the woman's hazel eyes and held her gaze for a long few seconds.

When he turned to look at Lydia she frowned but she did not say anything to him. Instead she turned to Jerusha. 'Will you be all right today? Until your father comes to fetch you?' She nodded. But Rees did not like the way she stared at the floor, the picture of unhappiness.

Lydia collected Joseph and Sharon from the classroom and joined Rees outside. 'I wish we could send her to the Shakers,' he said, 'but I don't dare, not with a murderer targeting the Sisters.'

'Why didn't you let me handle this,' Lydia said.

'What?' Rees said, looking at her in surprise. 'It was taking too long.'

'Because Babette will be even crueler to Jerusha now,' she said. 'And Babette will take more care to hide her bullying so that every time Jerusha reacts to the torment she will get the blame.'

For a moment Rees did not speak. He did not like to admit it but he saw the truth of Lydia's statement. 'It's easier being a boy,' he said at last. 'A boy's method for resolving quarrels is a much better one: a fistfight settles the matter.'

'Although the physical battles might be censured in a boy it is also expected,' his wife said, darting a quick glance at her husband. 'For a girl?' She shook her head and sighed. 'It will be even more difficult for Jerusha now. That is why I agreed to this meeting with her mother. I hoped . . .' She stopped.

'Babette has pulled the wool over her mother's eyes,' Rees said, experiencing a wave of guilt.

Lydia glanced at her husband. 'I understand from the widow that Babette's mother was raised in one of the wealthier families in town. A shopkeeper, I believe. A farmer's son turned her head and she married beneath her. She wants something better for her daughter.'

'That doesn't excuse Babette's behavior,' Rees said. But he felt helpless. Raising girls was so much more difficult than boys. Would he face this with Nancy and Sharon as well? 'I'll drive you and the babies home,' he said aloud, 'before I go into town to speak to Constable Rouge.'

TWENTY-SIX

Although Rees parked his horse and wagon in the inn's yard, he did not go inside and look for Rouge. Instead he climbed the fence and went down the road to the livery. He did not want to think about how much the loss of the mule and the saddle would cost him. But when he crossed the yard he saw the mule in the paddock.

The livery owner stepped outside. 'Hey you,' he said. 'My mule came tearing down the mountain yesterday. What happened? And what'd you do with my saddle?'

'It's up in Josiah Wootten's barn,' Rees said. 'I had to leave quickly, more quickly than I wished to.' He turned to stare at the mule. 'You got a good animal there. I'm glad he made it back.'

'What happened?' the livery owner asked again.

Rees hesitated; he didn't want to admit he'd fallen off. 'Wolf pack,' he said at last. 'He bolted.' That was true as far as it went.

'I see,' said the other man. Rees thought he probably did. 'You gonna pay me for that saddle?'

'I'm going to try and get it back first,' Rees said. 'But I have to go back up Gray Hill.'

'You make sure you do that. Otherwise it's three dollars.'

Rees thought that price was too high but opted not to argue now. 'You'll get it back,' he said and turned to go. He was glad he didn't have to pay for the mule as well. He had almost no cash money left from the weaving trip he'd taken down the coast, culminating in Salem, two years ago. He hoped to find some more custom this coming spring; in fact, he must. Otherwise he and his family would be struggling to make ends meet.

He walked back to the tavern. This time he kept to the street instead of climbing the fence. As he walked around Bernadette's house, the midwife herself came through the door. 'Mr Rees,' she said. He halted and looked at the door. 'I believe I owe you an apology.'

'You do?' he asked in surprise.

She nodded. 'Hortense confessed the whole sorry tale to me,' she said. 'Now I know her affections were engaged by that mountain boy.'

Rees nodded. 'Yes. Granny Rose told me Hortense and Jake met on one of her visits to the Bennetts.'

Bernadette twisted her hands together. 'Come inside by the fire,' she said. 'I don't want to talk, outside here on the porch, where any passerby can hear my shame.'

He hesitated briefly before going up the stairs and into the midwife's house.

Bernadette took up a position in front of the fireplace. Rees was reminded of his previous visit here when the midwife stood in exactly the same way. She'd been angry with him then. Now she held out her hands pleadingly. 'I pray you will forgive me for my ill-temper,' she said.

'I understand,' he said. 'I have daughters.' He thought of the meeting with Babette and her mother earlier this morning and sighed in his turn. Bernadette looked at him with sympathy.

'It can be difficult,' she said.

'What did Hortense say?' Rees asked.

Bernadette's eyes filled with tears. 'I'm sorry,' she said, swiping the back of her hand over her face. 'I was so angry at her for developing an affection for that boy.'

'Yes?' he said encouragingly.

'But . . .' She stopped short, her cheeks coloring.

'What did Hortense tell you?' Rees said, stifling his urge to shake the woman.

'Mr Wootten, Jake's father, tried to force himself upon my daughter.' Bernadette kept her face averted. 'He caught Jake kissing Hortense and said if she was old enough . . . well . . .'

'But Jake came to her rescue,' Rees said.

'Yes. How did you know?' She looked up in surprise.

'I heard about the fight,' Rees said. 'Jake is a good lad.'

'He may be but I will not allow my daughter to wed an illiterate mountain boy,' Bernadette said in a fierce tone. 'I vow, Hortense will remain in Quebec until she is married. And that will be soon, I hope.'

Rees could not tell if she were serious or not. But he suspected she was.

'That still doesn't explain the murder of the Sister in Zion,' he muttered. 'Unless Wootten saw her in that gray cloak and tried to have his way with her. As he attempted with Hortense.'

'And when he saw the woman was not my Hortense . . .' She swallowed.

'He strangled her. And we would never know the identity of the murderer if another Sister hadn't seen him.'

'I hope you catch this monster,' Bernadette said.

'I will,' Rees said. 'Don't worry. I will.' As soon as he was entirely persuaded Josiah Wootten was the murderer. He was not exactly sure why he was not one hundred percent convinced but some niggling questions remained.

When Rees entered the tavern Rouge shouted from behind the bar, 'What did you think you were doing, going up Gray Hill without me?'

'I couldn't wait,' he said.

'Right.' Rouge scowled. 'Because you can handle everything on your own.'

'I learned some new information,' Rees said, looking around him. 'I spoke to the Wootten boys. And your sister confided something Hortense told her.' Rouge eyed the weaver for a few seconds.

'Hmmm. I feared there was more to my niece's tale – more that she did not wish known.'

'I want to speak to that storekeeper again. Mr Morton. Will you accompany me today?'

'Why do you want to talk to that sour old coot?'

'Because one of the daughters of the Wootten family ran off with him before she got dragged back home by her father. I want to know what he can tell me about that family.'

Rouge regarded Rees. 'Ran off with Morton?' he asked in surprise. 'I can scarcely credit it.'

'I don't blame her,' he said, recalling the dirt-floored little cabin and the bruises on Jake's face.

'You really believe Josiah Wootten killed that Sister?'

'Not for sure but I think it's likely. Wootten certainly terrified Hortense. And there's the death of another of the Wootten girls and her babe. But I don't want to go up that mountain again without company.' He almost confessed his experience with Josiah Wootten as well but decided against it.

'Wootten threatened you, did he?' Rouge grinned knowingly.

Rees nodded, not trusting himself to speak. He didn't want to admit that he had not only been chased down the mountain but that he had had to be rescued by a woman, the midwife Granny Rose.

'He's a vicious old bastard,' Rouge continued. 'Not one to cross.'

'We should take our rifles,' Rees said. 'And maybe Thomas can accompany us as well.' He thought they should take as many men as possible.

'Wootten really put the fear of the devil in you,' the constable said, smiling. 'Don't be embarrassed. Not many men in this town would go up against him.'

'You know him then?' Rees asked.

Rouge shrugged. 'Barely at all. But there are stories . . .' His smile faded. 'And you're right. We will take our rifles. Not Thomas though. He's cooking today and it will soon be noon. I don't want to lose the custom. People seem to like his food.'

But Thomas, who'd been listening, pleaded to join them. Although Rees did not understand all of the French, he caught enough to know that Thomas was bored. But Rouge refused, not entirely for selfish reasons. He did not want to leave Therese alone in town. Anti-French sentiment was still running high and she was just a girl. So Rees drove in his wagon with Rouge on his own horse. Rees could not help remembering his first journey up Gray Hill with the constable. It was only a few days previously but so much had happened since then that it seemed as though weeks had passed.

TWENTY-SEVEN

Although no wagons or buggies were pulled up to the general store, a couple of male customers stood inside. Rees thought the two men were father and son. The older one did all the talking with Morton as they dickered over the price of flour. Morton glanced once at the new arrivals and then ignored them until his two other customers left.

'What do you want?' he asked in an unfriendly voice.

Rouge turned to nod at Rees.

'I understand you ran off with one of Josiah Wootten's daughters,' Rees said.

Morton hesitated, frowning as though he did not want to answer.

'We're trying to find a murderer,' Rouge said, leaning toward the other man.

'You'd best tell us what we want to know.'

'I've met Wootten,' Rees said. 'He came after you, didn't he?'

Morton blinked several times and looked away. When he returned his gaze to the two men, he said sharply, 'There was no running off. Me and her were going to get married. It was all respectable.'

'You knew her from the store?' Rees asked.

'Known her since she was five years old. Tried to court her a few years back – until her daddy did this.' He gestured to his leg. 'Once I got the store, though, I seen her all the time. With her mother sick and her sister not right in the head, Bathsheba were the one who came down.'

'What do you mean, her sister wasn't right in the head?' Rees asked, his voice fiercer than he intended.

'She could hardly talk,' Morton said. 'Mainly grunted. Had that funny face.' He gestured at his own grizzled countenance. Rees nodded slowly.

'When was this?' Rouge asked. 'When did you and Wootten's daughter plan to marry?'

Morton sighed. 'It were February. We knew her family wouldn't

like it so she met me here in the store. We were planning to drive
down to town and get married. Spend the night.' He forced a grin.
'We knew they'd have to accept we were married then.'

'What happened?' Rees asked.

Morton lifted one shoulder in a shrug. 'Her father caught up to
us halfway down the mountain. He threatened me.' He rubbed his
chin and Rees guessed Wootten had done more than threaten. 'He
told me he'd kill me if I ever looked at his daughter again and
dragged her home kicking and screaming.'

'Did you lie with her?' Rees asked bluntly.

Morton shook his head regretfully. 'Didn't get the chance, did I?'
He heaved a heavy sigh so redolent with onions Rees stepped back.

'You haven't seen her since?' he asked.

Morton shook his head. 'Not since she run off,' he said
regretfully.

'I don't understand,' Rouge said. 'Rees told me she had a baby.'

'That was the sister,' Morton said. 'She and the baby died.'

Rees tapped his finger on his lip. 'So who was the father of her
baby?' he asked.

Morton shrugged. 'Only God knows. She tried to follow
Bathsheba, you see, so the fool girl was alone on the road. Some
man took advantage. A'course they all blamed Bathsheba. I wasn't
surprised to hear she'd run off again.'

'And when did she run away?' Rees asked, trying to get the
timing straight.

'Right after her sister and the baby died.' Morton chewed his
thumbnail. 'Must have been October. Or November. Yes, that's it.
Wootten came down here, screaming and threatening to kill me.
But I didn't know where she was. Still don't. I hope she's safe
though.' His forehead furrowed with worry and Rees realized
Morton genuinely cared for the girl.

'Do you have any idea where she could have gone?' Rees asked.

The shopkeeper shook his head. 'I wish I did. Wootten went
around to all the cabins on Gray Hill and she weren't anywhere.
I just hope she's safe.' His voice trailed away and Rees nodded.
Where would a young girl go? Friends or relatives – but Wootten
would have found her then. There was nowhere else unless she
had fled to Zion, the Shaker community in the valley. Rees thought
of Pearl and her eager description of the man who had killed the

Sister. Did Wootten suspect his daughter was hiding with the Shakers? Perhaps that was why he'd gone to Zion, not to recover Hortense as Rees had once thought, but to take back his daughter. And Pearl had seen him. Rees had to talk to her again.

'I hope you find her,' Morton added.

They talked for a few minutes more but as Mr Morton had nothing more to add Rees and Rouge started back down the mountain.

By the time they reached the tavern the sun was beginning to decline in the sky. It was long past dinner time; Rees would have known that even without his pocket watch. He was famished. When Rouge offered him a meal, Rees accepted eagerly. Therese wiped off a table with a sour-smelling rag and both Rees and Rouge sat down to wait.

'I suppose we have to look for the girl now,' Rouge said glumly.

'I have an idea about that,' Rees said. He stopped speaking while Therese brought him a mug of coffee. When the cream and sugar chunks were deposited on the table as well, he continued. 'I think she went to Zion.'

'The Shakers?' Rouge's initial surprise melted into acceptance. 'Of course she did. There's nowhere else.'

'In fact,' Rees continued, 'I believe she's calling herself Pearl now. She was one of the girls who found the body of her murdered Sister. And she identified her father.'

'By name?' Rouge asked.

'No, not by name. She described him though. To increase the drama of the situation,' Rees added, his voice going acid.

'Did Wootten see his daughter?'

'No. I don't know. Maybe.' Rees hesitated, thinking. 'If Wootten saw her, he must now know where she's hiding. Besides, Pearl saw Jake, her brother.' He recalled the girl's fear. 'Yes.' He drew out the word as he pondered. 'Jake might have seen her as well.' Would the boy tell his father? Rees wasn't sure. 'Pearl knows she isn't safe.'

'Do you think Wootten will go after her?' Rouge asked. 'Probably.' He answered his own question.

Rees nodded. 'I think he did once already. And the Sister in Hortense's cloak got in the way. We should warn the Shakers to watch for him.' He imagined Brother Jonathan confronting the brutal Wootten and shuddered. 'We better hurry.' Despite the hollowness clenching his belly, he wished he had not agreed to dinner. He still had to collect his children from school. And it would be dark in a few hours. When Therese delivered the plates to the table, Rees took such a big mouthful of steak he almost choked. Rouge thumped him on the back.

'Perhaps you shouldn't hurry quite so much,' he advised.

They both ate quickly. As Rees put on his coat in preparation for leaving, Rouge said, 'I'll catch up to you.' He nodded, knowing that Rouge, on horseback, would travel faster than the wagon.

'I must stop at school to collect my children anyway,' Rees said.

Eating dinner had cost him precious time. Harnessing Hannibal to the wagon devoured another twenty minutes or so. When he finally climbed up into the wagon seat he knew he would be late. He hoped Jerusha and her siblings had had the good sense to wait.

Slapping the reins down upon Hannibal's back, Rees pushed the gelding forward as fast as he would go. Still, as he'd feared, school had already been dismissed. Most of the children were already gone although he spotted Babette, loitering by the road as though waiting for someone.

Rees's children, Nancy, Judah and Joseph anyway, were standing with the widow on the steps. From a distance it appeared she was protecting them within the circle of her arms. But where was Jerusha? Then Rees saw her red cloak surrounded by several older boys.

The wagon had barely rolled to a stop before he jumped out and begun to hurry. His sore ankle throbbed with the sudden impact but he ignored it. 'Jerusha,' he shouted. 'Hey.' Two of the boys looked up. Seeing a very angry father bearing down upon them they fled toward the road. He made as if to follow but they easily avoided him and ran down the lane. He saw Babette run out to meet them. Their laughter floated through the still air to his ears.

Rees turned back to Jerusha. 'Did they hurt you?' he shouted as he ran to her side. 'Are you all right?' She sat up. Her cloak, her dress, her face and her hands were coated with mud. Dropping on one knee, he reached out for her. She was sobbing and tears streaked her dirty face. 'Was that Babette's brother?' he asked. She nodded.

'And his friends,' she quavered. Rees helped her up. What should he do now? Putting an arm around her shoulders, and transferring mud to his greatcoat, he walked her back to the widow.

'I'm sorry,' she said. Rees's stifled his first impulse – he wanted to shout accusingly at her for allowing those boys to torment his daughter, but the old woman looked frightened herself. 'I was very glad when those rough brutes left school for good,' she said, her panicky breaths separating each word.

'Babette was at the bottom of it,' he said.

The widow nodded, biting her lip. 'I always wondered if she was as sweet as she seemed . . .' she began, her voice trailing away. Her bosom in its plain black dress rose and fell with the intensity of her sigh. 'I don't know what to do.'

Her admission sent a wave of sympathetic understanding through Rees. He knew she didn't want to expel any of the children. The fees supported her and she was probably barely surviving as it was. 'I don't either,' he said. 'Let me talk to my wife. Maybe there is some solution that will answer.' He didn't see one now but sometimes Lydia was able to find some compromise.

The widow nodded, tears forming in her eyes. Rees looked away, embarrassed. 'Come children,' he said, stretching out a hand to the three youngest. 'Let's go home.'

TWENTY-EIGHT

Jerusha refused to sit in the wagon bed with her siblings. Instead, she sat on the front seat next to her father. Although she was no longer weeping uncontrollably, her body still quivered with hiccups and every now and then she sniffled. When Rees reached out an arm to pull her close she stiffened slightly and then relaxed against him. She was, he thought, still just a little girl.

'What happened?' he asked.

'Those boys were waiting for me outside,' Jerusha said, her voice hoarse with tears.

'Now wait a minute,' he said, trying to speak gently. Something was not right. 'That can't be the entire story.'

Jerusha stiffened once again and then all the air went out of her. 'No,' she said. 'Babette and I quarreled again. I-I slapped her,' she admitted.

He nodded, not quite sure what he should say. 'I understand why,' he said at last. 'But you shouldn't do that.'

'But why not? If Simon were here . . .' She broke down into sobs once again. Rees knew he was in over his head. This time he kept silent.

By the time Rees reached the farm Constable Rouge was already there, sitting at the table and eating eggs. 'Oh no,' Lydia cried when she saw the wet and muddy state of Jerusha's clothing.

'Babette's brother,' Rees explained, pushing the children to his wife. 'We'll talk about this later.'

Lydia's mouth tightened and she nodded. Her nod seemed more of a threat than agreement but she changed the subject. 'Constable Rouge just finished telling me about your visit to Morton's shop on Gray Hill,' she said. 'And Mr Wootten's daughter.'

'I think she ran away to Zion,' Rees said.

'That would explain why Mr Wootten and Jake were both seen in Zion,' she said, her forehead puckering.

'Yes,' he agreed. 'Once they knew Pearl was there, they went after her.'

Lydia turned around to Jerusha. 'Change your clothes, my dear. We'll speak about the school later this evening. But now I must ask you to watch the babies for me while I accompany your father to Zion.'

'Do you think this is wise?' Rees asked in a low voice, pulling his wife to one side.

'Jake and his brother know Hortense is no longer with us,' she said. She turned to her daughter. 'You understand how important this is, don't you?' she asked.

Jerusha nodded. 'Of course. I can do this.' She squared her shoulders.

'But I don't want any of you to go outside,' Lydia added. The girl nodded, her expression serious.

Rees was surprised to see how his daughter pulled herself together to handle this responsibility. Was it because watching the younger children was familiar? Or was it because she wanted to prove to herself she was strong and capable and that she could be trusted to care for her younger siblings? Whatever the explanation, he was very pleased.

While Jerusha ran upstairs to change into dry clothing, Lydia collected her own cloak. As soon as the girl returned to the kitchen, in a clean dress and with her face and hands freshly washed, Lydia nodded to Rees and went through the door.

'What happened to the girl?' Rouge asked as they crossed the yard. 'She was muddy.'

'She is being bullied by one of the other girls in school,' Rees said. 'I arrived just as Babette's brother and his friend were pushing her into a puddle.'

Rouge nodded slowly. 'Do you think it wise to leave her alone here?' he asked, darting a sideways glance at Lydia. 'Maybe her mother should remain here.'

Of course, Rees thought. The constable always demonstrated discomfort and a certain suspicion in the presence of Rees's outspoken and capable wife.

'Jerusha needs to feel not only useful but competent,' Lydia said. Her stiff tone told Rees that she understood what was really behind Rouge's question but preferred to reply only to the spoken words. 'Being put in charge of her younger brothers and sisters will help her recover her confidence.' She turned to look at Rees. 'But we will have to find a more permanent solution.'

'I know. We can't have her coming home every day in dirty clothing.'

'Besides, she no longer wants to attend school.' Lydia's forehead wrinkled. 'I confess I am not quite sure what we should do.'

Rees nodded. He wavered between allowing his daughter to stay home – God knew Lydia needed the help – and insisting Jerusha remain in school. He couldn't help remembering how excited she'd been at learning to read.

'But for now, tell me why we are returning to Zion to speak to Pearl?' Lydia's question broke into Rees's thoughts.

He assisted her into the wagon. 'I think she may be Josiah Wootten's daughter,' he said. He patted his horse. Poor Hannibal was shivering in the cold; Rees had forgotten to throw the blanket over the gelding and then had remained inside far longer than he intended. 'At the very least, I'm certain she knows something.'

'I, for one, would not blame her for running away,' Lydia said.

'I don't,' Rees agreed. 'But her father is searching for her. That's why he went down to Zion in the first place – to look for her. And then he saw Hortense . . .' Lydia shook her head.

'Perhaps . . .' Her voice trailed away. Rees looked at her curiously. But before he could ask what worried her Rouge spoke.

'Enough talking,' he said, kicking his horse. 'Let's go,'

During the summer the Shaker Brothers tended the fields and their livestock. But with the beginning of the cold weather, they went inside, devoting more time to making the brooms, whips, boxes and baskets they sold to the World. Rees found Brother Jonathan in the wood shop. When Jonathan looked up and saw not only Rees but also Lydia and Constable Rouge behind him, the Brother's expression changed from mild surprise to alarm.

'Oh no,' he said. 'What's wrong now?'

'Nothing serious,' Rees said quickly. 'But we must speak to Sister Pearl again.'

Brother Jonathan regarded first Rees and then Rouge. 'Why?'

The constable looked at Rees.

'It's possible,' he said cautiously, 'that Pearl knows more about the Wootten family than she has confessed to us. If so, we need to know it.'

Jonathan put down his tools. 'Very well. Wait here. Allow me to find Sister Esther. She'll know.' When he went outside he shut the door even though it was almost as cold inside as out.

A few minutes later Jonathan returned with Esther behind him. She smiled at both Rees and Lydia. 'Brother Jonathan says you are looking for Sister Pearl?'

'Yes,' Rees said.

'She should be in the laundry today. Follow me, please.'

Rees and his two companions followed the Shaker Sister down the main road to the little bridge. The traffic on the main road had trampled the snow flat and the warm sun had melted large patches down to the dirt. But when they crossed the stream and turned toward the laundry house the going became much more difficult. Here, in the shadow of the trees, the snow had not melted and in some places the drifts lay knee deep. Rees extended his arm to Lydia.

The smell of wet cloth penetrated the tree break surrounding the shed, reaching all the way to the bridge over the stream. And, when Rees and his companions broke out of the trees, they saw that despite the snow all the branches and bushes were festooned with sheets. Esther went directly to the laundry and opened the door. She turned back and gestured impatiently.

It was almost impossible to walk inside the small structure. The space was crowded with racks, all draped with damp body linen drying in the heat from a fire blazing in the fireplace. A line of irons marched across the brick hearth.

One of the older Sisters came forward to greet them, her brows lifted. 'What are you doing here?'

'We're looking for Sister Pearl,' Esther said.

'Oh, she never came today,' the Sister said.

'Never came?' Esther repeated, her voice lifting in a question. 'But where is she?'

The other Sister smiled slightly. 'I don't know. I certainly did not think much of her absence. Pearl dislikes the laundry and escapes the work as much as she can. This is not the first time she did not arrive for her chore.' Rouge's sudden gust of knowing laughter attracted everyone's disapproving attention. When Rees frowned at the constable he shrugged, grinning. He clearly assumed he understood everything now. 'I planned to discuss this problem with you; Pearl's behavior exhibits serious disobedience,' the Sister continued.

'But she was here yesterday?' Esther asked.

The laundry Sister nodded. 'Yes. But she might as well not have been. I caught her staring into space, lost in a daydream, several times.'

'Excuse me,' Lydia said, moving forward. 'Do you think she was daydreaming? Or was it possible she had something on her mind?'

The Sister offered Lydia a cold smile. 'Does it matter? She was not working. "Hearts to God, hands to work." Pearl has great difficulty with the second half of that lesson.'

'Who might know where she's gone?' Rees asked.

The Sister hesitated. 'Glory might,' she said finally. 'They share a room.'

'Of course,' Rees said with a nod. 'The girls are friends.'

'Everyone here is both friend and family,' replied the Shaker in a repressive tone.

'Thank you,' Esther said, with a quick glance at Rees. 'Is she here? Or assigned elsewhere?'

'Here. She arrived first this morning with a cartful of laundry.' The Sister nodded approvingly. 'She is a hard worker and will make an excellent Shaker someday.'

As she stepped away and disappeared in the direction of the large tub, Rees experienced a flashback to his arrival in Zion last year. When he had come to this building he'd found a body floating in the washtub. He shuddered involuntarily.

Both Esther and Lydia glanced at him. 'I'll fetch her,' Esther said.

While she went in search of Glory, Rees and Lydia stepped outside. Rees took in a deep lungful of the cold air; it had been almost too warm inside.

Footsteps thudded on the stone inside. Rees looked up as Esther and her charge stepped outside. Glory, her mouth turned down with reluctance, glanced at Rees and then quickly turned her gaze to her clasped hands.

Although Esther, an escaped slave who had found a refuge in Zion, was not a small woman, Glory was still several inches taller and probably a stone heavier. 'I told Sister,' Glory said, 'that I haven't seen Pearl since breakfast.'

'But you share a room?' Lydia asked.

Glory nodded. 'Usually we walk together to the Dining Hall but we didn't today.'

'Why not?' Rees asked.

'She left early. She said she had someone she had to speak to.' Glory raised her eyes from her hands and met Rees's gaze. 'She did that sometimes.'

'Who was it?'

'I don't know.' She paused but burst into speech once again when the three pairs of eyes trained upon her did not waver. 'I thought it might be one of the Brothers.'

'I knew it,' Rouge said loudly.

'You walked to breakfast alone?' Lydia asked Glory, ignoring the constable.

'No. I met some of the other Sisters and walked with them,' the girl replied.

'Did you see Pearl at breakfast?' Rees asked.

Glory bit her lip. 'I'm not sure. I think so. But she wasn't at my table. And we are not supposed to allow worldly concerns to distract us.'

'Just so,' Rees said, put off by the girl's pious tone.

'Where would Pearl go?' Lydia asked. 'I mean, if she wanted to be alone?'

Glory shrugged. 'I don't know. We weren't really friends. We're not supposed to have special friends,' she added virtuously.

Rees wondered if Glory made these solemn pronouncements because of Esther's presence or if she really believed them.

'So, after breakfast?' Lydia prompted.

'I went to the laundry shed,' Glory said. 'I'm assigned to laundry this week.'

Esther turned to Rees and Lydia and nodded slightly.

'Thank you,' Rees said.

'Go back to your work,' Esther said. As she watched the young Sister run back inside, the Eldress said, 'She doesn't know anything. She's been here all morning.'

'So where is Pearl?' Lydia said.

'Probably keeping some young man warm,' Rouge said. When three pairs of disapproving eyes turned to him he shrugged.

'We'd better find the girl, and soon,' Rees said, a hollowness forming in the pit of his stomach. He recalled only too clearly his search for another missing girl last year here in Zion. He had found her alive, that was true, but he still had nightmares of finding her dead.

'Before we believe the worst,' Lydia said, putting her hand on her husband's arm, 'maybe we should search her room?' Esther nodded in agreement.

'I'll meet you back here,' Rees said.

While the two women crossed the hall, Rouge and Rees went outside. They crossed the road and went up the steep hill by the smithy. Rees's ankle began to ache as he struggled up the steep incline. He began to slow down. Rouge reached out to grasp Rees's arm and draw him up the hill.

The cottage in which Lydia had been living when he had first met her appeared even more dilapidated than it had a year previously. With the winter's frost, all the flowers that had filled the front yard were dead, the tall stalks brown and dry and crackling in the breeze. Rees went up the flagstone walk. The door, swollen with the recent snows, was even more difficult to open than before. Rouge joined Rees in throwing their combined weight against the wooden panel. It finally exploded inward, the door jamb shattering from the stress.

Inside, except for the sound of dripping water all was silent. Even the swarm of bees was gone, although Rees suspected they had found a home nearby. When he peered into the small room to the side he found the source of the dripping water: the roof was no longer whole and melting snow came through the ceiling in one slow drip after another.

Of Pearl there was no sign.

TWENTY-NINE

Both men left the sad abandoned cottage and started down the hill to the village. Although only mid-afternoon, the sun and the temperature were already dropping. Shadows stretched across Zion's main street. Soon it would be dark.

As the men joined Esther and Lydia in front of the Dwelling House, Rees asked, 'Find anything?'

'Pearl's second dress and her cloak are gone,' Esther said.

'Do you think she's run away?' he asked.

'Maybe—' Esther began but Lydia cut her off.

'No.' Lydia shook her head, her cheeks flushed with the cold. 'I looked under the mattress and found these.' She held up a small bag.

'The girls aren't supposed to own possessions other than their clothing,' Esther said. 'When people join they contribute everything they own to the community.' Rees nodded. Pearl would have been expected to do the same. Yet, somehow, she had managed to hang on to her treasures.

'But the young girls try to keep the things they cherish,' Lydia said. 'And they hide their belongings wherever they can.' Rees took the cloth sack from his wife and spilled the items into his palm. A necklace of carved wooden beads, earbobs inset with red stones and a small Bible comprised the sum of Pearl's few possessions. Lydia fingered the wooden beads and then held the earrings up to the light. 'These are not glass,' she said. 'They are true gems; rubies, I think.'

Rouge leaned over Rees's shoulder for a better look. '*Mon Dieu,* they look expensive.'

'Pearl had them when she came to us,' Esther said, eyeing the earbobs.

'So why didn't she take them with her?' Rees said.

But Lydia's attention had shifted to the necklace of wooden beads.

'I expect she is meeting a boy,' she said, holding it up by one bead.

Esther stared at it. 'I've seen that previously,' she said, her forehead wrinkling. 'I just don't remember where.'

Rees inspected the necklace as well. He knew he had never seen it but still he felt a tickle of familiarity.

'This is a simple thing,' Lydia said, breaking into his thoughts. 'Not worth anything, not like the earrings. They are valuable.'

'That doesn't matter right now,' Rees said. He could see the conversation going off at a tangent. 'Where is Pearl? She can answer all of these riddles for us.'

'Probably no longer in Zion,' Esther said.

'We can't be sure of that,' he said. 'If she is still here – and caught outside . . .' His voice broke and he started again. 'We must find her. It's already growing dark.' And it was already cold. Once the sun set any creature caught outside could freeze to death.

Spurred on by the urgency in his voice, Esther collected several Brothers as well as a group of Sisters. While the men searched the barns, the orchards, the hired men's quarters and everything else outside, the Sisters scoured the Dwelling House, the School, the kitchen and all the outbuildings including the Weaver's House and the laundry.

By the time the searchers began returning to the center of the village, it was almost too dark to see. 'The girl is gone,' Esther said, as the searchers began drifting away to finish chores and prepare for supper. 'She's probably in Falmouth by now,' she added hopefully.

'I pray that is true,' Lydia said, her brow furrowing. 'But did she run away? Or was she taken? Surely if she'd chosen to leave she would have collected her bag of treasures.'

Rees nodded in agreement. 'Those earrings are worth many dollars,' he said. 'I don't believe she would leave them behind.'

'Do you think it is possible she went home?' Rouge asked. 'I mean, if she's Wootten's daughter, maybe she went back to the cabin in the mountains?'

'I suppose it's possible,' Rees said. 'But it is a long way on foot. And it's cold and there are packs of wolves . . .' He shivered involuntarily, recalling his own journey down the mountain. 'Even with the shortcuts.'

'Maybe one of her brothers came for her?' Esther suggested. 'We know at least one of the boys was here.'

'That must be what happened,' Rouge agreed.

'But Pearl seemed so frightened of Jake Wootten,' Rees objected. 'Why would that be?'

'She didn't want to go home,' Lydia guessed, her voice lifted in inquiry.

'And the sight of her brother searching for her scared her?'

Rees considered that and shook his head. 'I'm missing something,' he said.

'It's too dark now to continue the search,' Jonathan said. 'We will have to resume tomorrow.'

Rouge and Rees looked at one another. 'Meet here tomorrow?' Rouge asked. Rees nodded. But he hoped they did not find the girl's frozen body after a night outside.

As Rouge mounted his chestnut, Rees and Lydia crossed the street to the wagon. One of the boys had unhitched Hannibal upon Rees's arrival and was now quickly and efficiently reversing the procedure, harnessing him back up to the wagon.

'I don't like this,' Lydia said as Rees helped her into the wagon. 'I am very, very worried about that young girl.'

Rees nodded. 'Me too.' He thought of Jerusha. 'I hope everything is all right,' he muttered, and flicked the whip over Hannibal's back. The gelding broke into a trot.

The following morning, Rees was in the barn milking when he heard Jerusha screaming from inside the house. He picked up the pail and walked as fast as he could to the kitchen door. As he'd surmised, Jerusha and Lydia were standing opposite one another, the tension between them almost visible. 'She doesn't want to go to school today,' Lydia said, glancing at Rees. 'Again.'

'Please don't make me go,' Jerusha pleaded, her face wet with tears.

Lydia and Rees exchanged glances. 'I could use her help here,' she said.

'But she'll never be able to settle this if she hides,' Rees said.

'I want to go home,' Jerusha sobbed.

'You are home,' Lydia said.

'Home to Dugard where David and Simon are.' Jerusha wiped her hands over her eyes. 'Why did we have to leave? And why can't I go to school in Zion?'

'This is home for now,' Rees said. 'I'll drive you and your brother and sister to school and pick you up after.'

'No, no. Please don't make me go to school,' Jerusha cried. Tears and snot ran down her face. Lydia took her handkerchief from her sleeve and handed it to Jerusha. 'Don't you understand?'

'Go on, get ready,' Rees said.

'You want to be rid of me,' she shouted. 'Now that you have Sharon you don't love the rest of us anymore. Neither of you.'

'Why, Jerusha, that isn't true,' Lydia began.

Jerusha hurled the handkerchief at her mother and ran upstairs. The thud of her feet on the steps sounded loud as cannon fire. Judah and Nancy began to wail and after a few seconds of hesitation Joseph joined them.

Lydia turned a desperate glance upon her husband. 'Please help.'

'I'll see to Jerusha,' he said. As he followed his daughter up the stairs he wondered what he would say to her. He knew that any advice he might offer, based on the method – fighting – he had employed as a boy, would not work for her.

He could hear her sobbing although the sounds were muffled. When he went into the room she shared with Nancy he found Jerusha lying on her unmade bed with her face buried in her pillow. The heat rising from the fireplace downstairs in the kitchen barely warmed the cold air.

Rees sat down on the floor. She gave no sign that she knew he was present. After listening to her weep for a few seconds he cleared his throat. 'I know I'm not the best father,' he said, 'and I know the move from Dugard and then from Zion was difficult.' He paused, not because he thought Jerusha might want to speak but because he wasn't sure what to say. 'I was sorry too when Simon chose to stay with David. I miss him. I do love you and your brothers. I'm sorry.' He hesitated. She cried even harder. 'We will try to figure something out,' he said. She pulled herself up. Her face was red and swollen with tears. She crawled into his arms and as he held her to him she relaxed.

Gradually the wild weeping diminished to shudders and hiccups.

'Did you begin the quarrel with Babette?' he asked. 'That's what the widow told us.'

After a long hesitation Jerusha nodded. 'I threw a book at her,' she admitted in a very small voice. 'And then I slapped her.'

'A book?'

She nodded. 'It hit her and the pages came out. That was in September. She told me she was the one the widow always chose to help and to not even try. Then Babette smiled at me with that fake sweet smile. I could tell she didn't like me.' Jerusha heaved a sigh. 'So I threw the book.'

Rees nodded, wishing Lydia were here. He did not doubt that he would have reacted in exactly the same way as his daughter.

'And from then on you were blamed for everything?' he said.

Jerusha nodded against his chest. Then, exhaling a heavy sigh, she said, 'Well, not everything. Widow Francine spoke to Babette a few times. But mostly she scolded me.'

Rees hesitated, wanting to comfort his daughter but not sure what to say.

'Let's talk to your mother,' he said at last. 'Maybe you can stay home today.' He knew many parents would accuse him of being soft and encouraging disobedience but he understood, with painful clarity, her experience with Babette and her subsequent actions.

Oh, how he hated to see his daughter so upset. And she was in danger of losing her love of learning. That was something he did not understand; he had never been a scholar. But she had loved attending school in Zion.

'We'll see what we can do,' he went on. He did not want to explain exactly why she could not return to Zion. Jerusha – and her siblings – had already lived through enough frightening situations.

They went downstairs together. Lydia had succeeded in quieting the younger children and they were all seated at the table eating. She looked up. When she met Rees's gaze the worried frown puckering her brow smoothed out.

'I told Jerusha she could stay home from school today,' he said.

Lydia grimaced and shook her head at him but she did not contradict his decision. 'Very well. But I'll accept no excuses tomorrow.'

'All right,' Rees agreed, turning to smile at his daughter. She was safer here at home anyway. 'I hope the Shakers have found Pearl,' he added anxiously.

'Well,' Lydia said now, 'if Jerusha can mind the babies for a few hours, we can join the search for the girl.'

'Today we will comb the fields,' he agreed with a nod. 'Just in case Brother Jonathan and his fellows missed her.'

Lydia swallowed and managed a tiny nod. If they found Pearl in the fields she would likely be dead.

'It was very cold last night,' she said. Rees said nothing. He did not believe Pearl was still in Zion. He hoped she had gone home to the Woottens but he feared, considering the treasures found under the mattress, that something much worse had happened to her.

Nancy and Jerusha went outside together: Nancy to feed the chickens and gather their eggs while Jerusha fetched water. Rees returned to Daisy and sat down to finish his milking. In the peace of the barn, with no one clamoring for his attention, he was able to think. The jumbled pieces of his experiences this past week began to settle. And, as his thoughts sorted themselves into a rough order, he realized that at the center of the mystery stood the Wootten family. Of that he was certain, although he still didn't have all the pieces. Or rather he did, but so many people had lied to him that he couldn't winnow the truth from the false. And who, among those to whom he'd spoken, had told the truth? That was the question. Once he knew whose information he could trust he would be better able to separate out the false from the true.

THIRTY

When Rees and Lydia arrived at Zion, Elder Jonathan and several of the Shaker Brothers were already out in the fields, walking across the snowy ground and calling for Pearl. Although the recent storm had dropped a couple of inches on the ground, the dry stalks of last fall's harvest stood above the white like pins in a pin cushion. While Lydia joined Esther and some of the Sisters, Rees walked across the fields until he found Jonathan.

'We've covered all the property and the orchards near the village,' the Brother said as Rees approached. 'Now we are looking in the more distant fields.'

Rees turned to look in that direction. He had already driven down the road by these fields and parked his wagon in the village. Joining the men here meant walking back – toward the Ellis farm where Rees and his family now lived.

The temperature today was not bitterly cold but still, after two hours of walking slowly over snow-covered ground, the chill began to seep through Rees's coat and set his fingers and toes tingling. And they found nothing: no sign that Pearl or anyone else had come this way.

'The girl has run off,' Jonathan said, speaking with absolute certainty. 'She was a light-minded girl, more concerned with frivolity than honoring God.'

Although Rees thought Jonathan's assessment of Pearl's character essentially correct, he did not believe she had just run away. Wouldn't she have taken her treasures? In any event, now Rees – and Constable Rouge as well – would have to go up Gray Hill again.

He found Lydia enjoying a hot cup of tea in the kitchen. Since this was the domain of the Sisters, Rees, as well as the Brothers, waited outside until she donned her cloak and gloves. He thought longingly of hot coffee and the warm kitchen in which Lydia sat but he knew he would not be permitted inside.

And there was still the long, cold ride home.

'I spoke to Annie,' Lydia said as they walked across the road to the barn. 'She will be coming for a visit soon.'

He nodded, barely listening. 'I suppose you found no sign of Pearl,' he said.

'No,' she said.

'I didn't either.' He sounded grim.

She took his arm. 'And no one has seen her since breakfast yesterday.' Lydia directed an anxious look upon her husband. 'She's already been missing twenty-four hours.' She added in a lower tone. 'What if this was Jerusha?'

'I know,' Rees said, squeezing her arm against his side. 'Do *you* think she's run away?'

'I know that's what everyone else thinks. But of course she hasn't,' she replied. 'Not without her mother's earrings. Do you think she went home? To the Woottens?'

'Probably,' he said.

She heard the uncertainty in his voice and, pausing in the middle of the street, turned to look at him. 'You think her father took her, however unwillingly she wished to go?' Lydia said in a soft worried voice.

Heaving a sigh, Rees looked down into her blue eyes. 'Perhaps he did.' And Pearl would not have wanted to go; he was certain of that. 'But the alternative – that she started out on her own and got lost in the woods – is far, far worse.'

Lydia sighed.

They did not speak again on the journey home.

Rees helped his wife down from the wagon in the yard. 'I'll heat up the stew for dinner,' Lydia said. Rees nodded gratefully. Cold and tired and very hungry, all he wanted at the moment was a hot cup of coffee and something to eat. He led Hannibal to the barn and unhitched him from the wagon. He began walking the horse around the yard to cool him. Poor Hannibal had been worked very hard this past week. But Rees had barely completed one lap when Lydia ran out of the house. She'd taken off her cloak but did not seem to feel the cold. Her face was bloodless.

'Will. Will. Jerusha is missing.'

'What?' He almost dropped the reins but then thought better of it. He hurried Hannibal into his stall in the barn and closed the door. 'What are you saying?'

'I went into the house. Only Nancy and the little ones are inside. Oh dear God.'

'And the boys?'

'They're there. Sharon still needs her diaper changed. I didn't do it before I came outside.' Lydia buried her face her in her hands.

Seeing that she was distraught, Rees put his hand on her neck and guided her toward the house.

'Where is Sharon now? Is she all right?'

'Sitting on the floor eating a biscuit.' Lydia managed to smile. 'That child can always be quieted with food. Just like her father.' Rees could not manage a smile.

He took a quick look around the yard but saw nothing. 'Perhaps she's in the outhouse. Go on inside and I'll check.'

She nodded, some of the color returning to her cheeks. As she went up the steps Rees climbed the slope to the outhouse. A line of firs screened the shed but he knew even before he circled them and tapped on the door that the privy was empty.

Now even more worried, he retraced his steps to the house. When he went inside Lydia was changing Sharon's diaper. She looked up with hope but when she saw his expression her hands stilled. 'Oh no,' she murmured.

'Did you check upstairs for Jerusha?'

'Of course I did.' Lydia's voice took on a snap. But Rees had to search himself. He ran up the steps two at a time, as fast as his sore ankle would allow. But of course his wife was right; there was no sign of Jerusha. Fear began to spread cold fingers into his body. He couldn't believe she had willingly left her younger brothers and sisters alone.

He hurried down the stairs. 'Nancy,' he said. 'Nancy.' Seated next to Sharon, she was eating a big bowl of stew. She paused with her spoon halfway to her mouth.

'Where's Jerusha?' he asked, his voice rising. When Nancy froze and her expression changed to one of worry, he took a deep breath and forced himself to speak slowly and calmly. 'Where's your sister?'

'A man took her,' she said as gravy dripped onto the table.

Lydia uttered a quickly stifled gasp.

'A man?' The coldness in Rees's belly began to spread. 'What man? What did he look like?' Forcing himself to pretend to be calm he knelt by her chair. 'This is important, sweetheart. What color hair did he have? Red like mine? Or black like Constable Rouge?'

'Black. And long,' Nancy said. Her face crumpled. 'He was scary.'

'One of the Woottens,' Rees said, looking at Lydia. He knew even Jake and Jem would appear big and frightening to these little children. But it wasn't one of the boys, he was certain of that. The image that appeared in his mind's eye was Bernadette, saying with white-faced horror, 'He tried to force himself on Hortense.'

'She cried,' Judah said in his light treble.

Nancy nodded gravely. 'And shouted,' she agreed. 'She didn't want to go. But you'll bring her back, won't you?'

'Yes, I will,' Rees said. He rose to his feet. 'I have to go after her,' he said to Lydia. She nodded, biting her knuckle. He thought she was barely keeping herself from screaming.

'On dear Lord, what does he want with her?' She pressed her hands to her mouth, the teeth marks on her finger red against the white skin. 'What if he hurts her?' Tears flooded her eyes.

'If he touches one hair on her head I'll kill him,' he said simply although he hoped this situation would not come to that. 'I'll bring my rifle.'

'You'll need help,' Lydia said. She sounded as though she could barely force out the words and her voice was unrecognizable.

'I'll stop in town and tell Constable Rouge when I go through on my way to the road up Gray Hill,' he said. He knew there were faster paths up the mountain including the cleft Granny Rose had brought him down, but he was not sure of the entrances to any of them.

At least it was still daytime; he hoped he would not see the wolves.

While he fetched his rifle, powder horn and bag of shot, Lydia made him a mug of coffee to drink before he left and a napkin of bread and cheese to eat on the way.

He drank the coffee down in several swallows, too anxious to enjoy the beverage. It was lukewarm anyway. He picked up his food, kissed his wife goodbye, and went out to harness Hannibal once again to the wagon.

THIRTY-ONE

Rouge, busy with customers, tried to persuade Rees to wait. 'I'll join you shortly,' the constable said. 'It's dinner time.' He gestured to the crowded tavern. 'Maybe another twenty minutes?' But Rees shook his head, too frightened for his daughter to pause any longer than he had already. It had taken a supreme effort of will to stop and speak to Rouge for even these few minutes.

'I can't. She's up there all alone—' He stopped abruptly, too choked with fear to continue.

'You know another storm is coming?' Rouge asked. When Rees nodded the constable sighed. 'All right. I'll bring all the men I can round up,'

'I can't wait,' Rees said.

'We'll meet you there, at the Bennetts' place,' Rouge said. And then, quite unexpectedly, he reached across the bar and clapped his friend on the back. 'She'll be all right,' he promised, clumsily offering what little comfort he could.

Rees didn't speak; he couldn't. He managed a sharp ragged nod and then he turned and ran outside to his wagon.

The snow began falling before he made his turn onto North Road. At first just a few flakes whirling lazily down from the sky, the flurry rapidly intensified until Rees could barely see Hannibal's ears. If he had been on the road for any other reason he would have turned back. But his fear for his daughter pushed him forward.

By the time he made the junction with Gray Hill the falling snow was so thick and the wind so strong he could see nothing. 'It's a goddamn blizzard,' he muttered. He was already shivering with cold and his mittened hands felt like chunks of ice. And poor Hannibal! Rees could see the horse trembling, the shudders shaking his hindquarters in successive waves. But Rees would not give up.

Horse and wagon began climbing up the hill. Because the journey was now fairly familiar, the distance seemed shorter than it had the first time Rees had come this way. He passed the turnoff to the Bennett's place. With what he had learned about the Hill, this little farm did seem part of the valley. Although he could smell the smoke from their fireplace, he could see nothing of the cabin. Already more than an inch of snow covered the road and Hannibal was beginning to slip. If much more snow fell the accumulation would hold the wheels and the wagon would stop. Still Rees pushed on.

Then, as Hannibal rounded the first of the hairpin curves, the wagon lost traction and began sliding toward the edge of the road. The gelding shuffled back and forth as the heavy weight at his heels veered toward the woods. There was nothing Rees could do but sit there and wait for the inevitable crash.

Luckily for him, the thickening coating of snow on the track caught at the wheels and slowed the wagon. It merely bumped into a tree trunk. Even so, Rees had to sit for a minute, shaky and trembling. He knew this could have been much worse. Higher up, the road curved perilously close to deep woods, ravines and cliffs. Up there the wagon might have slipped off the road entirely and plunged into a chasm. For his own safety he needed to turn around. Even though he knew this was the sensible course to take he nonetheless hesitated for a few seconds. He did not want to accept it and abandon Jerusha.

At last, as a gust of wind bent him inexorably over, he surrendered. He climbed down on shaky legs and almost fell. Carefully, holding on to the wagon for support, he went around to examine the damage. The side of his wagon bore a large splintered patch but the tree trunk, except for the removal of the snow and a small white mark, was unharmed. Rees grunted. 'I was lucky,' he muttered. The wind snatched away his words, drowning them in the scream of the storm.

He carefully made his way around to the front of his vehicle. From there, holding himself upright with one hand on Hannibal's back, he crept forward to the horse's head. Crooning to the animal, Rees took hold of the bridle and very slowly they turned to face the foot of the mountain.

The descent was even worse than the climb. Rees measured his length in the snow several times and even Hannibal struggled. He slipped also but managed to keep his footing. The wagon moved in fits and starts as the wheels were either caught by deepening snow or moved freely in areas laid bare by the wind.

Although time was hard to tell in the white world surrounding them, Rees was sure several hours passed before they finally reached the bottom of the hill and the junction with North Road. As the uniform white surrounding him darkened to gray he knew night was coming.

Despite the bitter cold he paused for a few moments to rest. Both he and his horse were exhausted. Hannibal was blowing hard, his breath steaming out in a thick cloud, and his head hung low. But when Rees stared at the ground beneath his feet he saw that the snow here had been churned into ridges and deep ruts almost to the dirt below. A party of horsemen had come this far and turned around. He uttered a breathy tired chuckle; Rouge had made good on his promise although he too had been turned back by the weather.

Rees climbed into the wagon and turned on to the main road. The wagon juddered as the wheels slid sideways but stopped, caught by a rut. He exhaled a relieved breath in a cloud of steam and they started for home.

It was past nightfall when he turned at last onto Surry Road and still snowing hard. The white all around him maintained a certain glow so he could see somewhat. The road was invisible but Hannibal knew the way. And as they neared the farm, he began to walk faster. Rees would have missed the turn but for the horse who floundered into the lane, and stopped, unable to drag the wagon through the deepening snow.

Rees had to climb down from the seat and push the last few yards, through the gate and into the barn at last.

Although he felt dizzy with fatigue, he rubbed the horse down until he was completely dry and fed him before going inside to his own supper. Lydia met him at the door, her gaze going behind him. 'Jerusha isn't with me. I couldn't make it,' he said apologetically. Lydia tried to nod but couldn't. She bit her lip so hard a drop of blood formed. 'I will go back out tomorrow, as soon as the snow stops,' he promised.

'Of course,' she said. 'I don't want to lose both my husband and my daughter.' But as she stared at the dark window and the spinning snow outside her face twisted with anguish.

Rees spent a wakeful night. Every so often he would run to the window and stare out, hoping the snow had stopped. Finally Lydia, who woke every time he did, said, 'You might as well sleep. Even if it stops snowing you won't leave in the middle of the night. You'll be able to see even less. And Hannibal deserves at least a little rest.'

Rees nodded and returned to the comfort of his warm bed. How he wished he had bought a mule or another horse, despite the cost. He was not sure Hannibal, although still a young animal, would be able to make another journey as difficult as the one the day before.

He was back on the road at dawn with a lunch of bread and cheese and a jar of hot coffee. It was slow going. Although the snow had stopped at least a foot had fallen. The wind whirled it around, creating bare patches on the road but also deep drifts. Rees had to climb out over and over to shovel a path for Hannibal to follow.

When he reached town mid-morning the tavern was open but only Thomas was inside. Rees told Thomas where he was going and made the man swear he would pass on the message. Then he started out again, trying to follow the path already broken through the snow by other vehicles.

Someone had shoveled a lane from the turn off to Gray Hill as far as the Bennetts' place. Today he could see the cabin through the trees and wheel tracks went from the drive to the road.

He continued on. With the thick trees on both sides, the road had been protected from some of the accumulation. And as he climbed higher and the trees began to thin, much of the snow had been scoured away by the wind to the bare rock beneath.

It was almost noon when he passed Morton's small shop – it seemed very close to town now. He stopped and ate his bread and cheese and drank his cold coffee. He did not linger. It was too cold to sit and anyway he still had three or four hours ahead of him.

By the time he passed the turnoff to Granny Rose's cabin, the sun had begun its descent to the western horizon. Under the trees the light disappeared to a deep gloom. Rees knew he would still be on the mountain after dark, something he had not wanted to ever happen again. But he had to find Jerusha. His little girl must be terrified. He flicked the whip over Hannibal's back, more to give himself the illusion he was doing something than to encourage the horse to travel faster. Hannibal tried though, digging his hooves into the crusty snow and pulling forward.

They passed the spot where Rees had fallen from the mule: he recognized the tall pine nearby. Not far now. He saw now that he would never have made it to the shop, especially not with the wolves at his heels. The store was several hours away – and that was with Hannibal pulling the wagon.

As they climbed the steepest part of the mountain the scent of wood smoke touched Rees's nose, a familiar warning that he was approaching a human habitation. He was surprised; he thought he was still a distance from the Wootten family's cabin. The smell of wood smoke intensified as he climbed. Rees began to wonder about the size of this fire; the sweet smell of burning wood had become a thick and acrid stink. Hannibal began to toss his head and resist moving forward.

And now another odor had joined the heavy smell of burning wood: cooking meat. It momentarily transported Rees to his childhood and butchering time in the fall. Families went from farm to farm to help. Although most of the meat was cut up and put aside to smoke, the heads were boiled to make headcheese. The fat was cooked to render into tallow. And some of the pork was always roasted to feed the hungry helpers. That was what he smelled now.

Hannibal stopped at the final curve and refused to move another step. Rees could see that no amount of whipping would persuade the horse so he accepted the inevitable and climbed down from the wagon. Once he'd thrown the horse blanket over Hannibal and tied him to a fir tree, Rees began the stiff climb up the last incline.

The penetrating stink of smoke intensified and he could see it now too. Floating ash and cinders filled the smoky air. The sparks fell into the snow with tiny hissing sounds. This was not a pig roast. Rees began to hurry, lengthening his stride and leaning into the tainted breeze.

THIRTY-TWO

When he breasted the final hill and came into sight of the Wootten home he saw his worst fear. The cabin was ablaze and the fire had jumped to one of the pine trees. As orange and yellow flames consumed the branches, the pop and crackle of burning sap filled the hollow with sound. Mr Wootten was running back and forth in front of his home screaming, 'Mother. Sally. Oh my God.'

Rees turned to stare at the cabin. Long red tongues darted out of the windows. The front door was open as though Wootten had tried to run in to save his wife. If so the fire had driven him back. Flames stretched through the opening. The wooden planks on either side wouldn't last long. Even as Rees watched a narrow burning finger touched one of the logs and took hold.

And Jerusha was in there!

'Do you have buckets?' He turned to Wootten and shook him by the shoulder. 'Buckets, man. We must try to put out the fire.'

Wootten looked at Rees blankly, as though he'd lost the ability to hear and speak.

Swearing under his breath, Rees ran for the barn. Surely there would be buckets there, for oats and feed.

Hortense's stolen horse stamped nervously. Crooning to her, he began peering into each stall. He soon had two or three wooden pails; a very tiny number with which to fight the fierce fire consuming the cabin. As he peered into the last alcove, not a stall for there was a door at one end, a small quavering voice said, 'Father?'

'Jerusha?' He dropped the pails and stepped into the stall. A small hay mound shivered and broke as she stood up. 'Oh Jerusha, I was so worried,' Rees said, falling to his knees and pulling the girl into his arms. He held her to him so tightly she uttered a squeak of protest. Now that he had found her, the full weight of his desperate fear swept over him and tears rushed into his eyes. 'Are you hurt?'

'No. Mr Wootten put me in the room with Miss Sally. He said I had to help her.' Jerusha gulped. 'When the fire started she pushed me out the window. Told me to run and hide in the barn where I would be safe. She couldn't get through the window. She was too fat.' Her last words ended in a sob.

'You're safe now,' he said, his own words trembling. 'Everything will be all right.'

Jerusha sniffed and nodded against his chest. 'I knew you'd come.' She tipped her head back so she could look at him. 'Are you crying?' She sounded more frightened than ever.

Rees swiped at his wet eyes. 'I am just so glad I found you,' he said.

'Everything will be all right.' She repeated his assurance back to him as she stepped back. Now that he could see her more fully he realized she did not have her boots or cloak. Instead, large moccasins covered her feet and she wore a blanket over her shoulders. 'Miss Sally gave them to me,' she said, noticing the direction of his gaze. 'She was kind to me.'

'Yes,' he agreed doubtfully. 'You stay here. I'll help Mr Wootten—'

'Wait. I have something to show you. It's important.'

Rees hesitated, glancing involuntarily over his shoulder at the fire burning behind him. 'I can't now,' he said gently. 'Miss Sally is still inside the cabin.' He detached her clinging hands and, picking up the buckets, went out into the hellish orange glow.

The cabin was thoroughly ablaze now and a few buckets of melting snow would not be enough to conquer the flames. Still, even though it was too late for Mrs Wootten, he went to the side of the cabin where her room lay, and started throwing snow at the wall. Sally Wootten's room had had the protection of a door, but Rees did not doubt that once the shutters were opened and the waxed paper broken, that that wooden barrier had not stood for very long.

He'd thrown only a few buckets full of snow at the wall when other men joined him. He spared a quick glance at the two men: Jake and Jem. They hurled buckets of snow like madmen – two to three buckets of snow to every one of Rees's. Josiah Wootten joined them as well although he concentrated on the front porch. Rees wondered if the man had some notion that his wife would manage to escape through the front. As others arrived to help extinguish the blaze, and put out the fire consuming the fir tree behind the cabin, the hollow gradually filled with wagons and people.

Rees's arms and shoulders began to feel heavy and sluggish. He was tiring. Someone, he never knew who, pushed him out of the way and took his bucket. So weary he staggered, he made his way back to the front of the barn.

He had spent more time than he realized struggling to quench the fire; the last rays of the setting sun painted the tops of the trees with gold. But the thickness of the trees – and most of them evergreens – meant that the light didn't reach the ground. In the shadowy clearing the floating sparks from the fire glowed, pinpricks of orange and red.

The cabin was almost gone. The front porch and steps had fallen away from the burning building, and the wooden, shingled roof had collapsed. Only the small room attached to the eastern side – Sally Wootten's room – remained relatively intact. The Wootten boys had done their very best to coat that part of the cabin with water. In the increasing cold, the logs that made up the wall glistened with ice.

Although some of the structure remained, Rees was regretfully certain Sally Wootten had died either from the smoke or from the fire itself.

'Here, you're shivering.' Granny Rose came up behind Rees and threw his greatcoat over his shoulders. It smelled of smoke. Now he vaguely recalled tossing the heavy caped coat aside when he became too warm. He drew it around himself gratefully. 'Did Sally escape?' the midwife asked.

'I don't believe so,' he said. 'But she saved my daughter.' He had to stop speaking lest his thickening voice betray his emotion. Granny Rose patted his arm and he knew he had not fooled her.

He looked around for Jerusha now, wondering if she had come out of the barn. There were so many people here now and the dimming light made seeing faces difficult. Then he saw her, staring at the burning cabin in horror.

'Jerusha,' he called. 'Over here.'

She looked away from the fire but instead of approaching him she gestured at him. With a sigh, he crossed the trampled snow.

'Will you come and look now?' she asked insistently. He hesitated a few seconds before nodding. She ran into the barn to the door and pulled it open.

Steps dropped into a shadowy cellar that smelled of cold damp earth and rotting apples. 'I'll wait here,' Jerusha said in a trembling voice.

He turned a puzzled glance upon her before descending the stairs.

It would have been too dark to see but for the orange light from the fire spilling through the narrow window and onto a long table in the center of the room. Rees stared at the canvas-shrouded mound. He was almost afraid to approach it.

'Do you see?' Jerusha hissed from the doorway.

Without replying, he tiptoed toward the table. He could not help recalling a similar experience a few years ago; then the shrouded form had been his boyhood friend Nate Bowditch. Rees stopped. Taking a deep breath he forced himself to go forward. He stretched out a hand to throw aside the canvas but paused. Did he really want to know what was underneath that rough cloth?

He did not, but he had to. Steeling himself, he threw aside a corner. A pale moon face stared up at him. He took two sudden stumbling steps backwards and almost fell.

'Father?' Jerusha said.

'I'm all right,' He said, hoping she did not hear the quiver in his voice. 'I tripped.'

Gulping, he approached the body once again.

Someone had closed the girl's eyes and for that he was thankful. This then was the girl who'd died. Her face was wrong: heavy, slanted eyelids and a flat nose. She was here after all, just as Granny Rose said. Winter had come early and by late October the soil had already been crusty and too hard for digging a grave.

At least the freezing temperatures had kept the body from corruption.

Rees pushed down the canvas. On the girl's breast was another form, a tiny baby, within weeks of birth. So frail, so vulnerable. He could not help thinking of Sharon, his own daughter. He stepped backwards, huffing out a breath.

'What's happening?' Jerusha quavered.

'I see the body,' he said. Recalled to himself, he reached for the canvas but his hand stilled. Something about the baby – the delicate nose had been broken. Smashed flat by something pressed upon it, Rees guessed. Who would do something so terrible?

His gaze returned to the mother's face. This time, steeling himself against a surge of revulsion, he lifted one of the girl's eyelids. Red dots speckled the eye, still visible through the film of death. This had been murder.

Rees turned and heaved the bread and cheese he'd eaten into a corner.

THIRTY-THREE

'Rees? Mr Rees?' Granny Rose's voice came from the door. 'What are you doing down here?' Quickly, despite her long skirts and men's boots, she trotted down the steps. 'Where are you?' she asked, peering into the gloom.

Wiping his mouth on his coat sleeve, he straightened up and turned. 'Here.' He approached the table behind him. 'Look.'

She joined him and for a moment she stared at the uncovered face. 'Oh dear,' she said at last. 'How distressing. But you know that mothers and babies are frequently taken home to God.'

'This wasn't natural,' Rees said angrily. 'Look closer. Look at the baby.'

The midwife leaned over to examine the small head. With a heavy sigh, she drew a finger over the tiny skull. 'I see,' she said.

'The constable will have to be told,' Rees said.

'Yes. When he arrives.' The midwife raised her head and gazed into Rees's eyes. 'But you can't do anything more for these poor souls now. And Josiah and his sons are trying to rip down the cabin to rescue Sally. She might still be alive. They need the help of a strong man like you.'

He met her eyes and then nodded, ashamed. 'Of course,' he said, starting for the door.

Granny Rose flipped the canvas over the pale face and the pathetic bundle clasped to the chest and followed.

'What is your daughter doing here anyway?' Granny Rose asked.

'Wootten abducted her,' Rees said, clenching his hands into fists. 'I came after her.'

'She wasn't hurt?' Granny Rose said, clutching at his arm in alarm.

'No. Apparently he made a habit of taking girls to care for his wife. So Jerusha spent all her time with Sally. And she saved my daughter, by pushing her through the window.'

Granny Rose nodded as if a great many things made sense. 'I see. I knew she was sick. Of course he needed help with her. Especially with him away at the lumbering camp and the boys working and hunting.'

As they exited the barn, a party of horsemen scaled the knob on the track and rode into the hollow. It was Rouge, with three or four men accompanying him. Thomas rode pillion behind the constable. Rees turned to Granny Rose. 'The constable. I must speak with him about . . .' He jerked his head toward the barn and the bodies in the basement.

Nodding, she fell into step with him as he crossed the crowded yard.

The constable dismounted, looking at Rees with suspicion. 'Was this your doing?'

'Of course not,' he said, his voice sharp with anger and exhaustion. 'The fire was already burning when I arrived. And Sally Wootten saved my daughter's life.' He turned away from the constable, under the guise of looking for his daughter. The tangle of emotions inside him – anger, fear, relief – was so powerful it left him prey to easy tears. He would not allow Rouge to see them.

'Where's Wootten now?' Rouge looked around. Not a sensitive fellow, he seemed oblivious to Rees's emotions.

'Over there,' Rees said, pointing with his chin. Rouge stared at the three men: Josiah, Jake and Jem Wootten gathered together at the side of the cabin. The senior Wootten seemed shrunken somehow and he was weeping. Rees remembered his anger with his sons and how he had struck out at Jake. Now the boys were supporting their father who appeared too weak to stand.

Rouge tossed the reins of his horse to Thomas and started across the snow.

'Wait,' Rees said. 'There's something you should see – in the barn.'

'Later.'

'The bodies of Wootten's daughter and her child. They were murdered,' he said.

Rouge spun around. 'Are you sure?'

'Yes. Granny Rose will tell you.' Rees gestured at the woman standing by his side.

Rouge spared the midwife scarcely a glance before saying, 'They'll keep. I'll deal with Wootten and his sons first.'

'I'll want to speak with them,' Rees said.

'You can do that through the bars of the jail,' Rouge said.

'I don't think the boys had anything to do with it.' Rees met the constable's eyes defiantly.

'Huh. They must've known about his activities,' he said without sympathy. 'I want them all in one place until we've gotten to the bottom of this. Besides, they have no home now.'

Rees glanced at the smoking ruin. Only the small room added on for Sally Wootten remained.

Although neither Rees nor Rouge expected the Wootten men to go to prison quietly, taking them into custody proved to be more difficult than anyone expected. And it was not for the reason – wanting to keep their freedom – that Rees would have guessed either. No, Josiah Wootten wanted – was determined – to see what had become of his wife. He fought like a savage to free himself from Rouge's grasp while Rees and some of the other men sought to control the boys. Finally, nursing a bloody nose that was his prize from the scuffle, Rees said, 'Let them help bring Mrs Wootten out from the house. They won't be satisfied until then.'

The constable hesitated before finally nodding. At once all of the Woottens calmed down. The group, with Rouge and his newly sworn-in deputies following close behind the hill family so they would not run, walked over to the ice-covered wall. 'It looks pretty solid,' Rouge said at last.

'Maybe she lived,' Wootten said in such a hopeful tone Rees turned a look of sympathy upon the other man. A brute he might be but he clearly loved his wife. Rees did not think there was any chance at all that Sally Wootten had survived.

'We don't hear anything,' Rouge said, turning a meaningful glance upon the other men.

'She might have fainted,' Wootten said, glaring at the constable. 'She does that sometimes.'

Rees walked around to the back of the cabin. The fir tree that towered over the building still smoldered and every now and then a spark stung his neck. He tipped his head back to examine the pine; a black skeleton reaching into the sky.

Turning, he inspected the cabin. A sizeable chunk of the back had been reduced to a mess of charred logs. He could see through the openings into the interior. Most of the furniture had been reduced to ash, and flames continued to smolder.

He peered through the opening, focusing his attention upon the wall that had once separated Sally Wootten's room from the rest of the cabin. Although scorched, the blackened wood ridged by the heat, the wall seemed largely intact. He heard no sign of movement.

How could they reach Sally Wootten?

Rees looked around one final time. With the fire still burning in the main room, they could not go through to the door. Could they chop down this back wall? Most of the logs forming this side had been burned completely through. He ran his eyes over the entire wall, top to bottom.

Underneath this section, where the wall was completely destroyed, lay a small hollow. Dug down all the way to the dirt, the hole was surrounded by a ridge of blackened snow. Someone had set a fire here and a pile of wood ash and a few charred pieces of wood were all that remained. He stared at the scraps, not realizing for a few seconds exactly what this meant. Why would anyone build a fire here?

Then he knew. The blaze in the cabin had not been an accident. If Sally Wootten had died here, her death was murder.

The only question was: which of the Wootten men had murdered her?

THIRTY-FOUR

'We're going to have to pull this wall down,' Rees said, hurrying around the last standing wall to the crowd of men on the other side. 'We must. Mrs Wootten's room is intact.'

'She might still be alive,' said Mr Wootten, looking around. 'I tole you. She's alive.'

As Jake and Jem led several men into the barn for hemp rope and whatever other cords they could find, Rees crossed the trampled ground to Jerusha. 'Would you mind waiting a few minutes longer?' he asked her. 'Before we go home, I mean. I want to help . . .' He gestured backwards, at the men loudly discussing the best ways in which to attach the ropes.

'N-no,' Jerusha said. 'I suppose not. Is Miss Sally still inside?'

'I think so,' he said. 'We are hoping she is just unconscious.'

'She was kind to me,' Jerusha said, her gaze returning to the cabin.

He looked around until he saw Granny Rose. She was watching him and moved toward him at his gesture. 'Would you—?'

'Stay with your daughter? Of course.' Granny Rose smiled at Jerusha.

'We'll be pulling the wall down,' Rees said.

Granny Rose nodded. 'Sally still inside?' she asked.

He nodded. 'She is.' He could not say anything more, especially with Jerusha listening.

Granny Rose nodded. 'How did the fire start? Sally's bedchamber was closest to the fireplace. If the cabin caught from a coal or something like, her room would have burned first.'

'Not sure,' Rees lied, his gaze going to his daughter. Jerusha, her attention focused on the men fixing the ropes to the cabin wall, did not seem to be listening but he didn't want to take that chance. Granny Rose fixed her sharp blue eyes upon his face. He nodded at her.

'God have mercy,' she said, so softly he could almost not hear the words.

She put an arm around Jerusha and drew her close.

Rees hurried over to the gang of men. They had tied the ropes to the roof beam and to the logs surrounding the small window. He joined Jake, taking hold of the end of the rope and, at Rouge's signal, they all pulled with all their strength. The wall came away from the roof with such ease Rees almost went sprawling in the snow. The bottom, still pegged to the posts, had to be dragged away; the fire had not reached this wall or these posts and the logs were still securely fastened. Wootten was first there, his meaty hands grabbing the wall so tightly the knuckles went white. Rees could see the strain in the other man's back and shoulders even through his ragged coat and rushed to help.

The logs began popping away from the posts. When the opening split almost to the ground and Wootten could make it through he scrambled over the remaining pieces of log and into the bedchamber. 'Sally, Sally,' he began to shout.

Jake and Jem followed their father and then Rees, who muscled his way to the front of the group and pushed his way through to the inside.

The door was burned almost all the way through and the wall adjoining the main room of the cabin was charred by the intensity of the fire on the other side. But the flames had not consumed this room. Sally Wootten had made sure of that; the barrel of water by the bed was almost empty. She lay on the floor, her head toward the back wall, a jug clasped in her hands. Although one foot and the lower part of the leg were blistered – now Rees knew why he had smelled cooking meat – Sally had not burned to death. Smoke had overtaken her. Gagging, he pushed his way through the cluster of men and threw up in the snow. He had nothing left in his stomach so he only vomited bile. He did not think he would be able to eat meat for a long time.

Wootten dropped to the floor and cradled Sally's head in his lap. 'Wake up, Sally girl,' he said. 'Wake up.' Wiping his mouth, Rees turned and stared through the demolished wall. He knew the woman was not breathing but did not want to say so, not in the presence of a man so obviously overcome with grief.

Jake knelt by his father and put his hand gently on his mother's face. 'She's gone,' he said, his voice thick. He wiped the tears from his eyes. 'She's not alive.'

'She has to be,' Wootten said. 'The fire barely touched her. Come on, Sally. Wake up. Please wake up.'

Rees began to back up so he could leave the Woottens with their grief. As he turned to look for Jerusha, an anguished cry like the howl of a wounded animal sounded behind him. He shook his head at the crowd gathered there, the men who'd ridden up from town and some of the inhabitants of nearby cabins. 'She didn't live,' he said. A low mutter of sorrow rumbled through the crowd.

Rees tipped his head back and looked up. The last pink of daylight streaked the sky but it was already completely dark here. Some of the men had gathered a huge pile of sticks and dry wood in the middle of the clearing and lit it with a coal from the fire. People were gathering, stretching out their hands to the blaze. Rees joined Rouge.

'What do we do now?' the constable asked.

'We'll have to take the body out,' Rees said. Turning to look over his shoulder he added, 'In a few minutes. Allow them this time to grieve.' Rouge nodded. Like most of the men, and Rees himself, the constable was marked by soot. 'A word,' Rees said, touching the other man's arm and drawing him back. He looked at Rees curiously but followed him away from the fire, to a spot a distance from any other person. 'This wasn't an accident,' Rees said.

'What?' Rouge stared. In the gloom, the ash streaks looked like war paint against his white face.

'The fire was deliberately set,' Rees said. 'Come with me and I'll show you.'

He started across the snow but quickly realized that in the back of the cabin, under the trees, Rouge would not be able to see anything, Rees grabbed a long stick and plunged it into the heart of the fire. The tip began to glow and after a moment a small flame burst into being. 'Come on,' he said.

He picked his way cautiously underneath the still smoldering tree. With the upper branches consumed, some of the last light from the sky reached the ground.

The black stain on the snow was clearly visible. 'Look,' he said, shoving his makeshift torch at it.

'What?' Rouge asked.

'Don't you see? Someone set the fire.'

Rouge turned his gaze to the area. 'Someone dug down to the dirt,' he said, 'and built a fire?'

'Yes. It is almost the only place this could be done.' Rees gestured with his torch at the large rocks on either side of the hollow. 'The cabin was built over rock. Sally Wootten's death was murder.'

As another wild cry erupted from inside the cabin Rouge said. 'But I thought . . . didn't Wootten?'

'Maybe,' Rees said. 'Or one of the boys?' He did not want the murderer to be one of them so he added, 'But I don't think so.'

Rouge swore in French. 'I'll put all of them behind bars,' he said. 'For all we know, they're all in it together.' He turned and blundered through the gloom, toward the fire-lit hollow.

But Rees did not follow the constable. Instead he held the torch to the lower edge of the cabin once again and stared at the charred pit. Doubt about the Wootten men's guilt was beginning to creep in. Why would they risk destroying their home? Now they had nowhere to go. Besides, Wootten could have smothered his wife in the same manner as his daughter and her babe. Did that mean one of the boys was the murderer? But they had even more to lose than their father. Something did not make sense.

When he finally returned to the hollow he found Wootten and his sons tearing down the last of the cabin wall. 'They're getting ready to take Mrs Wootten out,' Rouge said in reply to Rees's question. 'They couldn't lift her over; she's too big of a woman. So the entire wall had to come down.'

In the reddish flickering light from the bonfire, the movement of the Wootten men looked to him like a scene from Hell.

Although Wootten and his sons shoved the bed aside and bent to their task, they couldn't lift Sally. As several other men from the mountain community ran to help, Rouge turned to Rees. 'I don't suppose you have your wagon? I want to bring the body down to town and let Doc look at it. Before they hide her in the ground,' he added grimly.

'I do have my wagon,' he said in a reluctant tone. He was not eager to collect the body and transport it to town, especially not with Jerusha beside him. But he supposed he could do it. There were the other bodies – those of the girl and her baby – as well. And he had to travel through town on his way home anyway.

Rouge nodded his thanks and both men turned to watch the crowd struggling to lift the body. After several minutes – time that were filled with grunting and cursing – Granny Rose climbed through the collapsed wall and pulled the quilt from the bed. 'Roll her on to this,' she said, 'and then you can pull her out.'

'She spent years working on that thing,' Wootten objected.

'It was something she loved doing,' Granny Rose said. 'What better end for it than that she should be wrapped in it and put to her rest.'

After a minute or two more of discussion, with no better idea put forth, Wootten took the quilt. As they struggled to roll Sally's body onto the covering, Rees turned to Rouge. 'We aren't needed here now. Come into the barn with me. I want to show you the dead girl and the baby that I told you about earlier.' Rouge took a flaming brand from the fire and followed him into the barn and the attached cold cellar.

At first the constable, casting a brief glance at the pale round face revealed when Rees thrust aside the canvas, seemed indifferent. 'Mothers and babies die all the time,' he said, repeating Granny Rose almost word for word. 'And you can see something is wrong with the girl. Look at her face.'

'There are red dots in her eyes,' Rees said. 'I have seen that before, in victims of hanging and suffocation. And the baby's nose is broken.'

Rouge uttered a heavy sigh. 'We don't know what happened. Maybe an accident?'

'You wouldn't be so calm if this was Hortense lying here,' Rees snapped. 'After all, she was taken to this house.'

Rouge stared at the other man for a moment before his gaze returned unwillingly to the body on the table. 'All right, if you insist.' he said at last. 'We'll take them into town to the Coroner also.'

'I'll fetch my wagon,' Rees said.

When they stepped outside once again, they found that the Woottens and the other men had succeeded in dragging Sally's body from the cabin. Rouge discarded the stick he'd been carrying. By now flames were beginning to run down its length to his hand. He picked up another, a thicker one this time, from the fire. Together they crossed the snowy yard to the track that led down the mountain.

Wolves howled nearby. Rees, his neck prickling, was glad of the constable's company and of the fire. It was difficult not to feel targeted by those intelligent hunters. As the two men approached Hannibal, the trampled snow around him bore mute witness to the number of times he had tried to flee down the mountain. His eyes rolling, he danced at the end of the leather strap. Rees was glad it hadn't broken under the stress.

By the time they returned to the hollow, the bodies had been dragged to the top of the road. Rees turned the wagon slightly so that when he stopped the corpses could be lifted directly into the wagon bed. Raising Sally took five or six men on the ground and Rouge and Rees in the wagon bed but the body was finally in place. He turned the corners of the quilt over her, covering her face. Then, as Rouge lifted the body of the young girl, Rees turned and knelt to take the sad cargo. He placed the daughter and baby on top of Sally.

'Where're you taking my girl?' Wootten asked.

'To the coroner,' Rouge said tersely.

'Why?' Wootten asked. 'She and the babe – they just died.' He turned his gaze away from the canvas-wrapped bundle as though he could not bear to see them. 'We planned to bury her in the spring.'

'Get in the wagon,' Rouge said. 'You and your boys.'

For a moment Rees thought the Wootten men would protest. But Rouge prodded Jake and Jem forward with his meaty hand and they climbed in. Josiah hesitated but then, his shoulders slumping, he joined his sons by the bodies of his wife and daughter and baby granddaughter.

Rees called for Jerusha. She took one look at the men in the wagon bed and scrambled into the front seat. He did not object; he did not want her anywhere near the Woottens. Thomas elected not to ride behind Rouge, squeezing in next to Jerusha.

Rees lit the lanterns on either side of the wagon and the party started down the mountain. When he glanced back over his shoulder, mainly to see that the Wootten family were riding as comfortably as possible, he saw the mountain community, with Granny Rose at the front, draw together behind the departing group.

Now that the sun had set, the air was bitterly cold. Jerusha snuggled close to Rees; he could feel her skinny body shivering. Wolves yelped in the distance but as far as he could tell none of the animals approached this large and well-armed party.

THIRY-FIVE

By the time Rees and Jerusha arrived home, it was well past nine. While Rees had delivered the Wootten men to the jail, and Mrs Wootten to the coroner, Jerusha had eaten in Rouge's tavern. Therese had made much of her. But the day had been a long one for her and she dozed most of the way home, her body heavy against her father's shoulder.

Lydia came running through the door as they drove through the gate. Rees knew she had been listening for their wagon wheels. 'Oh Jerusha, oh my dear,' she said.

'She's fine,' Rees said. 'She wasn't hurt. And she ate supper at Rouge's tavern in town.'

Jerusha climbed down, almost falling. Lydia put an arm around her daughter and led her, stumbling with weariness, into the house. Rees unhitched Hannibal, made sure he had food and water, and gave him a nosebag of oats. The last few days had been long and hard for the horse as well. Then Rees followed his wife and daughter into the house.

Only Lydia waited for him. Coffee perked over the fire and as he entered and shed his coat, she put a dish of eggs and bacon on the table. Rees realized how hungry he was. 'Where's Jerusha?' he asked as he began eating.

'I put her to bed in the front room,' Lydia said, putting a cup of hot strong coffee before him. Rees nodded as he dropped several chunks of sugar into the dark liquid and followed it up with cream. The first swallow was heavenly, hot and sweet.

'Why did Wootten take her?' Lydia asked. 'Was it from simple spite? Or for some other reason?'

Rees put down his cup and looked at her. Anxiety had worn grooves into her face and he knew she feared the worst. 'They didn't hurt her,' he said. 'Apparently Wooten has abducted young girls before because he needed help with his wife. She's been sick a long time.' He paused and then added, 'Although Wootten may have chosen Jerusha out of spite. Because of me.'

Lydia leaned forward and covered Rees's hand with her own. 'This wasn't your fault. After all, if you're right about Mr Wootten's motivation, he would have taken some other girl if he hadn't chosen Jerusha.'

'I suppose so,' he said, comforted. 'Anyway, Sally Wootten helped Jerusha escape. I found her hiding in the barn.'

Lydia blew out a long breath and sat back in her chair. 'Well, that is good news.'

He offered her a lopsided smile. 'Someone set the Wootten's cabin on fire. It's totally destroyed. And Sally Wootten is dead.'

'What?'

Rees nodded. 'Is there any bread?' Lydia rose to fetch the loaf. As she cut a thick slice, he continued. 'Her bedroom wasn't completely burned. She used her drinking water to wet the door and keep the fire out. The smoke got to her, I think. And we found another body.'

'What?' Lydia turned in alarm, the knife still held aloft. 'Who?'

'Another daughter of the family. The youngest. And her baby. They were murdered, Lydia. Smothered.' He paused and then added, 'Jerusha found them.'

'Dear Lord,' she said, breathing out the words. 'My poor daughter.' After a moment of silence, Lydia asked, 'Who do you believe set the fire? Mr Wootten?'

Rees shook his head uncertainly. 'I thought it might be one of the boys but now I'm not sure. They were doing everything in their power to rescue their mother. Besides, they – and Josiah Wootten – are all strong enough to strangle Sally as the Shaker Sister was strangled. Why set a fire and risk losing your home and all your possessions?'

Lydia considered that. 'Setting a fire is indirect. Maybe one of the boys couldn't bear to see Sally's face.'

'True,' Rees agreed. 'But they worked as hard as they could to pull her out of that cabin. Their home is just ashes. And the hams they put up are gone so they have no food for the winter. It doesn't make sense.' He shook his head.

'Who else would do this?' She wondered. Rees turned to look

at his wife, a terrible suspicion blooming in his mind. She met his gaze and he could see his own horror mirrored in her eyes.

'Pearl,' they said in unison.

'That does explain why it was a fire,' Lydia said, sounding reluctant. Rees understood; he didn't want to believe it either.

'And why Pearl is missing,' he said.

Lydia nodded. 'But why? Why would she murder her mother?' she asked.

'I don't know. I suppose she didn't want to go home,' he said. 'We know both Jake and his father went to Zion to look for her.'

'But that would explain *their* murders,' Lydia said as she took Rees's plate and brought it to the sink. 'Does that mean that Sally's death was accidental? Maybe Pearl was trying to murder her father and her brothers?'

Rees thought of the hollow dug beneath the cabin and the sooty snow. The fire had been set as close to Sally's room as possible. Still, it hadn't been set under Sally's room.

'Pearl is probably miles away by now,' he said. 'We may never know.'

Despite the long day and late night, he awoke early the following morning. He guessed he hadn't slept for more than a few hours. But the terror of Jerusha's abduction and now all the questions he had buzzing in his brain kept him from relaxing into slumber.

He crawled out of the warm bed. Lydia turned over with a sigh. He looked into the cot where Sharon slept. She was really too old to be sleeping in her parents' room but Lydia couldn't bear to put her in the room with Jerusha and Nancy. Rees covered her again – the room was very cold – before descending to the first floor. When he looked into the front room Jerusha was sound asleep under a mound of quilts. She had burrowed into a nest and even her face was covered. A wave of gratitude that she had not been harmed swept over him. She could have died in the fire that killed Sally Wootten. For a moment his legs felt too weak to hold him and he clutched at the rocking chair for support.

What had happened to Jerusha? He had not wanted to question her with the Woottens sitting in the wagon with them and the bodies. Jerusha said she had not been harmed and, to Rees's eyes, she did not appear terribly scared. Yet Hortense had been so frightened she'd fled barefoot into the snowy forest. And Josiah Wootten had strangled a Shaker Sister in the mistaken belief she was Hortense. Was it all about an attempted rape?

Rees went into the kitchen and stirred up the fire. Although dawn was still several hours distant, he lit a lantern and went outside to finish his morning chores. He needed answers. Jerusha had to tell him everything she knew.

In the quiet in the barn, with his head planted against Daisy's warm flank as he milked, he moved on to other questions. Jake had gone down to Zion in search of his sister. Had he found her? And how had he known she was in Zion? Was he in the habit of visiting her? Or had his father spotted Pearl at the same time she saw him murdering the Sister?

Rees shook his head in frustration. Too many questions. And he could not avoid one final worry, perhaps the most important of all. Where was Pearl now? There were no safe havens for a young girl other than family or friends or the Shakers, to whom Pearl had made her way. But she had not been found at any of those refuges.

Perhaps her father had seen her set the fire that took Sally's life? Rees paused in his milking. He knew Wootten was a rough and violent father; Jake bore the scars of a quarrel that had become physical. Had Wootten, despite Granny Rose's defense of him, attacked his daughter?

Daisy lowed and shifted her feet and with a start Rees began milking again. After speaking to Jerusha he would drive into town and question the Woottens themselves.

To his surprise, when he went into the house with his brimming pail of milk, he found Jerusha and Lydia sitting at the table together. The fire had already warmed the room and he removed his coat.

'Jerusha has something to tell you,' Lydia said. Rees looked at her. His daughter met his gaze, her eyes brimming with tears.

'I slapped Babette first,' she said.

'What?' Rees, whose thoughts had been focused on murder and the Wootten clan, stared at her in incomprehension. 'I thought you threw a book at her.'

'I did. But I also hit her. The widow chose her, you see. And then her big brother always came to fetch her from school. And Simon was gone. And my only job was helping Nancy and

Judah . . .' Jerusha's voice trailed away and she lowered her eyes to her lap.

Rees stared at her. He was not quite sure what to say. 'I told her we will take her to school to apologize to the widow Francine today.' Lydia said. 'On Monday she will apologize to Babette.'

'But she had a terrible experience yesterday,' Rees said.

'It's best she finish this as soon as possible,' Lydia said. 'At least with the widow.'

'Very well,' Rees said. A tear leaked out from underneath Jerusha's eyes and ran down her cheek. He felt sorry and reached across the table to take her hand. But he didn't dare contradict Lydia.

'We will hear no more of quarrels,' she said, staring hard at her daughter. Jerusha kept her head bowed.

Rees broke the moment of silence. 'What happened when Wootten abducted you?' he asked

'Nothing,' Jerusha's voice squeaked in surprise. 'I told you . . .'

'From the very beginning,' he said.

'He came to the door,' Jerusha said, raising her eyes. Rees had not known how she would react but she seemed glad of the change of subject rather than afraid. 'He said you wanted me and told me to fetch my cloak.'

'You didn't wonder why I would ask you to leave your sisters and brothers?' Rees asked. Jerusha bit her lip and shook her head.

'Then what happened?' Lydia asked. She poured another jot of hot coffee into her husband's cup.

'As soon as we went outside he threw a sack over my head and put his arms around me.'

'*He* threw it?' Rees repeated. 'The boys weren't there?'

'No. I don't think they knew he was going to kidnap me,' Jerusha said. 'When we got back to the cabin, Jake, the oldest one you know, started yelling at his father.'

'Where were you?' Lydia asked. Her voice was stiff with fright.

'In the room with Miss Sally. She told me to come with her.'

'Let's back up a bit, shall we?' Rees said, holding out his hand to stop the flow of words. 'How did you get back to the cabin? Buggy?' He knew he hadn't seen one.

'No. He had a horse. He threw me over it. I threw up.' Jerusha leaned into Lydia's arm, her cheeks coloring.

'Good,' Lydia said vehemently. 'I'm glad you didn't make it too easy for him.'

'Did Wootten tell you why he wanted you?' Rees asked.

'He said he needed my help, that his wife was sick and couldn't manage on her own,' Jerusha said.

'So what did you do?' Lydia asked. 'To help Miss Sally, I mean.'

'I kept her water barrel filled. She drank a lot of water,' Jerusha said, her voice rising with remembered amazement. 'And she made a lot of water too. I had to take her chamber pot to a barrel in the cabin. Either Jake or Jem emptied it several times a day. I helped her dress and I combed her hair.'

'Did they feed you?' Rees asked.

Jerusha nodded. 'That was another of my duties; I did some of the cooking. The night I was taken Jake had roasted a turkey but the next morning I cooked ash pone. Then I brought some food into Miss Sally.'

'She ate alone, did she?' Lydia asked.

'Mostly. She didn't walk good—'

'Well,' corrected Lydia.

'She didn't walk well. She said her feet and legs always hurt her. So I brought the food in for her and me and we ate together.'

'Where did you sleep?' Rees asked.

'In Miss Sally's room. She told me to share the bed but there wasn't really enough room so I took my blanket and slept on the floor. Right next to the chimney. It was warm there.'

Rees and Lydia exchanged a glance; Jerusha's experience was a far less frightening – or dangerous – one than either had supposed.

'Did anyone ever talk about other girls?' he asked.

'Like Hortense, you mean? Yes. She did what I did. And there was someone before her. A girl called Bathsheba.'

Rees rose and went to stand behind Jerusha. He put his hand fondly on her braided hair.

'Ouch, you're pulling my hair,' Jerusha said in a muffled voice.

He realized he had pulled the girl close in his spasm of relief. 'Sorry.' He relaxed his hold and took a step back.

'And how did you escape the cabin?' Lydia asked.

For the first time Jerusha's eyes widened in fear. 'The room was filling with smoke. When I put my hand on the wall it was hot. Miss Sally took her dipper and flung water all over the wall.

In some places it sizzled.' She shook her head, remembering. 'Then Miss Sally said, "Girl, no point in you burning to death in here. Can you climb through that there window?" So I said, "Can you get through?" And she said, "No, I'm too portly. You go on now." So she helped me climb up to it and she boosted me through it.' Her eyes filled with sudden tears. 'She was kind to me.'

'And I shall be grateful to her for the rest of my life,' Lydia said.

Rees nodded and for a moment they all sat in silence. Then Lydia said, 'However, although your father and I love you and are grateful to Miss Sally, that does not excuse your behavior. You engaged in fighting and quarreling and you lied to us about the causes. Your father and I will have to consider an appropriate punishment.' Jerusha, turning white, gulped and nodded.

Rees looked at Lydia. With her mouth turned down and her forehead furrowed she looked grim and unyielding. He hoped she did not intend to whip the girl.

'She has had quite a scare,' he began. But the words died on his lips under the force of Lydia's frown. He changed his speech to a cough instead. 'I will be driving into town,' he said. 'I intend to question Wootten and his sons. After all, there have now been several murders . . .' He stopped short, recalling the young girl and her baby lying on the table in the cold cellar. Why, that girl was only a few years older than Jerusha.

'Were the mother and her baby murdered?' Jerusha asked now in a soft voice, almost as though she could read his thoughts. When he turned to look at his daughter her eyes were huge in her white face.

'Probably not,' he said, striving for a light tone. 'Birthing babies is a dangerous business.'

'Will you take us to the school?' Lydia asked her husband. 'It is best we finish that chore first.'

'Of course,' he said, watching nervousness play across Jerusha's face. 'I'm driving into town anyway.'

'Go on, get ready,' Lydia said. As Jerusha left the kitchen Lydia added, 'Annie will be here soon. I asked her to help while we went out. She can watch the younger children.' She smiled tremulously. 'I don't plan to leave my children alone again . . .' Her voice broke. Rees touched her shoulder, understanding how frightened she'd been. Her face contorted with the effort of controlling her emotions. 'Then we will walk back,' she said, forcing herself to speak calmly.

THIRTY-SIX

When they drove up to Widow Francine's little house, she stepped outside and asked them in surprise, 'What are you doing here? There's no school today; it's Saturday. And I thought, after Jerusha's experience yesterday, she might stay home for a while.'

'You heard?' Rees asked as he climbed down from the wagon seat.

'Yes, I heard.' She directed a very sympathetic look upon Jerusha. The girl looked down at her hands, her cheeks coloring.

'She wasn't hurt,' he said as he helped Lydia to the ground. Jerusha followed, slow with reluctance.

'I think you have something to say to Mrs Francine, Jerusha,' Lydia said with a stern nod.

'I'm sorry,' Jerusha mumbled, staring at the ground.

'I don't believe Mrs Francine can hear you,' Lydia said.

'I'm sorry,' the girl said more loudly. 'I lied. I slapped Babette first.' For the first time she raised her eyes and looked directly at the teacher. 'But she was so . . . so . . .' Words failed her.

'Violence towards another is never acceptable,' Mrs Francine said, 'especially for a young lady. I expect you to behave with more decorum in future. You can apologize to Babette when you see her next.'

'That will be Monday,' Lydia said.

Although Mrs Francine didn't smile at Jerusha, Rees sensed the widow's sympathy. 'We will say no more about it. Now, why don't you go inside? I prepared a small packet of assignments for you. You can take it home and begin working on them.'

Jerusha nodded and quickly disappeared through the door.

'I apologize for my daughter's behavior,' Lydia said once Jerusha had disappeared inside.

Mrs Francine smiled slightly. 'I confess to feeling a certain sympathy with your daughter. Babette has learned to please those around her. She is already accomplished at influencing others to do her bidding and then they catch the blame. After several years teaching I am less susceptible to those pretty ways. Of course,' she added, 'none of that excuses Jerusha's behavior.'

'She lied,' Lydia said. 'To you and to us.'

'Of course she did. Almost all young girls lie. But I expected better of Jerusha and I was more disturbed by the lies than the slap. If she had told the truth, I would have punished her and that would have been the end to it.'

Drawing her shawl around her shoulders, the widow Francine turned and entered the house.

'I wonder who else is lying to us,' Rees said in a meditative tone after the woman had disappeared.

'That is precisely what I was thinking,' Lydia replied with a smile. 'Everyone? I daresay the real question is who has told us the truth?'

'Is there anyone we can exclude?' Rees wondered. He drew his wife toward the wagon.

'Hortense,' said Lydia. 'She lied to us several times but we know she could not have set the fire that murdered Sally Wootten. Hortense was gone by then.'

'We know why she lied as well,' he said. 'She didn't want her mother to know her abduction was a screen to cover her plans to run away with Jake.'

'True,' Lydia said. 'Hmmm. I think we should begin with Pearl.' She shot a quick glance at her husband. 'I can't help but feel that, if we had discovered the murderer of the Shaker Sister, we might have prevented Sally Wootten's death.'

He pictured Pearl. 'So, what do we know about her? She is Wootten's daughter Bathsheba. And she was one of the girls who saw her father strangle the Sister.'

'Perhaps,' Lydia said. 'I've been thinking about her. Remember, Pearl makes up stories and, in this case, she would have a good reason for doing so.'

'Yes. But Glory corroborated her tale,' he objected.

Lydia nodded slowly. 'Yes. But I wonder – Glory seems a lonely girl. She might agree with anything Pearl said.'

'They described Josiah Wootten,' he pointed out.

'That's true,' Lydia said, her face falling. But Rees, as he began walking toward his wagon, pondered his wife's suggestion.

'Neither girl mentioned the wound on Wootten's face. We both know how obvious it was – we saw it. It would have been easily seen, even from a distance.'

'Exactly,' she agreed, her eyes sparking with renewed excitement. 'And Pearl is the leader. What if Glory supported the story because Pearl is her friend?'

Rees considered that. 'I see. They found the body but didn't see Wootten strangling the Sister.'

'Seeing the murder occur made a better story than just stumbling upon the body,' Lydia agreed. 'Much more satisfying for Pearl.'

Nodding slowly, Rees said, 'They probably saw Wootten running away. Except for the wound, the girls described him exactly.'

'Yes.' Lydia agreed. 'Besides, if Pearl is the Wootten daughter, she would know what her father looks like. Even from the back.'

'Of course she would. And she'd recognize her brother as well. So when she saw Jake she feared he would compel her to go home,' Rees said.

'That explains why she ran away,' Lydia said.

'Of course,' Rees agreed. 'But we still don't know where she is.'

'Or who the murderer is,' Lydia said, her brow creasing with frustration. 'Josiah Wootten?'

'I don't know,' Rees admitted glumly. He wanted it to be Wootten but wasn't convinced that was so. 'It could just as easily be one of the boys,' he said after a moment of thought. 'But which?'

Lydia offered him a sympathetic smile as Jerusha came out of the school and ran towards them. 'We'll see you at home,' she said.

When Rees arrived at the jail he found Granny Rose there before him. She had a basket of ragged coverings that she was pushing one by one through the small barred window and a pail of soup. From the few drops remaining in it, he deduced that the Woottens had already eaten their breakfast. A moment later proof arrived in the form of dirty wooden bowls turned sideways and squeezed through the bars.

He pulled up beside her mule. When he climbed down from the wagon seat and approached the jail, the midwife turned with a slight smile. 'Will Rees,' she said. 'What are you doing here? Came to check on the prisoners?'

'I'm glad you're feeding them,' he said. 'I was worried.' He didn't want to answer her since his motives for visiting were far less altruistic.

She nodded. 'When the constable is finished with them, send the boys to me. I'll care for them until a new cabin is built.'

Rees noticed the obvious exclusion of Josiah Wootten; even Granny Rose's kindness did not extend so far. Rees didn't blame her. 'How are they doing?' he asked, tilting his head to the jail.

'Better now, I'd guess. But you can ask them,' Granny said. She put the bowls into the basket and picked up the almost empty pail.

'Will you be feeding them regular?' Rees called after her as she began walking toward her mule.

She turned. 'Probably. Although, by the grace of God, they won't be here long.'

Rees approached the barred door. 'What do you want?' Wootten asked belligerently.

'We didn't hurt your daughter,' Jake said quickly. He was huddled under a blanket with only his face showing.

'I know,' Rees said. 'She said Sally was kind to her.' Jem uttered a sob and Jake turned so Rees could not see his face. 'That's not why I'm here.'

'Then why?' Wootten asked angrily. His hair stood out in spikes around his head and sticks and leaves clung to his beard. He seemed even more a wild man than before, but Rees found himself pitying the other man whose red-rimmed eyes spoke of a night of grief.

'I have a few questions,' he said, gentling his tone.

'Come to lord it over us, huh?' Wootten said.

Rees sighed. Wootten's combativeness was both frustrating and exhausting. 'No. I just want to ask some questions,' he said.

'And why should we answer any of them?' Wootten asked.

'No one else cares that you're in here,' Rees said, his own temper fraying. 'You can rot in here as far as most people are concerned. But I want to know the truth. I want to know what happened. I'm your only hope of release.'

'Ahh,' said Wootten, flinging out a dismissive hand, 'you don't care about us.' He turned and went to the stone ledge at the back.

'I care about Sally,' Rees said. 'She was murdered. That fire was purposely set. And, if you are not the guilty ones, maybe you can go free.' Even Josiah Wootten had no response. After a few seconds of silence Jake approached the barred door.

'What do you want to know?'

'Jerusha said she was abducted to care for Sally,' Rees said.

'That's true,' Jake said. 'Jem and I – with our chores – we couldn't manage. And someone has – had to be with M-Mother—' his voice broke and steadied – 'almost all the time.'

Rees's gaze traveled to Wootten. He grunted. 'I couldn't do it,' he said. 'I had to hunt so we could eat. Anyway, in two or three months I'll be leaving for the lumber camp. Cutting trees for the spring drive. Besides, it's woman's work.'

Rees turned his gaze back to Jake. 'So you took Hortense,' he said.

'I already tole you,' Jake said.

'And he were sweet on her,' Jem said. 'And she were sweet on him.'

'Puppy love,' Josiah Wootten said from his position on the stone bench.

Jake turned a look of such virulent anger on his father Rees wondered that Wootten hadn't been found dead.

'Tell me, Jake,' Rees said in a conversational tone, 'does your father know Hortense is carrying your child?' It was a guess but he saw by the flush that colored Jake's cheeks that he'd surmised correctly.

'She what?' Wootten said from the back. 'That's not possible.'

'How far gone?' Rees asked the boy.

'She said coming on to two months,' Jake admitted in a low voice. Rees spared a glance for the father. Wootten, blinking rapidly, looked as though he couldn't believe his ears.

Rees wondered if Bernadette suspected her daughter was pregnant. Of course she did; that explained her rush to spirit Hortense away to Quebec and marry her off to someone more suitable.

'So Hortense and then Jerusha,' Rees continued aloud. 'Who cared for your mother before then?'

'Our sister,' Jem said.

'Pearl?' Rees asked.

'Is that what she's calling herself now?' Jake asked.

'Selfish biddy ran off,' said Wootten.

Jake's face contorted and Rees knew there was more to this story.

'Before or after the birth of the baby?' Rees asked.

'After. Bathsheba was supposed to care for them too,' Wootten said. 'But when they died she run off.'

'Did you father your daughter's baby?' Rees asked, staring hard at Josiah Wootten. 'And then kill her and her baby to hide your shame?'

Wootten rushed forward, his face red with rage, and although he couldn't reach through the bars between them Rees involuntarily stepped back.

'You been listening to gossip?' Spittle flew from Wootten's mouth as he leaned forward, clutching the bars. 'I never touched my daughter. And nobody killed them. I looked at them one morning and they was simply dead.' He glared at Rees. 'That old woman on the mountain has nothing better to do than tell tales.'

'I didn't hear anything from Granny Rose,' Rees said, not entirely truthfully.

Wooten grunted dubiously. 'Huh. Well, the ground was already frozen so we put 'em in the cold cellar till spring.'

Rees considered that for a moment while the cold seeped through his boots and coat. Did he believe Wootten? No, he did not. Wootten was lying about something. But it was more important now to find Pearl. 'Did your daughter Bathsheba flee to the shopkeeper Mr Morton?' he asked.

'Not this time,' Wootten said. 'I made sure of that when she run off with him last winter. Morton will never look cross-eyed at the girl again, not if he knows what's good for him.'

'First place I checked,' Jake said to Rees. 'But he said he hadn't seen her.'

'We watched him,' Jem added. 'For weeks. He didn't go nowhere.'

'And we never saw her,' Jake agreed.

'So you went to Zion to look for her,' Rees said, turning to Jake.

He nodded. 'Looked for her,' he said. 'Never saw her. Couldn't find her anyway.' His voice rose in annoyance. 'All of those women look the same.'

'But your father had already gone to Zion,' Rees said, puzzled.

'No, I didn't.' Wootten almost spat out the words. 'I never went near there. Never guessed she'd run somewhere with such unnatural folk.'

Rees wasn't sure he believed that. Turning back to Jake, he asked, 'Would you have brought her home?' He wanted to say dragged her home but guessed Jake would take offense.

'Maybe,' the boy replied. 'Probably. To care for Mother. We couldn't do it, you see.'

Rees did see and for a moment he experienced a sharp sympathy for Pearl. What kind of life was this for a young girl, trapped in that cabin with not even the hope of a home and family of her own someday.

And poor Sally. She must have known what a burden she'd become for her family.

'Where were you when the fire in the cabin started?' Rees asked.

'Hunting,' said Wootten.

'All of you?' Rees asked.

'All of us,' Jake said.

'Together?'

'Of course not,' said Wootten as though Rees was stupid. 'Scare the game away.'

'We saw the smoke,' Jem said. 'Started running.'

'But you just said you weren't with your father or brother,' Rees said.

'No,' Jem said.

'Jem caught up to me when we started coming up the mountain,' Jake said.

'And your father?' Rees persisted, staring at the older man.

'What difference does that make?' he shouted.

'He were already there,' Jake said.

Rees looked through the bars to the three men inside. They'd separated and gone their own way into the woods. Any one of them could have returned to build the fire under the cabin and lit it. It would have caught and burned slowly. By the time the fire began in earnest the Wootten men would have been far away. And when they returned – seeing the smoke – Sally Wootten would be dead. And so would Jerusha.

'My daughter could have died in that fire,' he said, his voice trembling.

For a second or two the men inside the jail were silent. And then Jake said, 'We're right sorry about that.'

'She lived,' Wootten said. 'Sally saved your daughter's life.'

'Sally saved *your* life,' Rees said to Wootten. If she hadn't pushed Jerusha through the window and the girl had perished, Rees would probably have killed Josiah Wootten with his bare hands.

He stepped back from the jail. He wanted to believe Josiah Wootten was the murderer but reminded himself that Sally's care weighed heavily on the boys too. They'd said as much. And there was still the fact that Wootten and the boys could have murdered his wife in a way that would not have destroyed their home.

It all came back to Pearl.

THIRTY-SEVEN

'Just because Josiah Wootten sobbed and carried on when you saw him at his burning cabin,' Lydia said when Rees described his talk with the Wootten men, 'that doesn't mean he is innocent of setting the fire.' She put a heel of bread and a block of cheese in front of him. 'Supper won't be ready for another half hour or so.' Rees nodded. As he cut a piece of cheese and put it on the bread, Lydia continued, 'After all, Wootten has the lumber camp to go to. Maybe he didn't care about the cabin. Or what happened to his sons.' She returned to the fire and stirred it up. She had put a ham into the oven to bake and the aroma was almost more than Rees could take. He felt like taking the meat out now and devouring it. Lydia had brought a bunch of beets up from the cold cellar. The greens had been eaten when the vegetable was first picked and now the dark red globes waited to be peeled and sliced.

For the moment they had the kitchen to themselves as the children were engaged in their evening chores. Jerusha had been sent for water. Nancy was collecting eggs and Judah was supposed to be gathering wood. Joseph had insisted on tagging along. Rees was not sure how many eggs or how much kindling would make it inside the house; through the stout walls he could hear childish laughter. Even Jerusha had abandoned her pretensions to adulthood and was running around shrieking with the other children. From what he could hear, Rees suspected a wild snowball fight was in progress.

'It will be dark soon,' Lydia said, staring at the back door. 'The children should come in. We have to rise early for church.'

'Oh, let them play a few more minutes,' he said. He was enjoying the peace.

'And they'll be wet and cold.'

'Dinner will warm them up.'

Lydia did not speak for a few seconds. She lifted a beet and carefully began paring the skin from the burgundy flesh below. 'I think Mr Wootten tired of caring for his ill wife,' she said at last.

'That's true,' Rees agreed. He had seen men behave with apparently genuine grief at the death of a loved one – even when the murder had occurred at their hands. He added reluctantly, 'I suppose I could say the same about Jake and Jem.'

'I hope neither one of them is guilty of murder,' she said, speaking his thoughts. The beets had stained her fingers and the palms of her hands a deep red and she took a rag to wipe away some of the color.

'What do we know for certain?' he asked his wife.

'Wootten and his sons were abducting girls to care for Sally,' she replied.

'Once Pearl ran away,' Rees said.

'And then Hortense, despite her feelings for Jake, ran away,'

'Because Wootten attempted to interfere with her,' he said.

'Josiah Wootten bears the blame for that,' Lydia said in a sharp voice.

Rees did not say anything for several seconds. He understood. Wootten's wife was seriously ill. Then a young and pretty girl came into the house. Although he hoped he was a better man, he understood the temptation Wootten faced.

'I see you excuse his behavior,' Lydia said in a stern voice.

'No,' Rees said. 'I neither excuse nor condone. But I understand it.'

'A man and his base nature,' she said in such a judgmental tone he had to pause before he spoke. He did not want to argue with his wife over Wootten.

'The fight between Jake and his father makes perfect sense,' Rees said instead. 'Desire and jealousy are a potent combination. Now I know why, when Hortense ran away, both Jake and his father went searching for her.'

Lydia nodded, lifting her eyes from the beets. 'Then Mr Wootten saw the Shaker Sister and thought she was Hortense,' she said; almost, Rees thought, with relief. 'He rushed up and tried to strangle her.'

'He said he never went to Zion,' Rees said. Lydia sniffed disbelievingly. 'And he would have known he had the wrong woman when he saw her face. He should have left her alive.'

'Unless he didn't want her to tell anyone he'd been there.'

Rees considered the defiant man in jail with his damn-your-eyes attitude. 'Would he care?' He shook his head. 'I don't think so. Wootten has no reputation to protect.'

Lydia stopped slicing beets, pausing to think with the knife up raised. The dark red juice ran down her arm and dripped on the table. 'Oh dear.' Dropping the knife, she grabbed a towel and began sopping up the juice on her arm. 'Maybe he wanted to protect his wife's feelings? Well, wouldn't he? I know I would be heartbroken to hear something similar about my husband.'

Rees moved to her and dropped a kiss upon the patch of her forehead revealed by her cap. 'You never will,' he promised.

Smiling she pushed him away. 'But wouldn't he want to protect Sally's feelings?' she persisted.

'Maybe. But that assumes someone would travel to the cabin to tell her.' Rees hesitated, thinking about the woman who was a virtual prisoner in her room. 'Maybe not,' he said, contradicting himself. 'She probably knew about Hortense anyway, since Wootten's attack took place only a door's width away. And when Jake confronted his father, well, the noise of the fight would surely have penetrated her refuge. Besides, Hortense was in the room with Sally Wootten.' Lydia stared at her husband.

'She knew,' she said. 'She must have.'

'Wootten had no reason to strangle Hortense,' he said. 'Not to keep the secret anyway.'

'Maybe he planned to revenge himself upon her for her refusal,' she said in a dry voice.

Rees looked at her, wondering what she had experienced to occasion that darkly knowing tone. 'Perhaps.' He considered Wootten, a man given to anger – but sudden quick outbursts, not planned revenge. 'When I accused him of visiting Zion, he told me he had never been to Zion.'

'And you believed him?' Lydia asked in amazement. 'He lied to you.'

Rees did not reply. He wasn't sure he believed Josiah Wootten – but wasn't so sure he didn't either. Wootten's denial had seemed genuine. 'We're missing something important,' Rees said now.

And then the opportunity to continue reviewing the case ended with the entrance of the four children, their cheeks red with cold. Their laughter filled the kitchen as they dropped the snowy sticks in the wood pile. Rees, who could barely think with all the noise, escaped upstairs to spend some time weaving.

When he awoke in the early hours of morning, Lydia was already gone from the bed. He rolled over into the cooling hollow to peer into the cot by the bed. Sharon was missing as well but he could hear her high treble voice. Rees scrambled out from under the warm quilts. He quickly donned socks and slid his feet into his shoes. He added breeches and two shirts, one a heavy woolen one, over his body linen. He decided no number of shirts would be enough to keep him warm and hurried downstairs. Although he tried to step quietly, his footsteps sounded very loud in the still house.

When he entered the kitchen the fire was blazing on the hearth. Lydia was sitting at the table with a cup of tea watching her small daughter play.

'I've set up the coffee pot,' Lydia said, half-turning in her seat. 'If you want coffee, put it over the fire.'

With a nod, Rees arranged the pot on the spider and pushed the pot nearer the flames.

Then he joined his wife at the table. 'Couldn't sleep?' he asked.

'I've been thinking about Pearl,' she said. 'Something about her – well, her disappearance – bothers me.'

'What, exactly?' he asked. He too had been worrying about the fate of someone lost in this cold weather.

'I don't know. But I'm not so sure she ran off with a young man,' Lydia said.

'Why?'

Without speaking, she brought a handful of something from her lap: the earbobs and the necklace.

'She would have taken them, if only to sell. I know she would have. These earrings would fetch a good price.' She held one up and the red stone sparkled, as crimson as a drop of blood. Involuntarily Rees flinched.

'But Esther said Pearl was interested in the boys,' he said. 'She told me Pearl hangs out the window and smiles and waves at the boys any chance she sees.'

Lydia nodded, but not as though she agreed. 'Daniel said none of the boys were missing – and none of the Shaker Brothers either. So who?'

Rees stared at her for several seconds. 'We've got something wrong,' he said at last. She nodded in agreement. 'But what? I keep thinking that Pearl is the key. If we understand Pearl, we will understand everything.'

'Do you think one of the Wootten boys found her and dragged her home?' Lydia asked.

'Then where is she?' Rees asked. 'I swear, she was not there when I went after Jerusha. And our daughter never mentioned another girl.'

Lydia chewed her lip. 'Perhaps she saw her opportunity and ran?'

'Where would she go?' he asked, wondering if he would need to visit Mr Morton again. At least Rees need not fear meeting Josiah Wootten this time.

Lydia stared into space for several seconds, the necklace clutched in her hand. Finally, surprised to find herself still holding the beads, she stared down at them. 'These were made with love,' she said. 'Look. They are all carved.' She held out the necklace to her husband. He had assumed the beads had been crudely made but now he saw one was carved into petals like a rose and another indented with circles. He reached for the necklace. Each bead was different, carefully carved and polished.

'It must have taken a long time to carve this,' he said, once again experiencing that twitch of familiarity. 'I wonder . . .' Lydia turned to look at him. 'Jake Wootten carves,' Rees said. 'I saw him working on a wooden bowl.'

'Of course,' she said. 'He carved it for his sister. That's why Pearl has it.'

Rees nodded. 'That makes sense.'

'No it doesn't,' Lydia said fretfully.

'It doesn't? Why not?'

She did not reply. Instead she stared into space, her facial expressions changing with her thoughts. Finally he asked, 'What are you thinking about?'

'Laundry.'

'What?' Rees gaped at her.

'We have to go back to Zion.' She looked at him. 'I have to check on something.'

'But today is Sunday,' Rees said.

'I know,' Lydia said. 'But I suspect the Sisters did not finish all of the wash. When I was a Sister we almost never finished it all.' She paused. 'I hate to miss church but we must. I'll leave Jerusha to watch her younger brothers and sisters.' She added with a twist to her lips, 'I am not so afraid with the Woottens behind bars. And I want to leave as soon as we can.'

'The Shakers will be attending services in the Meeting House.' Rees said, thinking of the questions he might consider asking and couldn't if they were busy.

'That may be for the best,' Lydia replied with a cryptic smile.

Morning chores meant they did not get on the road for another three hours, despite their intentions. When they drove into Zion the main street was empty of people. Although Rees still found the silence of this community disconcerting, he was accustomed to seeing the Brothers and Sisters walking through the village, on their way to chores or to the Dining Hall. The empty streets felt strange and he was glad to hear the singing emanating from the Meeting House.

'Let's drive as close to the laundry shed as we can,' Lydia said. Rees turned a quick glance upon her. A furrow had formed between her brows and as he watched it deepened. She was clutching at the side of the wagon and he thought that if not for her gloves he would see her white knuckles. Something, some thought, was making her tense but he knew she wouldn't tell him until she was ready.

They crossed the bridge but once on the other side Rees pulled Hannibal to a stop and climbed down. Although no snow had fallen the previous night, the temperatures had dropped below freezing and the vegetation crunched beneath his feet. He draped the horse blanket over Hannibal and then helped Lydia alight. In silence they walked through the glade to the laundry shed.

Usually a hive of activity, all was quiet now. But, as Lydia had predicted, the Sisters on laundry duty had been here working here yesterday. A few pieces of body linen and a couple of sheets, all frozen solid, festooned the leafless bushes. She pushed open the door and stepped inside. Rees followed. The fire had been banked and a line of cold irons waited on the hearth for the Sisters to return.

'What are we looking for?' he asked.

'Dirty laundry,' she said. 'I am almost positive it has not been done. Yet. At least, I pray not.'

Rees turned a look of bewilderment upon her. She did not notice. She moved purposefully toward the large baskets in which the Sisters brought the washing to the laundry. Most were empty but there were still a few full ones at the back. She began hurling sheets, towels and other linen items to the floor. 'What are you doing?' he asked.

'Looking for something. I may be wrong. I hope I'm wrong.' She went from basket to basket until an enormous pile of laundry lay upon the stone floor. Finally, at the rearmost basket, she found what she was searching for. 'Look.' She held up a handful of towels. All of them were stained dark.

'Blood,' Rees said.

Lydia nodded. 'There are only a few items in this basket besides these towels. Of course, there may be a perfectly innocent explanation for the blood but I don't think so. There's too much of it, for one thing.'

'What do you mean?' he asked. But the words died on his lips as his thoughts raced. 'Something else was in the basket,' he breathed in understanding.

'*Someone* else,' she corrected him. He stared at her. 'What if Pearl did not run away with a boy? She didn't take her treasures. That's bothered me from the very beginning. I kept thinking that if she had simply run away, well, she would have taken her valuables. They were important to her. If she didn't take them, then there had to be some other explanation.'

'You think she's dead?' Rees said. This was exactly what he had feared. Lydia nodded. 'But where is she? We – I mean the Shaker Brothers and myself – searched the entire village.'

'But you were looking for a living girl, not a body,' Lydia pointed out. He gulped. 'What's more, I think her body is somewhere here, around the laundry.' When he did not respond, she added, 'Her body was brought here, to the wash house, in the laundry basket. Pearl cannot be too far away.'

'Surely the Sisters would have seen her . . .' he began. But perhaps not. Not if Pearl had been carefully hidden. And she would have been hidden in a laundry basket. Rees looked at his wife. 'We must search the wash house.' She shook her head but followed him into the next room.

Although the laundry was not very large, it was full of hiding places. They turned over all of the coppers, looked into the cupboards and peered under the ironing tables. Nothing.

'I think,' Lydia said, 'we need to search the area around this wash house. If she is dead . . .' Her words trailed away and she met Rees's gaze with an anxious frown.

He thought of the steep hillside behind the laundry. It dropped to a stream below and was a handy location for the disposal of unwanted items. He sighed. He should have thought of it before. 'The hill behind the laundry,' he said. 'I'll climb down and search.'

Lydia joined him as he walked around the wash house to the steep slope at the back. Hillocks of dead grass and large stones protruded through the snow. 'Be careful,' she said. He nodded. Even during the summer this hill was difficult to navigate. Now, with snow covering the uneven ground and ice slicked over the stones, both the descent and the climb back up would be difficult.

He began inching his way down the hill.

Dirty wash water was sent down the hill by way of a hollowed-out log. With the cold temperatures, the most recent evacuation of water had left a large icy streak descending down the slope.

He was careful to stay well away from it; he did not want to slide all the way down to the stream below.

Using the leafless branches of the scrubby trees that somehow managed to cling to this hill as supports, Rees picked his way down. When he was about a third of the way and had stopped to rest – he was breathless and his thighs were beginning to ache – he saw something fluttering below. Something dark. 'Oh no,' he said involuntarily. Now he began to hurry, his feet slipping in the snow. He fell twice but he barely felt the impact before he was up again. His injured ankle began to ache.

Dusted with snow, the object disappeared into the white landscape, invisible to even a cursory search. But Rees, with each step closer, became more and more certain that he was approaching a body. The fluttering cloth that to a quick glance could appear as leaves or a discarded rag resolved into a corner of a dark blue dress.

Finally he stood over the snow-covered mound. When he used his handkerchief to brush away the snow he revealed Pearl's white face. She was dead and he thought she had been for some time. Abandoned in the cold, her body displayed no signs of corruption. Except for the bluish tint to her skin and lips, her face was unmarked. Her cap had fallen off somewhere and the dark red wound in her blond hair glittered with crystals of ice.

Rees turned and began the long climb back to the top. 'I guess Pearl could not have started the fire that killed her mother,' he said. Lydia nodded mutely. The only sound was the clicking of the carved beads she held tightly in her hands. He stared at the necklace and thought, *Jake Wootten.*

THIRTY-EIGHT

B rother Jonathan was not pleased when Rees pulled him out of services. The Elder was unhappier still when Rees guided him down the steep hillside behind the wash house. But his irritation faded when he saw the body lying in the snow. 'Oh dear,' he said. 'Oh dear.' Looking up at Rees, he added, 'How long has she been here?'

'I don't know,' he said. 'Days, I suspect. It's been cold. She's frozen almost solid She could have been here since we first found out she was missing.'

Jonathan shook his head with dismay. 'All right,' he said. He paused and Rees guessed that the Elder was considering leaving the body here until later, after prayers. But he thought better of it; death trumped even the services to God. 'We'll have to bring her up,' he said.

Within the hour several of the Shaker Brothers had been called in to assist Rees. They were struggling to bring the body up the hill and to the front of the wash house. Although Pearl had been of slight build, her dead weight and the uneven and snowy terrain meant removing her to the top of the slope involved six men. Rees did not think Rouge would be available but a boy had been dispatched to town to alert him nonetheless.

By the time Pearl's remains had been brought to the top, Rees was sweating. They had almost lost the body once. It threatened to tumble down the hill, when one of the Brothers had fallen over a snow-covered tree root. Rees had wrenched his shoulder grabbing at the body, preventing the slide down the slope by catching the full skirt. It was a great relief to reach the flat ground by the building. Rees stood aside when the Brothers carried the slight figure around to the front.

Esther, and some of the other Sisters, waited there with Lydia. Louisa stared at the motionless body on the ground with avid curiosity but Glory, her eyes filling with tears, turned away. 'Oh no,' Esther said. 'Oh no.' Taking her handkerchief from her cloak pocket, she smoothed it across Pearl's waxen face.

'She's not wearing her cloak,' Lydia said quietly to Rees.

'She was killed inside,' he replied. She nodded.

'I suppose the young man she was seeing murdered her,' Esther said sorrowfully.

'But she—' Rees stopped speaking abruptly when Lydia put her hand on his arm.

'Not now,' she said so softly he could barely hear her.

Male voices sounded clearly from the path and within a minute or so Rouge and Thomas appeared.

'I thought you would be at Mass,' Rees said.

'I should have been,' Rouge replied. 'I overslept. I daresay God had a plan for me today.' His gaze went to the still form lying on the ground. 'What happened?' He sounded both resigned and tired.

'This is the missing girl,' Rees began but Jonathan, directing a frown in his direction, stepped forward.

'We all assumed she had left our order for a man,' he said.

'And you think he didn't want her?' Rouge said. When Jonathan nodded, the constable added, 'Maybe the man was one of you.'

Jonathan took a quick step backward. 'Of course not,' he said.

Esther, her caramel-colored cheeks damp with tears, stepped forward. 'Although Pearl was forward and pushed herself at Daniel and other young Brothers, we never saw any special or inappropriate relationship. Most of the Brothers seemed embarrassed rather than intrigued. So we—' and here she gestured to Jonathan and Daniel standing behind the older Elder – 'assumed she had met someone from the World.'

Rouge glanced at Esther then quickly away again. He was not accustomed to women, and colored women at that, speaking directly to him as though they were equals.

'You don't have any idea who she might have been seeing?' Rees asked, stepping into the sudden awkward silence. 'One of the hired men perhaps?'

'We only have the one at present,' Jonathan said, 'and he is an old man more interested in his supper and his beer than in any young girls.'

'No idea at all,' Esther said.

Lydia took the jewelry from her pocket and stared at it thoughtfully.

'I'll bring the body back to town,' Rouge said. 'The coroner must examine her.'

'She is one of ours,' Jonathan argued. 'We'll put her in the spring house and bury her when the weather turns and the ground warms.'

'She is a murder victim,' Rouge said, although he knew there was a question of his jurisdiction over the Shaker community. His predecessor had been more circumspect about entering Zion even when a violent death occurred, but he was cut from different cloth. This was not the first time he had quarreled with this community over whose authority took precedence. 'She needs to be examined. Especially considering the circumstances of her death.'

'No doubt this was an unfortunate accident,' Jonathan said, his voice weakening. Rees eyed the other man sympathetically. The Elder must know he stood on shaky ground.

'No doubt she hit herself on the head and threw herself down the hill to the creek,' Rouge replied with heavy sarcasm.

'Someone else could have hit her,' Jonathan replied, his voice rising. 'Someone from outside this community. Rees will tell you; those brutish Woottens have been seen creeping around our village.'

Rees nodded. 'That's true,' he agreed. But would Jake – or any of the Woottens – know the location of the laundry? And especially that behind this building was a steep hill dropping down to a stream? He doubted it.

'They are in jail.' Rouge's deep voice interrupted Rees's furious thinking.

'But Pearl disappeared before the Woottens were taken,' Jonathan said.

'So, are you saying Josiah Wootten is not guilty?' Rouge asked in confusion. 'Or is he?'

'Of course he is,' Jonathan said. 'He took her before they were imprisoned.'

'I don't think so,' Rees said. 'Moreover, Josiah Wootten claims he's never come into Zion.'

'He's lying, of course,' the Elder said.

'Maybe,' Rees agreed. There was that word – lying – again. 'But I don't think so,' he added reluctantly.' Of almost everyone I've met, he has the least reason to lie. He does what he wants and devil take the hindmost. And that includes the abduction of

Jerusha and the other girls.' He sighed. It didn't seem right that a man like Josiah Wootten could be honest.

'But he wouldn't stick at murder,' Rouge said.

'Maybe not,' Rees agreed. 'But he wouldn't lie about it afterward either. He'd tell you the truth and dare you to do something about it. Josiah Wootten doesn't care what we think. But the murderer of both the Shaker Sister and Pearl, well, he doesn't want to be discovered. I think he has something to lose.'

'Is it one of the Wootten boys then?' Jonathan asked.

'Maybe,' Rees said, trying to imagine the links between the victims.

'We still don't know who's guilty?' Rouge cried, his voice rising with frustration.

'Where's Lydia?' Rees asked suddenly, looking around at the faces in the group.

'She was just here,' Esther said. She glanced behind her as though she expected Lydia to appear.

'In the laundry?' Jonathan suggested.

'She wouldn't leave now,' Rees said, examining the crowd once again. He strode to the laundry and peered inside, thinking – hoping – she had gone in to sit down. But when he called her his voice echoed. He looked in the drying room and the alcove where the ironing took place but they too were empty.

He went outside, hoping she had reappeared. But she wasn't there. Rouge turned. Rees realized he must look worried; the constable put a hand on his shoulder. 'I'm certain she has just wandered off,' Rouge said.

'This is a Shaker community,' Jonathan added. 'Nothing will have happened to her.'

'How can you even say that?' Rees asked waspishly. 'There have been two murders here in the last week. And that does not count the previous murders these past few years.'

'I'm sure she's fine,' Esther said, breaking the awkward silence.

'Did anyone see her leave?' Rees asked, his gaze moving rapidly from face to face. Most of the community had elected to remain at services but there were still a group of Brothers and Sisters here. Everyone shook their head.

'Maybe she went to your wagon,' Rouge suggested.

'Maybe,' Rees said. He started down the path to the road, and his wagon, at the end. As soon as he went round the curve and the vehicle came into view he knew that Lydia was not there.

Now seriously alarmed, he looked into the springhouse. It was, of course, empty; why would she go in there? He started up the main thoroughfare through the village, so terrified that the murderer had taken her he could barely think.

Three of the Shakers were walking to the white Meetinghouse at the end of the street. Rees recognized them. They'd left services and now had chosen to return. He trotted toward them. 'Hey,' he called out. They did not turn around or give any sign that they heard him. 'Listen,' he shouted more loudly. Still no reaction.

Rees began to run. He knew they were aware of him; they visibly increased their speed.

He caught up to them as they separated; the Sister to ascend the women's stairs and enter through their door as the Brothers approached the entry on the other side. He grabbed the arm of one of the Brothers. He wrenched his arm free and frowned at Rees.

'Have you seen my wife?' he asked. 'Dark blue cloak. Red hair.'

The Brothers shook their heads and hastened up the steps. Rees turned and looked around. The street was empty.

Where could Lydia have gone?

THIRTY-NINE

As Rees began walking south, back to the end of the street and the laundry, he heard a faint cry. He spun around, his eyes searching the area. Nothing moved. And anyway, he thought, the sound had been muffled, as though it came from inside one of the buildings. He began to jog toward the Dining Hall and the kitchen behind it; when his family had lived in Zion, Lydia had frequently worked with the Sisters. But when he peered into the Dining Hall, automatically entering through the Men's door, it was empty.

There was only one woman in the kitchen and she shook her

head – no one else was here – while she shooed Rees away. He ran back to the village's center and looked around. He was truly frightened now and perspiring despite the cold air. His gaze went from building to building; he could think of no reason why Lydia would have gone inside any of them. Although he listened for another cry, he heard only the faint sound of singing and the sound of rhythmic thumps as the community sang and danced during the service.

Rees turned toward the Dwelling House. He could not imagine why Lydia would choose to go inside but he could think of no other possibility. He ran up the steps and went inside.

At first he did not see Lydia, only one of the Sisters at the back of the hall on the women's side. Her back was shuddering with effort. Hearing a panting gasp, Rees hurried forward. Just a few steps forward and he saw that the Sister was Glory. And her hands were clutched around the throat of another woman: Lydia. Blood suffused her face and she clawed at Glory's hands. Although scratches bloodied the girl's pale skin, she had not relaxed her hold. Rees hurled himself at the struggling couple.

First he attempted to wrench Lydia from the other woman's grasp but, although he freed one hand from Lydia's throat, Glory simply backhanded him across the face. She was far stronger than he'd guessed and he staggered back. She replaced her hand on Lydia's neck. Rees could see the tendons and sinews of her hands protrude as she squeezed.

He ran back to the struggling women. He put one arm around Glory's collar and the other on her well-muscled upper arm. He pulled with all his strength, shouting involuntarily for help. Although she was strong, Rees was stronger and after a few seconds she began to thrash in his grasp. He pulled harder until he felt both of her hands tear at his arm. Fortunately for him, his heavy coat shielded him from the worst of the scratching.

'It's over,' he said, hurling the girl away from him. Two large steps took him to his wife and he pulled her into his arms. 'Oh God, Lydia.' Her cap had come off in the struggle and her auburn hair tumbled down her back.

'It's her,' she said in a hoarse voice. 'She's the murderer.'

With a scream, Glory launched herself at Rees's back. He felt her hands circle his neck, scrabbling for purchase. He let go of

Lydia and turned to strike at Glory, woman or no. Fear and rage lent strength to his blow and she went down to the floor.

'Rees, stop. What are you doing?' Jonathan, followed by several of the community as well as Rouge, ran into the Dwelling House. He approached the girl lying splayed upon the floor but hesitated, stopped by the restrictions governing strict separation of the sexes.

As Esther approached, Rees held up a hand. 'Stop. She's the murderer. She was strangling Lydia.'

'Now, wait a minute,' Jonathan said when everyone was settled in the Elder's office. 'Surely you are mistaken, Rees. Glory could not kill anyone.'

'Of course not,' Rouge said.

Rees glanced at the girl. Seated between Lydia and Esther, she visibly shrank in upon herself and stared down at her clasped hands. Rees guessed she was trying to appear small and delicate, and far too weak to attack anyone.

'Because she is a woman?' he asked. 'I promise you, I fought with her and she is as strong as many men.'

'She did this,' Lydia said, raising one hand to her bruised throat. She still sounded hoarse. 'She would have murdered me but for my husband.'

'Why?' asked Jonathan, his voice and his posture betraying his doubts.

Lydia looked at Rees and spoke to him. 'The jewelry nagged at me. There was such a difference between the carved beads and the ruby earrings.'

'Those earbobs came from Pearl's mother,' Jonathan said.

'Exactly,' Lydia said, shooting him a glance. 'We knew Sally Wootten, and it was clear she would not own such expensive trinkets. At first I thought Pearl might have stolen them. But then I remembered Esther had said Pearl was brought by her mother. So it had to be the beads that were significant. And my husband guessed they were carved by Jake Wootten.'

'I don't understand what's important about a bunch of carved beads,' Rouge said.

'They are Glory's beads,' Lydia said, turning a glance upon the girl. 'She told me the beads belonged to her while she and I were standing over Pearl's body earlier today.'

'So?' Rouge said.

'What did you say?' Rees asked his wife. 'That now you understood everything?'

'Something like that,' she admitted with a reluctant smile. 'Anyway, Glory promised to explain everything, once we were away from the crowd.'

'I don't understand anything,' Rouge said in irritation.

'Glory is Josiah Wootten's daughter,' Lydia said. 'It was never Pearl.' Rees eyed the young woman. Now that he was looking for it, he saw the resemblance to her father.

'Bathsheba,' he said.

'Don't call me that,' Glory said angrily. 'I hate that name.'

'What?' Jonathan said, staring at her.

'You had almost all the care of your mother, didn't you?' Lydia asked, directing a look of sympathy upon Glory. 'And then when your younger sister gave birth to a baby . . . well, it was just too much for you.'

'It wasn't fair,' Glory burst out.

'But the beads,' Rouge said. 'What do they have to do with it?'

Rees wanted to hit him. Lydia had Glory talking and with the constable's unfortunate outburst the girl frowned and shut her mouth.

'Jake gave Glory the necklace,' Rees said, striving to keep his voice as soft and gentle as Lydia's. 'He made them for her. Out of love. Isn't that right, Glory?'

'But why did Pearl—' Rouge began. Rees reached over and clamped his hand on the other man's arm. He felt like putting it over the constable's mouth but Rouge, after a glance at Rees's expression, stopped talking.

'Did Hortense deliver your sister's baby?' Lydia asked.

Glory nodded. 'Yes. She and Jake . . .' She stopped abruptly.

'That's why you strangled the Sister,' Lydia continued. 'You saw the gray cloak and assumed it was Hortense.' She paused. Glory stared at her hands and did not speak. 'You feared Hortense might see you,' Lydia continued.

'I knew if she said anything I would lose my place here,' Glory said. 'I thought the woman in the cloak was Hortense so I grabbed her from behind. Then, when she fell, I saw her face.' She blew out a gusty sigh. 'I knew that Sister wasn't Hortense then but she knew me. She'd seen me in the village. I had to kill her.' When no one spoke, silenced by horror, she rushed into speech. 'If anyone knew who I was or if I lost my place here, my father would take me back home. I couldn't go back, I just couldn't.'

'Pearl and Louisa didn't see your father kneeling over the Sister, did they?' Rees murmured.

'No. But I said I'd seen him. I knew Pearl would pretend she'd seen him too.' Glory smiled slightly and Rees felt a chill sweep over him. 'She always wanted to be the center of attention. And she did exactly as I expected. She told everyone she'd seen the murderer.'

And that, Rees realized, was why none of the girls had described Wootten with the wound across the face. Glory didn't know about the fight between Wootten and Jake.

'But Pearl knew the truth,' Lydia said so quietly Rees could almost not hear her.

Glory nodded. 'She threatened me. She told me she would tell if I didn't give her my necklace.' Glory bit her lip. 'Then she wanted me to help with her chores. We were on laundry that week and she hated it. Hated ironing. I could see it would never end. I'd belong to her as much as I did to my parents. I couldn't have that. So I . . .' She stopped and looked at Lydia.

'You hit her?' she asked.

Glory nodded. 'She didn't go to the wash house that day and Sister sent me to find her. She was mooning about our bedchamber. She taunted me. I had a flatiron in my hand and I lost my temper and I hit her. I didn't mean to kill her. It just happened. When I bent down to look at her she was dead.'

'So you put her in the laundry cart and wheeled her to the wash house and told Sister you couldn't find Pearl,' Lydia said. Glory nodded.

'And later that night you returned and dumped the body down the hill,' Rees guessed.

'I didn't mean to kill her,' Glory muttered.

'Did you mean to kill your mother?' Rees asked.

'What do you mean?' Jonathan asked. He was pale and his hands were shaking.

'Someone set the fire that destroyed the Wootten's cabin,' Rees said. He returned his gaze to Glory. 'You could have hiked up there, built the fire, and returned to Zion with no one the wiser.'

'That would have taken too long,' Rouge objected. 'Someone would have noticed her absence.'

'Not if she didn't take the road,' Rees retorted. 'The hills are covered with trails. 'Shortcuts. I suspect Glory knows quite a few of them.'

'I didn't mean to kill my mother,' she said in a low voice.

'Your father then,' Rees guessed. 'He was the target.'

When Glory did not reply Lydia spoke. 'Jake did see you when he visited Zion, didn't he? Were you afraid he would tell?'

Rees stared at the girl. So Glory had intended to murder her brother, the one who had carved her beaded necklace for her. 'He kept your secret, Glory,' Rees said in a harsh voice. 'He told me he hadn't seen you. Jake loved you.'

'I'm done talking,' she said, staring at the ground.

'It's jail for you,' Rouge said to Glory as he stood. 'And hanging. I'll let the rest of your family out. But you'll take their place.'

Then Rouge turned a questioning look upon Rees. At first he did not know what the constable wanted. Then he realized Rouge had ridden to Zion on his horse and had no way of removing Glory to town. Not without Rees's wagon that is.

He sighed heavily and nodded.

'I'm coming,' Lydia said in a tone that brooked no argument.

'Why does this happen to us and our community?' Jonathan asked. 'These are problems of the World.'

Rees turned and looked at the Shaker Elder but did not speak. Taking in all who found their way to Zion was a saintly action but only the most naïve would not expect a few bad apples in the barrel. After all, people were people and the high level of goodness expected by the Shaker ethos was simply not attainable for most.

'I'll accompany the girl,' Esther said. 'I'll ride in the back with her.'

Rouge nodded in agreement. Within half an hour the party started for town, Glory restrained by some stout ropes and tied to the wagon bed besides.

FORTY

Rouge opened the jail. 'Get out,' he told the three men inside. 'You're free to go.'

Jem stepped out first, swathed in several old bed coverings. The one draped over his head made him appear like an old woman in a shawl. Jake followed his brother. Rees's heart broke to see them so worn and pale, aged beyond their years. Then Josiah Wootten stepped out, shivering with cold and dirty. But, although his rebelliousness was just a shadow of its former intensity, he remained defiant.

'Bathsheba,' he said, his eyes lighting on his daughter. 'What are you . . .?' The words died in his throat when he saw the ropes binding her arms. 'What . . .?' His gaze moved to Rouge. 'Why is my daughter here?'

'She's the murderer,' the constable replied. 'She confessed to the murders of the Shaker Sister.'

'And your wife,' Rees said. 'She set the fire.'

Wootten's hands clenched. 'No. That can't be true.' He looked at his daughter, his expression horrified. 'It ain't true. Tell them, Bathsheba. Tell them.'

Glory stared at her father for several seconds and then she smiled. The angry cruelty of that expression sent a shudder through Rees's body. 'But it is true,' she said. Shock sent Wootten two stumbling steps backward. 'You wouldn't even let me marry. You came and took me away from Mr Morton.' Once she began speaking, the words tumbled from her mouth almost without her conscious volition. 'I couldn't marry, no, I had to take care of my mother. Forever. And then it was *my* fault when my sister was got with child.'

'You knew she had no sense,' Wootten argued. 'But you went off and left her—'

'Caring for my mother was difficult enough,' Glory said, leaning forward. 'But then, my sister and her baby?'

'Who else was goin' to do it?' Wootten broke in.

Rees, hearing the grooves in this well-worn argument, stared at the other man. Had he forgotten what his daughter was accused of doing?

'I could see I'd be trapped in that cabin taking care of someone for the rest of my days. I had to get out,' she shouted.

'Now, don't raise your voice to me, girl,' Wootten said. 'You've always been defiant and I don't like it.'

'Why did you smother your sister and her baby?' Rees asked, his voice cutting through the quarrel. Wootten gulped as he remembered of what crimes his daughter was accused. 'Why didn't you just leave them behind, as you did your mother?' For a moment he thought Glory wouldn't answer.

'She saw me leaving.' Her words suddenly burst out. 'She was always after me. "Get me water",' she mimicked in savage garbled words. "I'm hungry. I need a change." She saw me going to the door with my cloak in my hand and she told me I couldn't leave. I had to care for her and the baby. She started that whine of hers, louder and louder until I knew she was going to wake everyone up. So I went to the bed and I put my hand over her mouth. But she struggled and made that grunting noise of hers. So I knelt on her chest. I didn't realize the baby was there. Until I felt it underneath me and by then . . .' She stopped short and turned her face away. It was the first time Rees had seen her express remorse.

Tears began streaming down Lydia's cheeks. And Rees, imagining those deaths in the dark and fetid cabin, felt like weeping too. He tried to console himself with the thought the baby would not have survived anyway without her mother. It didn't help.

He spared a glance at Wootten and his sons. Shock and horror contorted every one of their faces. 'Please, God. It can't be,' Jake muttered. Rees was startled to see tears in Josiah Wootten's eyes. But not surprise. Despite his denials, he'd suspected his daughter all along.

Rees felt an unwilling pity stir within him. How would he feel if this was one of his daughters? It was too terrible to contemplate.

'Tell them you didn't do it,' Jake pleaded with his sister, his voice raw with emotion.

'But I did do it,' Glory said. 'And I'm glad.'

'She confessed,' Rouge said unfeelingly.

Rees saw the exact moment when Josiah Wootten made his decision. His expression hardened and he said, 'I did it. I killed my daughter and her baby.'

'Oh, and did you strangle Pearl?' Rees asked.

'A course I did.'

'She wasn't strangled,' Rees said.

'He didn't do it,' Glory said in an icy tone. Rees felt Lydia shiver against his arm. 'I don't even know why he's saying that.'

'I'm trying to help you,' Wootten said, his voice cracking.

'I don't want your help,' she said. The years of pent-up resentment and anger colored her voice with rage. Wootten flinched.

'Why did you set the fire that burned down the cabin?' Lydia whispered. 'You were out of it by then.'

'But I wasn't,' Glory said. 'Don't you see? My mother was still alive. Jake knew where I was hiding. If my father found me he would drag me back home.' She glared at her father. 'I wasn't safe.'

'I don't understand. What did I do that was so wrong?' Wootten asked. And Rees, who had thought this man nothing more than a brute and a villain, felt his eyes moisten at the desolation in the other man's voice. Glory turned her back on him and walked into the jail with her head held high. Rouge slammed the door behind her. Rees jumped at the finality of the metallic clang of the lock sliding home.

There was a moment of horrified silence.

'We won't let you starve,' Wootten said, turning to the barred door of the jail.

'She is one of our community,' Esther said, straightening her shoulders. 'Even if it lasted for only a short time. We will ensure she's fed and warm, at least until . . .' Her words ran down.

'I want to go home to my children,' Lydia said suddenly.

'So do I,' Rees said, turning toward his wagon. He couldn't wait to see them.

Both he and Lydia were silent for the first leg of the journey. Rees's thoughts circled around Wootten and his daughter. By God, he pitied the other man.

'So much anger and bitterness,' Lydia said at last. 'I feel sorry for the girl.'

'I do too,' Rees said, smiling at his wife and reaching over to take her hand. 'I feel sorry for them all. But mostly I pity Wootten. He blames himself. He'll spend the rest of his life living with regret.' Rees knew how terrible that felt. He regularly prayed he would not add any more regrets to those he already owned.

Lydia nodded. 'I know,' she said so quietly he could barely hear her.

When they reached the farm a little while later, an unfamiliar wagon and two horses were parked outside the kitchen door. Rees felt his heart sinking. What new crisis had arisen in his absence from home? He jumped down and went around to assist Lydia. She had already climbed down on her own and was starting for the door when it suddenly opened. Jerusha ran through it. She had no cloak and her cheeks were flushed, but she was smiling.

'Guess who's here?' she shouted.

And then Simon and David appeared, with David's wife behind them. David's cheeks had hollowed out and he looked older than he had just a short while ago. Simon had grown at least an inch and looked to be all long legs and arms. He ran into Lydia's arms as David took two strides to reach his father. 'We've come for Christmas,' he said. Rees knew he was grinning like a fool but he couldn't help it. He was too happy to stop.

AUTHOR'S NOTE

Wolves

People have been frightened of wolves and wolf attacks for thousands of years.

Although I read several sources that claimed there has never been any documented wolf attacks in the US, many of the memoirs and other anecdotal sources describe such occurrences. One very popular tale from upstate New York describes a wife's defense of her husband with nothing but an axe. Of course, there is no way of telling which is the truth, so I opted to keep the belief appropriate to this era.

Diabetes

Although diabetes is thought of as a modern disease, Type 1 Diabetes has been a long-time human companion. In 1552 BC Hesy-Ra, an Egyptian physician, documented frequent urination as a symptom of a mysterious disease that also caused emaciation. (It can also cause weight gain since ravenous hunger is a feature of diabetes as well.)

Around this time, ancient healers noted that ants seemed to be attracted to the urine of people who had this disease. Centuries later, people known as 'water tasters' diagnosed diabetes by tasting the urine of suspected diabetics. If urine tasted sweet, diabetes was diagnosed. To acknowledge this feature, in 1675 the word 'mellitus,' meaning honey, was added to the name.

By the 1800s, physicians began to see that dietary changes could help manage diabetes. Some of the suggested diets, consuming only meat and fat or large amounts of sugar seem unhealthy to us now. Exercise was also added to the treatment when doctors noted that diet control and exercise kept diabetic patients alive for longer. Diet and exercise are still recommended as part of the treatment today.

Despite these advances, before the discovery of insulin, diabetes inevitably led to premature death. Then, in 1889 Oskar Minkowski and Joseph von Mering, researchers at the University of Strasbourg in France, showed that the removal of a dog's pancreas could induce diabetes. In 1910 an English physiologist Sir Edward Albert Sharpey-Schafer's study of the pancreas led him to the discovery of a substance that would normally be produced in non-diabetics: insulin. And in 1920, during a series of animal experiments, Frederick Banting, a physician in Ontario, Canada, first used insulin to treat diabetes. Banting and his team successfully treated a human diabetic patient with insulin in 1922.

Why does diabetes occur? No one really knows. One theory suggests that a tendency towards diabetes confers some evolutionary advantage in the same way that carriers of sickle cell anemia have some resistance to malaria.

The Shakers

The evangelical offshoot of the Quakers, the United Society of Believers in Christ's Second Appearance, the Shakers (a contraction of Shaking and Quakers) reached the shores of the New World in 1774. Begun by a woman, Mother Ann Lee, the Shaker Sisters enjoyed equal status with the men; a privilege unknown outside the faith. Mother Ann Lee was venerated among the Shakers and those that died were said to 'go home to Mother'.